Not Too Old

Also by Ann Tonnell

How Sweet the Sound

A Mountain to Coast Romance
Not Sorry

Not Too Old

Ann Tonnell

Desert Palm Press

Not Too Old

A Mountain to Coast Romance Book 2

By Ann Tonnell

©2023 Ann Tonnell

ISBN (book) 9781954213715
ISBN (epub) 9781954213722

Desert Palm Press
1961 Main Street, Suite 220
Watsonville, California 95076
www.desertpalmpress.com

Editor: CK King
Cover Design: Rainbow Glittershine Artworks
Photography: A. Beall

Printed in the United States of America
First Edition May 2023

Acknowledgments

My sincerest appreciation goes to Lee Fitzsimmons and Desert Palm Press for continuing to give me a chance to tell the stories of these strong women. At DPP, we are at various stages as authors, and yet, still lift each other up. A special nod to Ellen Hoil and Jazzy Mitchell for their work on the DPP livestreams. It's been good to share our works virtually, and I know it's no small feat for them. If you haven't done so already, please pick up books by my DPP author colleagues.

Please consider supporting our collection of prequels and sequels in *Tales from Under the Desert Palm*. All proceeds from the books sale go to True Colors United, an organization that helps find solutions to youth homelessness, focusing on the experiences of LGBTQ young people.

A hearty thanks to readers GLI, Debralee, and content expert, Jennifer Wolfe.

No book is ever complete without its cover. Thank you to Rainbow Glittershine Artworks for your patience with my numerous requests and for your thoughtful suggestions.

There is never enough love for my editor, Christina Wood Martinez. She continues to guide me toward a manuscript that I would feel confident to submit to a publisher. I hope she truly recognizes the importance of her endeavors to that end. I sure do. Speaking of editors, CK King is remarkable in shaping my growth and keeping the work oh so much tighter than it would have been. You wouldn't be reading this book if she hadn't provided her expertise.

As always, I must recognize my most patient supporter, my wife, DL. She never complains (at least to me) as I follow this author path. She picks up my slack (not anything new, though), and she tolerates my weeks of writing retreats and hours of solitude.

Last but not at all least, thank you to all of you readers and reviewers. Readers, you make these books possible. Without your support, our stories would remain in our heads.

Dedication

To Marian Gordin
1944 – 2022
Friend, Reader, Activist, Editor, Publisher
Always Supportive, Always Exacting

Preface

As a Mountains to Coast Romance, *Not Too Old* features fictional characters who spend time in or live in coastal North Carolina. Like *Not Sorry*, it also features fictional characters from that book's small, North Georgia mountain community. While the books stand alone, they are companions. Please enjoy this second Mountains to Coast Romance.

Chapter One

GEEZ. HOW STIFF CAN an ol' gal get? Isn't retirement supposed to be relaxing? The past three months had been anything but. Samantha Avery pushed open the car door and pulled herself out and into a standing position. "Oof."

She had spent at least two weeks of each of those months at her mother's place in Wilmington, North Carolina. The seven-hour drive—seven and a half with a stop—was tiring and boring. Even listening to lesbian romance novels on audiobook barely lessened the onerousness of the trip. She knew a few more stops to walk and stretch her back would help, but she didn't want the trip to be any longer than it already was. The trade-off in time saving was that every joint in her body was stiff when she arrived and had to climb the outside stairs to her mom's second-floor apartment. Sixty-four seemed so much older after each trip. *Ugh. I may be as strong as a bull, but my knees don't understand that anymore.*

Sam arrived, as usual, at four p.m. Luckily, it was early spring and only eighty degrees today. Unloading her suitcase, bicycle gear, pillow, cooler, cooking supplies and daypack with computer and other electronics, made for three trips. Ida, who lived a few doors down from her mom, sat in the white, plastic chair on the stoop for her afternoon smoke, holding court at the top of the stairs.

"Hey. How you doin? I heard you agroanin' down there. And you walk like I do up those steps. Your knee bothering you?" Ida asked. "How's your mom?"

"Luckily, the knee is better. Just stiff from the trip. Not so sure about Mom, though. She's hanging in there, I guess."

"Heh, heh. Yeah. I noticed she answered something kinda weird the other day. Just like my mom. Early dementia. She lives with my sister now. You're good to come stay with her. I saw your brother and that cutie visit her yesterday. She's a mess."

"Oh, Sasha. Yes, she is a mess. Keeps us young though, eh?" Sam opened the stairwell door for the final load into the hallway outside her mom's apartment door. "See you soon, I'm sure." The heavy, metal door closed with a thud. She opened her mom's door, ever unlocked, and rolled her suitcase in.

Her mother, Bea, eighty-eight for another few months, was slumped over her dining table with her head in her hands. *Yep. There's that rise and fall of the shoulders. She's still alive. How, I don't know...or understand.* Sam put the third bag into the guest bedroom, then walked back into the combined dining and living room. *I should wake her. How can that slumped position be comfortable?* Perky and outgoing were not the terms that described who Bea was becoming...at least when they were alone. It had to be hard knowing you had lost so many long-term friends, those folks with whom you'd shared the bulk of your life. Bea seemed despondent at times, as if the weight of the eighty-eight years was too much to endure. But she refused the antidepressant that had been recommended by her doctor. Bea's arm slipping on the table startled her awake. Sam gave her mom a hug.

"Hey there, stranger. Mind if I stay awhile?"

"Oh, you're here! I love you so much." Bea hugged back as tightly as she could. "I'm so glad you're here."

"Your lunch pills are still in a cup," Sam said. "Do you need some water?"

"Yes, I guess so." Sam handed her mom her well-worn water bottle. Bea tilted her head back, dropped the pills into her mouth, chugged a few swallows of water, and returned the cap to the bottle.

"Mom, have you lost some more weight? You feel like a bag of bones."

"Ha. I am. Look at this." Bea pulled a hunk of flab under her arms. "Now, how long are you going to be here?" Bea ran a finger along the dates of the calendar that served as a placemat. She stopped at today's date, and frowned, as if trying to figure out a puzzle.

"Ten days this time. I leave on the second. See, I wrote it on the calendar," Sam placed her finger on the date.

"I wasn't sure because no one ever tells me anything. I have to look at this so that I know," Bea said sharply.

"Yes, Mom. That's why we write it down for you." She tried not to sound annoyed. She had only been there five minutes and was already exasperated. She knew she needed to work on that. Being tired, she tried to cut herself some slack. She needed a big glass of water, but she wanted a big cocktail. She also knew she needed to work on *that*.

Is that me in twenty-plus years? Sam shuddered. *If only we had both taken better care of ourselves, things might be different,* she thought. Fifty pounds lighter and three sizes smaller than she was while she was still working, retirement had obviously helped her health. While

2

she walked several miles on the days she wasn't cycling, she knew she should add some free weights and yoga or stretching to her workout. She'd brought her bicycle this time to take advantage of some of Wilmington's extensive bike paths.

She had spent two years as a single lesbian after leaving a long-term, committed relationship. She hadn't even been on a date in years. Not that some friends hadn't tried to fix her up. She wasn't sure if she had passed her prime dating presence, or if she was simply too picky. Yeah, when she first moved back to the South, she'd certainly found her neighbor, Liz, attractive, but Liz was happily coupled with Monty. Even so, Sam still rolled down the car windows and played some cool tune in the hopes of piquing the interest of a bored soccer mom or athletic lesbian at a stoplight. Even when she was cycling along the beach roads, she never passed anyone other than couples or young, college-aged students. The latter would likely not have given her the time of day. She was surely an old lady to them. Unseen. Unwanted. Uncool.

The weather was supposed to be nice though, so she would try again. *Better than going to bars, isn't it?* She knew the question was rhetorical. She wasn't confident she would ever find companionship from a non-organized bicycle ride.

"Where are you going now?" Bea asked as she looked up from her calendar.

"I'm going to try to give Tom a little break and get two loads of laundry done." Sam pushed the door open with her backside. *You know...the never-ending pile of soiled sheets and pants.* She couldn't say that aloud. Her mom had declined. She had stopped reading several years ago. She slept most of the day or stared at an old movie. She had even cut back coloring in her books. She couldn't do her laundry. She could barely dress herself anymore, and she needed help to bathe. Falls had become more frequent, especially as she fell asleep on the edge of chairs, her bed, and the commode.

"Oh, he'll appreciate that." Bea turned again to the calendar, running her finger across it, apparently reading each item again.

"I know. I'm sure he never thought he'd be doing so much laundry as a part-time job." Bea's apartment door shut behind Sam as she moved the clothes through. She often found the complex's laundry room, which was centrally located on her mom's floor, a welcome sanctuary when she'd been at her mom's for several days. Bea's buddies would sometimes stop in to visit while the clothes were in the machines. Today, she set an alarm on her watch so she could go back to the apartment and start preparing dinner. Sam smiled to herself, although she sympathized with her brother, Tom, in this effort. She cooked for Tom when she was in town—the least she could do. That and preparing Bea's clothing.

She always put together sets of clothes for her mother for two weeks at a time, with two pairs of sleep clothes for her to change into. Regardless, Bea always slept in whatever clothes she put on that day. She didn't change until the next morning, unless her briefs overflowed, which happened several times a week. That would warrant another pants change.

By the time Tom and Sasha appeared the pizza was coming out of the oven.

"Just in time, I see!" Tom gave Sam a big hug. Sasha dropped her bag on the floor and joined in the hug.

"Yay! Pizza. See, Dad, I told you it would be pizza tonight. It's always pizza the night Sam arrives."

"Yeah. That's because I've already driven seven hours, done two loads of laundry, put out clothes for the next two weeks, mopped the floor, cleaned the bathroom, and bought groceries. What'd you do today, Miss Missy?"

"Don't be so grumpy. I've been at school all day. Did you get ice cream?"

"Does a bear poop in the woods?"

"Dad. Did you hear that? She didn't say the s word that she usually says."

"Sasha, are you going to come here and give me a hug?" Bea spread her arms as the nine-year-old flew into them and gave her a kiss on the cheek. "And don't think you're going to get away without a hug either, Tom." She tilted her head to the side.

"Not a chance of that." Tom walked up and pulled Bea up into his arms.

"You know the worst thing about getting old?" Bea frowned as Tom released her.

"What?" Sasha asked.

"You just don't get enough physical contact. I miss hugs and snuggling with your granddad."

"Tell me about it," Sam added, shaking her head.

"Oh, hush. You're not old. Just wait." Bea waved her hand in Sam's direction dismissively.

"Hmph." Sam sliced the pizza and pointed to the paper plates. "I'm not sure I remember how snuggling feels."

"I can tell you this. It'll come right back to you when the time comes. Don't you worry one bit. I was with James Garner in my dreams again last night. Mm. I was sorry to wake up."

"TMI, Mom. TMI." Tom grimaced and shook his head. "Sam, as usual, we appreciate your coming down." He leaned in and whispered, "I really needed a little break. It makes it so much nicer to spend more time at home."

"I know. I can't imagine...day in and day out, working full time...with a kid...and a mom," Sam replied in a whisper.

"I just figure, after everything she's done for us—"

"Agree wholeheartedly," Sam interrupted. "I'm just glad we all pitch in, but I know the burden is on you since you live here."

"Anyway, thanks for coming, Sam." Tom took his plate and stepped into the living room.

Everyone's appreciation helped Sam feel a little livelier. Sasha was a spitfire, talking a mile a minute about her third-grade's field trip to the aquarium. She liked to roll across Sam, kissing her, hugging, and sitting in her lap.

"Sasha, let's put everything away," Tom said. "Plates in trash. Glass by the sink. Tell Sam and Grandma good night. It's a school night, so we need to get home to watch Rachel's show before you hit the sack."

After they left, Sam washed and put away the dishes. Oh, the life at Restful Roost, as Sam called it when joking with her mom. *Nothin' could be finer than to be in Carolina*, Sam sung to herself sarcastically.

Bea's extra bed was a relatively cheap, unsupportive mattress. The apartment temperature was kept close to seventy-eight degrees. *Thank goodness it's going to be in the low forties tonight.* Sam opened the bedroom window a few inches. She was used to fifty-five at night at her home in the North Georgia mountains in the winter...seventy in the summer.

She loved the North Carolina coast; she had grown up here, but like much of Georgia, it was much too hot through the spring, summer, and fall. Above 3,000 feet it was always at least ten degrees cooler. That's the way she wanted it.

"Shit." She pulled her phone from the bedside table. She texted her neighbor and good buddy, Liz. *Made it. Heading for some Zs. Sorry it's late. Got caught up in the fam.*

Glad you're there safely. Mwah, Liz's text returned.

Sam read for ten minutes before feeling sleepy. As she drifted off, she heard a muffled Barry Manilow singing Bea to sleep. Sam was grateful for the tinnitus that drowned out the CD playing in the other room.

Chapter Two

EVEN THOUGH SHE HADN'T slept well, Sam managed to get up and have the coffee brewed by eight. She poured herself a cup and the remainder into a carafe for her mom. She set out her mom's cup, complete with three heaping, pink spoons of artificial sweetener and a spoon ready to stir it in. Sam would be on the bicycle before her mom's rise after ten. Bea would only have to pour the coffee and roll it on the walker seat to her spot at the table. She wouldn't eat until Sam returned or until her meal from Senior Services arrived just after eleven.

Sam parked in her favorite lot along the beach, retrieved her parking pass from the machine, and walked it back to put on her windshield. To her surprise, the parking service woman was writing her a ticket. "Hey, I was right there getting the pass. Here it is," Sam said, holding the pass up and opening her door.

"Oh. That's *your* car?" The attendant curtly pointed to Sam's Honda Element.

"Yes, and I walked right in front of you as you gave a ticket to that guy," Sam pointed. "I know you saw me."

"Sorry. I'll void it right now." Parking Lady was likely a little younger, quite a bit taller—five-foot-eight maybe—slimmer, short and graying hair, dark skin, and freckles. Her uniform included a polo shirt and boat shoes with socks. Her dark-khaki shorts revealed a knee brace, and Sam noticed what appeared to be a knee-replacement scar on the other knee, but she looked very athletic. Attractive. Actually, *very* attractive. Sam couldn't tell if she was a sister-friend or not, but she easily could have been.

"Thanks for that. I mean, the time stamp would have shown I was standing right here, but I'm glad I don't have to hassle with challenging it." A beat passed. "I guess not everyone is cheery getting a ticket."

"Not at all," Parking Lady replied curtly. "Everybody around here knows you pay to park—March first through October thirty-first. They just push it."

"You know, I've had problems with the machines in the past, and the telephone parking system doesn't always work seamlessly. The voice instructions ask for the parking spot number, and the spots aren't numbered in this lot." Sam pointed at the unnumbered pavement. "It's a bit irritating to know you're expected to follow directions that aren't clear. Hope I'm not getting myself in trouble. You know, I want to ride, not argue."

"Okay, then." Parking Lady slapped the ticket pad lightly against her palm. She turned her head up and then back toward Sam and raised her sunglasses to the top of her head. "Nice bike. Enjoy the ride and be safe."

"Thanks, I will. See you next time." Sam snapped her helmet strap. As a smile spread across Parking Lady's face, Sam returned the smile through a squint. Sam headed north and would make that short loop before heading the longer route to the south end, around Harbor Island, and back north to the parking area.

Heading north, she saw Parking Lady in the lot near the fishing pier stoplight. Parking Lady gave a little wave and a smile. *Whoa.* Sam waved back. *Maybe she's nicer than I thought. Maybe I will see her again sometime. Hmm. Maybe what, Avery. Just ride, okay.*

The headwind all the way north dropped Sam's average speed close to three miles per hour, but it was good to have the workout. The sun was warm and the breeze was chilly. She was glad she'd worn a long-sleeve jersey. Upon the return to her car, she locked her bike back to the rack, removed her helmet, and swapped her riding shoes for Crocs. Since there was a half hour left on her parking pass, she decided to walk out to the beach itself to see the ocean. The wind fueled some nice wave action, and their sounds were calming. As she walked back to her car door, Parking Lady drove up in the service's UTV.

"You made it back in time," she shouted as Sam reached for her car door handle.

"Ha, ha. You thought you'd get to give me a ticket after all?"

"Nah. Just thought I'd see if I could get a rise out of you." Parking Lady turned off the engine. "My name is Deb, Deb Martin."

"Sam Avery. Nice to meet you." Sam stepped to the UTV, pulled her bike glove off, and shook Deb's hand. "Glad I made it. You know, nothing can center me quite as quickly as the sounds of the ocean— waves crashing and rolling, sometimes with the tinkling of shells, but now I'd better get out of here before my pass runs out."

"I'd let you slide today." Deb looked over the rims of her sunglasses.

"I bet you say that to all the girls." Sam smiled, crossing her arms in front of her as she leaned against her car.

"Not everyone."

Sam watched Deb slide out of the UTV and walk toward her. *Okay, she's definitely flirting. Isn't she?* She couldn't see Deb's eyes, but she thought they were checking her out. *Woah. Is this happening?*

"You staying around here a few days? I see your Georgia plate."

"Yeah. My mom lives in Ogden." Sam pointed her thumb over her shoulder.

"Maybe I'll see you again, then."

"Weather's supposed to be nice tomorrow. I should be here again, same time."

"Good. It's a date." Deb tapped her sunglasses in a mock salute. "See you then." She smiled, jumped back into the UTV, and drove off.

Sam felt a stirring of excitement. *Now, Avery. Don't go there just yet.* It was the first action she had seen in years. She was going to do whatever it took to see where it might lead. She damn sure wasn't getting any younger. And if someone was halfway interested after seeing her in bike shorts, it was a good sign. She cranked up DNCE and sang about cake on the drive home.

Her imagination had her sprinting up the concrete steps to the second floor at her mom's building. On step five, her knee reminded her she wasn't even in her fifties anymore. "Shoot," she said out loud. Still, she had a little pep in her limp up the remainder of the steps. And as she helped her mom get into the shower, she was singing to herself.

After hours of going through her mother's closets and bagging up clothes that had long gone unworn, Sam took a carload to the donation center. Hopefully, someone who'd lost items in the recent hurricane would be able to use these. Even six months later, there was still evidence of destroyed or damaged homes. One of Bea's buddies said they were, just now, reopening her church's school gym, having housed a group of families whose homes had to be rebuilt. Sam wished she had done this purging a few months ago.

It was late afternoon, and Sam headed downstairs to check her mom's mailbox. She heard voices coming from the outside stairwell. Three of the residents were talking to Ida. Sam peeked through the thin, rectangular window and noticed that Ida and another woman were smoking. The other two ladies had koozies around what looked to be beer cans. Sam pushed the door open and stuck her head out. "Y'all having a party out here?" They turned and laughed.

"Yeah. Smoking and drinking," one of them answered.

"Come join us," Ida offered.

"Aren't you Bea's daughter? How's your mom doing?" the one Sam recognized as Barb asked.

"Same. Hanging in there. You're Barb, right?"

"That's right. One of the three Barbs."

"Yeah, sure. Let me tell Mom I'm out here. She thinks I've run to the mailbox." Sam popped her head in her mom's door, and her mom was asleep at the table. Sam grabbed a beer from the refrigerator and a koozie from the stash in her mom's cabinet, headed back out and took a place along the stairs, leaning back against the bricks.

"We were just sayin' how we noticed you're coming more often...and for longer," Barb said. Ida nodded.

"Yeah. You know how it goes." Sam looked at her can as she popped the top and took a slug. "So, have y'all all been here a long time? I think Mom has been here...what, ten years now, maybe more?"

"She has, ten years and a week," one of the ladies answered. "I'm also a Barb, but they used to call me Toots when I played softball, so that kind of stuck. I came the week after your mom came. She was so nice to me, making me feel welcome. Special lady. And your name?"

"Sam. Samantha. She *is* a special lady. I'm going to try to remember all y'all. So, you're Toots, Barb, Ida, and—" Sam nodded to the fourth of the group.

"Peg. We're all old softball players. Emphasis on old. Probably a good sight older than you!" They all chuckled.

"Oh, I don't know. I'm not quite a year from Medicare, so probably right there with ya."

"Close," Toots said. "But we're still two to eight years older. Did you play softball?"

"Nah. Actually, I never played any sport unless it was for a class. I've only hiked, biked, or walked. I did enjoy racquetball for a short while, but it got so popular, you couldn't find courts anymore. Then I was working all the time."

"Work does get in the way sometimes," Ida said.

"I live near a lake now, so I have a little kayak that I paddle around sometimes."

"Where do you live in Georgia?" Peg asked.

"It's a little unincorporated town in the North Georgia mountains...Suches. You probably haven't ever heard of it, but it's between Dahlonega and Blairsville. Some people have heard of those."

"I've heard of Blairsville," Peg replied.

"And Atlanta," said a couple of the others in unison.

"It's a little cabin in the woods, but it's near the Appalachian Trail."

"Oh, wow," a few said, again in unison.

"I wish I could still hike...or play softball." Ida shook her head.

"Yeah, not happening now," Barb replied. The others nodded.

"It was good talkin' with y'all. I'm sure I'll see y'all around, but I want to go check on Mom. She's probably wondering where I am, if she's awake."

"C'mon back anytime. You know where to find us," Peg said.

Whatcha know. Trying—twice in one day—to talk to strangers.

* * * *

The next morning, Sam made her mom's coffee and put it in a carafe for her. She left a note that she had headed to the beach for a bike ride, and that the coffee was ready to pour. She said she'd be back by one-thirty for lunch. It was another beautiful day, just as the forecast had promised. She wore her nice jersey and made sure all her accessories matched, in case Deb Martin actually did show up. Sam was locking her car and getting ready to hit the start ride button on her tracking app, when Deb's UTV pulled into the lot. She gave a little wave as she parked. She strolled toward Sam, slapping her ticket book as she walked. Sam chuckled to herself as she noted this pad slapping must be a habit. *Already noticing this woman quite a bit, Avery. Yep.*

"I had to check a couple of things in a lot on the south end. Was afraid I might be too late to catch you before you headed out." Deb pushed her sunglasses down as if to get a better look at Sam.

"Here I am, though. Good morning." Sam couldn't stop a smile as she felt her face redden. "Another beautiful day, eh?"

"Sure is. Look. Would you like to have a drink with me this evening, Sam?" Deb asked.

"Why not? Mom has bingo, and she wouldn't miss it for the world. She has to be downstairs by six. I could probably make it by six-fifteen. Would that be okay?"

"Close to my bedtime." Deb tapped a questioning finger on her cheek. "But, sure, that's great. Why don't we meet up at Bull's Bites and Brews? Are you familiar with it?"

"Uh...sure." *Am I really doing this?* "I've never been there, so yeah, that'll be great. Six-fifteen then." Sam started her map program and pushed off, hoping Deb hadn't heard her gulp.

"I'm looking forward to it." Deb adjusted her sunglasses. "Ride safe!" She called and gave a little wave.

What the fuck just happened? Am I going on a date? Really. Crap! Sam did the full island twice, but also added Harbor Island into both loops to make a nice twenty-miler. Man, did she need to burn off her nerves. During the ride, she tried to focus on keeping a certain speed or cadence, but she found herself preoccupied with the thought of her date, albeit an informal date. She wondered what she should wear. She knew the place was pretty casual, as were most beach venues, but she wanted to make a good impression. *Why can't I just let this unfold? Why is it such a big deal? Maybe because you haven't had a date or been with anyone in so many years, you dork!*

She thought back to her breakup two years ago. Seemed so much longer. Okay, so not one of those horrible breakups with fights regarding property or money. Amicable in that way, but stressful nonetheless. And then the loneliness. Had she been alone long enough she wouldn't want that sort of involvement again? Her buddies back home had tried to fix her up with someone at a holiday gathering last year. The woman ended up not coming due to unforeseen issues. Such a disappointment after finally allowing herself to look forward to a potential date. After that, she felt raw. Now she faced a full-on date...with a complete stranger. *Shit.*

She seems like a nice enough lady, although you really don't know. You've spent all of ten minutes, max, with her. She's good looking, though. You gotta give her that. God. I hope she doesn't smoke. Shut up, Avery. Just go have a drink with the lady.

Chapter Three

BEA DIDN'T PRY TOO much, though Sam could tell she was curious where she was headed.

"Like I told you, I'm going to check out that newish place near the pier, Bull's. Tom said he hadn't been. I just want to check it out. The menu looks pretty good. I looked at it online."

"Be careful." Her mom tilted her head and squinted. "I mean, be careful, but have a good time. Okay?"

"Mom. I will. Now I want you to win big at bingo." Sam kissed her on the cheek and headed out.

"Oh, I intend to...if I don't have to call the game. Let me get myself out of the door with this contraption." Bea blew out a big breath as she pushed her walker toward the door.

"Maybe they'll let you have an out this time." Sam knew that the group was sharing the calling duty since her mom had become so forgetful. One of them admitted to Sam that Bea had fallen asleep while calling two games, and someone had to relieve her both times.

Sam decided on a pair of cargo shorts and a gray, short-sleeve T-shirt. The long-sleeve Oxford overshirt, left unbuttoned, added a little style and protection in case the air conditioner was cranked up. She opted for her gray sneakers and ankle-length socks. Casual, but neat, and possibly nerdy with her color matching, but she didn't care. She checked the mirror one final time to ensure her short hair was nicely spiked. When she pulled into the beach parking lot, she saw Deb was waiting outside, across the lot from the pay station.

"Hey, Sam. I already printed you a parking pass. Here. Put it on your dash," she called as she walked to meet Sam at the car.

"Dang, thanks. I guess it pays to know the parking people around here." She smiled at Deb. "You look nice." The blue polo shirt matched her eyes perfectly.

"Thanks. You too." Deb returned the smile. "Come on in. I'm sort of a regular, so don't be put off by the stares, okay? I'm apologizing in advance."

"No worries." *No worries my ass. What have I gotten myself into?* Deb held the door for Sam and then motioned her to a table toward the back of the room.

"What would you like to drink? I'm having Jack and Coke."

"Sounds great. How do things work here? Order at the bar or do we have table service?"

"I was going to order at the bar, but they'll bring the drinks with some menus if you'd rather."

"Sounds perfect, since I've not been here before." Not only were the server and bartender checking her out, but also two tables of four were looking at her. They nodded at Deb as she beamed.

"Damn. You weren't kidding, girl." Sam furrowed her brow when Deb slid into her chair across the table.

"Again. Sorry. They usually see me at the bar. And always alone. Always." Deb shrugged. "Not many friends for the person who hands out tickets, I'm afraid."

The server, a woman who was probably in her mid-forties with straight, bleached-blond hair, brought their drinks and a couple of menus. "The usual tonight, Deb? Or maybe your friend will need a few?"

"A few. Thanks Jules," Deb took the menus and handed one to Sam. They perused the one-sided list. "Stick to basics, if you're interested in my advice. Fish and chips are pretty good. Burgers okay. Fish tacos good. The oysters? Not sure. Haven't tried them. I have a feeling they're pretty good because a lot of the regulars order them."

"Thanks. I'm a bit of a food snob, but I wasn't expecting four stars or anything here." Sam laughed as she put her napkin in her lap. "But they have one of my favorite Maine beers and my current favorite champagne. You can't go wrong with either of those," Sam noted. The menus back on the side of the table, Jules headed straight back and took their orders—two fish and chips with ranch dressing for the fries.

Deb sipped her drink, looking at Sam. "So, what do you do besides ride a bike?"

"And take care of my mom? I'm a retired nurse, and I pretty much do what I want. I enjoy traveling, camping, hiking. I have a little fold-up kayak that I use on the lake near where I live. I like fishing too, but just for relaxation. I haven't had an opportunity to really catch much, but I don't care. It's fun. And recently, I've been dabbling with writing," Sam answered. "What do you do besides give out parking tickets and frequent Bull's?"

"You just slid that writing thing in." Deb looked a bit perplexed. "What did you mean? What do you write?"

"If I told you, you'd probably laugh." Sam took a big slug of her drink.

"Try me," Deb replied, then took a big slug herself.

"Lesbian romance novels...maybe. We'll see how it turns out."

Deb coughed and covered her mouth with her napkin, laughing. "Are you kidding me?"

"Told you."

"God, you're cute when you smile. And your dimple."

The warmth from her reddening face traveled lower than she was expecting. Sam took another slug of her drink, averting her eyes from Deb's.

"You *are*," Deb insisted. Sam blushed again. She was grateful when Jules brought their food and Deb was forced to look away.

"You were supposed to be telling me what *you* do," Sam said.

"Early retirement. Taught for twenty years. Mostly health and girls' PE. A little science here and there across the years."

"Oh wow. Now that was probably interesting."

"Ha. You could say that. Mostly middle school. You know, just as hormones begin to rage, but anyway, I wanted to keep doing something, so I picked this up to help out with expenses. It's part time—nine to one. I have four months off—November through February. Allows me to keep my place down here, and I usually rent out the little bottom apartment during the summer. That helps pay the taxes and upkeep. I do all right." Deb motioned for another round. "I want to hear more about your writing. Where can I read it?"

"You can't. Yet. I'm not published or anything. That's why I say dabbling." Sam laughed. "So, you live here at the beach then?"

"Changing the subject again?" Deb chuckled. "Yes, it's here. I ride my bicycle to work on Harbor Island, unless it's raining. Then I usually drive. I love it here."

"God, who wouldn't?" Sam replied. "I'd love that life. I'd love living here."

There was a lull as they ate. Jules brought refills.

"Hey, we didn't toast. To lesbian romance." Deb's expression was hard to read. They clinked. Sam smiled and shook her head, looking down at the table, face warm again.

"Look now. Don't reveal my secrets. I'm talking to you, not anyone else." Sam kept her tone serious. "I hope it'll work out, but it's okay if it doesn't. I started writing, since I've been spending so much time at my mom's. I call it escape fiction, because writing serves as an escape for me."

"You slay me with that smile, you know? I hope it's okay I say that."

Sam nodded. "It's nice to hear. Thanks." She felt the warmth again, lower. "So, where is your place from here?"

Deb beamed. "Really, just a few blocks from here. That's the reason I'm a regular. I walk. Makes it safer if I have one too many, you know. Anyway, it's on the sound side. An older place. Quiet street. Porch faces the sound."

"Damn. I'd enjoy sitting on your porch some time. I love looking at the water. So restful."

"Any time. Come on back, or I'll give you my number and address," Deb said.

"That'd be nice. I wish I could come tonight, but—" Sam started.

"Sure! Why not? Oh yeah. I guess your mom would worry." Deb looked a bit dejected.

"I shouldn't drive right now. Maybe we could walk there and back?" Sam suggested. "Mom will be down there at bingo another hour or so, knowing her."

Deb beamed again and nodded. She motioned for Jules to bring the check. Sam reached into her purse and pulled out her wallet, and Deb held up her hand. "No. This one's on me, Sam. Please."

"As long as you let me treat next time." Sam nodded her okay for Deb's request.

"Next time for sure." Deb locked their gazes. *Okay. Officially attracted.*

As they strolled, Deb pointed to different houses and reeled off stories of the owners.

"I grew up on the island and know most everyone who's been here for more than twenty years." Deb stopped at a weathered, two-story, cedar shake house. The under-house, two-space carport had a small room at the back, which Sam assumed to be the rental unit. "This is mine." Deb led them up a set of steps on the right side of the house to a large, covered porch.

"This is beautiful, Deb. What a treasure!" Sam rested a hand on the back of a rocker and pushed it back and forth. The neatly mowed lawn extended to the bulkhead. Rippled reflections of lights from docks danced across the water, and the breeze brought salt into Sam's nose. With a deep breath, she whispered, "God I love the coast."

Deb opened the screen door. "Come in?" she offered.

"I hope you'll give me a tour sometime soon, but I'd love to sit out here for a while, if that's okay." Sam said. "This view...it's captivating."

Deb walked around to one of the other rockers. She motioned for Sam to sit.

"Glad you like it out here. I typically sit out here until bedtime," Deb said.

"God I could sit out here all night," Sam said, rocking. "You know, it's been a long time since I've been on a date."

"But you must've had relationships. I mean, we're a little old to be just starting out."

"Yeah. Of course. I was in a couple of long-ish relationships. My first, eleven years. We grew up together from college, you know. Lived together. Then another one, three and a half years, living apart. Good buddies, but just should've stuck to that. Then my last, longer. Twenty. Just grew apart. I moved back south, but there were dates in between some of those. You?"

"Oh yeah. A couple in college. A few here and there. One semi, off and on, for twelve or so years. Sounds like the one of yours...should have only been friends. Actually, we still are, I mean the best of friends, in a way. I just focused on teaching. And summer softball. Didn't mind not having to talk relationship trash in the teachers' lounge."

"Ever worry you'd be found out when you were teaching?"

"Yeah. That's what I mean. Why I avoided couple status or dating. You know. Don't ask, don't tell. Even worse, really."

"I always worry for friends who are teachers and if their identity is going to trip them up if some narrow-minded parents complain."

"Of course."

"But must be a little better these days...at least here. My niece said the principal at her school is gay and that everyone knows it."

"That's incredible. Glad to hear it's getting better." A beat passed. "So, your niece...that means you have a brother?"

"Two actually. Tom lives here. He's the baby. The one with the niece. Jeff, the middle child, lives part of the year in Bohol, in the Philippines."

"Wow. You're the oldest, huh?"

"Yep. And bossy, too. Just ask them."

"Ha, ha! I can see that...the way you had no problem spouting off at me the other day." Deb chuckled.

"Yeah. Sorry. What about you? Siblings?"

"Hah. Just me."

"I know I should head back," Sam said after a lull and stood up. Deb stood to join her.

"I'll walk you back to the car."

"It's okay. I don't mind walking alone."

"Do you mind if I walk with you, though?"

Sam shook her head. "Not at all." She felt herself blush again. "I had a nice evening."

Deb leaned and kissed Sam softly. "Me too." Sam pulled Deb's arm gently. Deb leaned and kissed Sam again, this time more firmly. Sam gave an audible sigh as a jolt replaced the prior warmth.

"Your lips are as soft as I thought they would be when you smiled," Deb whispered.

"How soft?" Sam closed her eyes and Deb leaned in again. As they kissed, Sam wrapped her arms around Deb's waist and pulled her close. *Shit. I don't want Mom to worry, but I don't want to leave.* Her chest heaved with an audible sigh.

"Oh God. I've got to go, Deb." She pushed herself against Deb's body.

"That's not getting you where you need to go, but you're sure headed where I'd like you to go," Deb whispered. She kissed Sam again. Their tongues touched and Sam moaned softly. Deb moved away just a little. "Come on. Let's get you back to your car."

"I know I should," Sam whispered. "And thank you for not talking me out of it. Let me get your number." She entered the number into her phone and Deb escorted her back to the car. They didn't speak on the walk. Sam loved the feeling of Deb's hand on her waist as she guided during a turn or stop. When they arrived at the car, Deb stood close behind Sam as she opened the door. Sam leaned back against her, lightly. She swooned when Deb slid her arms around her and pulled her close.

"I'll text you when I get home." She turned around and Deb softly kissed her again.

Sam was throbbing. She grinned at Deb, who was standing at the parking spot with her arms crossed in front of her, watching her pull away. *Whoa. What on earth? That kiss was so hot!* She could not remember such full, rich lips sending such an intense message. And so quickly. *Geez.* She was wet, warm, and throbbing, and she was pretty sure if they had kissed one more time she would have come right then and there. She wondered if Deb felt the same. She started planning how she could have a night with Deb. Would her mom care if she spent the night away?

Bea was back from bingo, and Sam tried to make small talk, describing the restaurant and the food. She told her mom she was tired and headed back to her room. She fell back on her bed and pulled out her phone.

Home. Had a lovely night. S. Sam held the phone and looked at the screen. When it buzzed with a call, it startled her. "Hi," Sam said softly.

"It *was* nice. I can't stop feeling your lips," Deb whispered. "I am on fire."

Sam sighed. "You'd better stop talking that way. Me too. I hope you don't think I am this easy all the time."

Deb chuckled. "All I know is that I did not want to stop kissing," she whispered. "I love the way your mouth feels. Just thinking about you...I would love to feel you in my arms again."

"We'll have to work that out. Hopefully soon."

"That'd be nice. I think it's supposed to rain tomorrow, so I guess you won't be riding."

"Not in the rain, no. But soon. I'll call or text tomorrow?"

"Yeah. Sweet dreams."

Sam wasn't sure she could sleep...or do anything productive for that matter. She ached, still throbbing. She remembered when their tongues first touched. She imagined Deb's tongue on her breast, her lips gently sucking her nipple. She wet her fingers, and slipped her hand under her shirt, then under her bra to her breast. She sighed and moaned quietly. Her hips were already moving as if Deb were there. She imagined Deb's tongue providing the stimulation and stifled a moan.

As she drifted off, she figured she could tell her mom a friend was staying down at the beach and had invited her to spend the night. Bea would certainly understand that Sam wouldn't want to drive home after drinking. Her mind settled, she picked up her phone and texted Deb she'd see her tomorrow, if that worked.

The text returned quickly. *My house. Six-fifteen. I'll have wine, cheese, hors d'oeuvres. We sit on the porch or...whatever.*

Look forward to it.

Me 2. (wink emoticon) was the reply. Sam held herself in a hug as she fell into a deep sleep.

Chapter Four

"WHAT THE FUCK WAS that?" Deb slammed her feet into her shoes the next morning as she prepared for work. *What were you thinking? Kissing her on a first date? Really? But she wanted it. Oh shit. She wanted it. Are you crazy? What the fuck, Martin?* Deb was freaking out. She changed her sheets and tidied up the bathroom and bedroom. All this had to be done now so she would have time to throw together some snacks she'd pick up at Roberts' supermarket on the way home and shower before Sam arrived. *What an idiot!*

Deb debated whether to call and cancel or buck up and see it through. She would have never done that in the past, and especially after that date last year. "Take it slow, Deb. Don't rush it. She'll understand that, right?" she counseled herself aloud. *Hell, not after that smooth move last night!* "What a jerk you are, Martin. Way to go." This chatter continued until Deb stepped out onto her porch to lock the front door.

A great blue heron stood on one of the pilings of the channel's bulkhead in her front yard. She stared in awe of her best friend's appearance. Angela had died almost ten years ago. She'd considered the great blue her spirit animal. *Amazing.* When things seemed almost too much to bear, Angela would turn up, usually flying across her path, or standing, as she did today, just being.

"So glad to see you today. Yes, I'm being hard on myself...again. I get it. Go with the flow, take it slow. Love you, but I'm going to be late if I don't get out of here." With that, the bird's neck pulled in, then stretched back out as its wings lifted and carried Angela across the channel.

She quickly unlocked the two Kryptonite locks from her blue, twenty-one speed Cannondale road bike. She fastened her helmet and pant leg bands, and threw her messenger bag across her shoulder, then jumped on her bike. Deb rode south on Lumina Avenue toward Causeway Drive. As she rode, she thought again of Sam. *Why shouldn't I go for it? As long as she doesn't see me as a predator, it should be fine. It's not like we're given any guarantees how long we have in this life. I'm not, that's for sure.* Deb arrived with just minutes to spare before her shift began. As expected, her supervisor glanced up at the clock as she walked through the door.

"Boss," Deb acknowledged, nodding her head. Jim Edgecombe had been the senior-most parking official for several years. While parking services were contracted by a large Atlanta-based firm, there were numerous frontline workers who took care of the day-to-day operations. He was a good twenty years younger than Deb, and he probably looked at the clock every shift out of habit. Evidently, tardiness was one of his pet peeves. Deb had never been tardy in the two years she had worked there, so it was a little irritating that he still checked the clock each time she arrived. She knew she wasn't the problem, but his habit still irritated her. Never once had he complimented her timeliness. Nor had he ever given any staff person a kind word that she could remember. She swallowed her irritation, checked her assignments, and headed out on her rounds. *I love my job. I'm good at it, but this is why people leave their jobs—no appreciation. Yeah. You're just nervous. You know those things shouldn't bother you.* She blew out a breath.

As expected, it rained a few times during her shift. The steam inside her rain jacket did nothing to help her not-so-sunny disposition. If she hadn't needed to burn off her anxiety, she would have driven. Whenever she was stressed about the upcoming evening or miffed at a soggy ticket pad, she brought up the image of today's beautiful, great blue heron. *Breathe in and breathe out.* She tried not to let thoughts of Sam break her concentration.

Luckily, there was only wet pavement to deal with on her way home. She stopped at the island's only long-standing, family owned grocery to pick up a few items for the evening. By the time she arrived home, she was ready for a shower. Her knee brace, shoes, and socks were soaked from the rain. The rest of her clothes were soaked from sweating under her rain jacket. Her skin was itchy with the salty, sandy layer deposited from the workday and bike ride home.

The warm water streaming through her hair and down her body relaxed tense muscles. She had become accustomed to seeing the flat chest and two scars marking the double mastectomy. Almost. The thought of undressing in front of yet another potential girlfriend, who'd take off running, was almost petrifying. *I know. Take it slow. It's all right. Enjoy the moment.* The lightly shaping prosthetic bra beneath her tank top offered a small shield. A long-sleeve button-front, boy-short briefs, and jeans were her familiar buffer. Should she nap in her newly donned outfit? Since she hadn't slept well the night before, she figured she owed herself a quick one. She was sure the lack of sleep had not helped her disposition. Yes, a brief nap would be helpful.

Her alarm woke her from a light sleep. A gentle rain made a steady pattering on her metal roof. *Perfect. Nice for snuggling and sitting on the porch.* She prepared a small spread of finger foods and dips. When she heard Sam's steps heading to the porch, she took another deep breath and let it out. *It's going to be all right.* She proactively opened the gate at the porch as Sam approached under her umbrella. Warmth spread through Deb's body.

"Hiya." She took Sam's umbrella and shook it out before closing it. "Come in."

Sam averted her eyes, blushing. "Hi to you, too."

Deb motioned for Sam to come into the house, then followed her in. "Look. Last night…" She looked into Sam's eyes. "Oh shit. Sorry. Let me take that wet coat."

Sam laughed and removed her coat, handing it to Deb.

"Wow. You…you look amazing. I mean…wow." Deb hung Sam's coat on a hook, shaking her head. A white Oxford shirt, unbuttoned to reveal the start of Sam's cleavage, complemented a mid-thigh khaki skirt. Sam walked up close to her and put a hand on Deb's arm.

"What was that about last night?" Sam whispered as she pressed against her.

Deb leaned and kissed Sam, pulling her closer. Sam pressed her pelvis into Deb.

"Look," Deb started, after she pulled her lips away. "I need to slow down. I don't want to, but I need to. Don't take it the wrong way, please. I just don't know what came over me."

"I hope you have a fire extinguisher then," Sam joked. "Or a cold shower. I admit you have me wanting a whole lot more."

"Yeah. Like I said…I mean…if I think of you…" Deb looked at Sam's mouth, sighed, and kissed her again, hard. She found her tongue and Sam's breath grew ragged. "Oh, jeez." Deb paused again.

"I know, but I can't slow down if we keep this up," Sam whispered as she pulled Deb's face back to her. Another kiss and Sam moaned as Deb's tongue found hers.

Deb pulled herself away and braced against the table. "I am wet and aching to feel you, but I have to slow down. I have to, Sam. I have to." Tears welled in her eyes.

"What is it?" Sam said softly. "Talk to me."

Deb wiped her eyes. "Can we have a drink, eat a bit, then talk…or more?" She ran a finger along Sam's cheek.

"You can't touch me that way though...that way or any other way..." Sam laughed. "Not if you want me to function. You are so damn hot, girl."

"Let's hope you think that later..." Deb said softly. *Shit. Shut up, Deb. Are you hell-bent on sabotaging this?*

"Come on now. Stop. You're beginning to scare me. Are you a vampire or serial killer?"

Deb laughed and shook her head. "No. Let's just eat, okay?" Deb waved toward the table.

They each made plates, and Deb poured some Blanton's over ice and brought the glasses out to the porch.

"Blanton's, eh? Dang. It's good, but it's pricey. You must have quite a retirement."

"Ha. You see this is only half full. I've had it three years. Only bring it out when very special company comes to visit."

"I sure am glad I made the cut. I typically sip nice bourbons, also. I like Jack, too, though."

"Yeah. I love a good sour mash. And of course, Jack and Coke. Can't go wrong. Other drinks? Beer? Cocktails?"

"Dirty martinis, but I tend to stay with vodka rather than gin. If I have gin, I like a gimlet, but those are strong."

"Yes, they are. And gin gives me a weird, fast buzz. Only want those if I feel safe...usually at home."

"Me too." Sam leaned to toast Deb's glass again.

"Now for beer, a porter or milk stout. Guinness...but draft only. Not a fan of all the sours and IPAs everyone seems to brew these days."

"Yep. Glad we have similar tastes."

"You tried any of the breweries here? There are so many now."

"Only Wrightsville. I've had some good brews there."

"Whoa." Deb stood to refill empty glasses and listed to the side. "Either I've had too much, or my porch is swaying." She held onto the back of the rocker. When it moved, she lurched forward to correct the slip, almost falling.

"Come on." Sam led Deb back inside. "You have a seat here on the couch, and I'll bring in the plates and glasses and lock the door. Sure you're not dehydrated?"

"Maybe. Do me another favor, would you? Pour me a glass of water, and please make sure the alarm by my bed is set for seven and is turned on." Deb asked. "I've never been late, but I don't feel confident in my bedtime prep skills this evening."

"Sure. Of course." Sam brought in the dishes and put them in the sink, then checked the alarm clock. She returned to the living room with a glass of water for Deb. "I was tempted to call you from your bed, but I thought better of it." She stretched out on the couch and pulled at Deb.

Deb slid in between Sam's legs. She closed her eyes and sighed as she lowered herself, lightly, onto Sam and pulled her skirt up. They kissed deeply, and Sam arched her pelvis up to rock against her.

"This isn't slowing down," Sam whispered, running her tongue along the edge of Deb's ear. "Not one bit."

"Will you come into my room with me?" Deb asked softly. She slid off the couch and stood, then pulled at Sam's arms to help her up.

"Slowing down?" Sam asked.

"Doesn't look or feel like it." Deb smiled. She walked Sam backward into her room, pushing her against the bed and lowering her to the mattress. Sam pulled herself up and onto the bed's center. Sliding her hands to pull Sam's skirt up again, Deb turned Sam onto her side and slid in behind her.

Sam pushed her pelvis backward into Deb and reached behind her to pull at Deb's neck. Deb leaned around to meet Sam's lips. She sighed into Sam's mouth as she found her tongue. Deb's right hand unbuttoned Sam's shirt, and Deb slid her hand under Sam's bra, caressing her breasts and down her midline to her wet panties. "These need to come off, I think," Deb whispered into Sam's ear and worked the panties down Sam's legs.

"Oh God, yes, please." Sam's words came on rapid breaths as she arched and rocked her hips. Deb relished the wild abandon playing against her body. She slid her left arm under Sam and found her nipple. Sam thrust her head backward onto Deb. She was enjoying the feel of Sam's body pressed firmly against her and slipped her fingers into wetness with light strokes.

Sam sucked in through her teeth, moaning. "Oh please. *Please,*" Sam cried softly. Deb could feel Sam pulsing on her fingers as she came. Deb held her fingers still and slowly withdrew them. She pulled Sam's skirt off and removed her shirt, then removed her own button-front shirt and jeans. Sam stirred.

"Come back here, you. My turn, okay?" Sam pulled at Deb's arm.

"I really need to get to sleep." Deb slid in behind Sam, rubbing her back. "You okay with a rain check?" Was this going to be awkward? She hoped Sam would be relaxed enough that it all seemed normal.

"Mmm. I guess so. Gotta admit I love the way I feel right now." She pulled at Deb's neck and brought her around for a good-night kiss.

"Stay relaxed and we'll both sleep." Deb leaned back and kissed Sam's shoulder. She wondered how long this would last. Her self-pep talks hadn't diminished how nervous she was. Here she had found the first potential prospect in more than a year and she was terrified of the rejection. She spooned with Sam until she heard the slow, rhythmic breathing of Sam's sleep. Only then did she allow herself to drift off.

When the alarm rang, Deb was on her other side, and Sam was behind her. Deb felt the warmth of the arm draped across her chest. She stiffened, hoping Sam had been asleep and hadn't discovered her secret. She slipped out of bed and into the kitchen to start her morning routine. She would let Sam sleep until eight and wake her to dress and leave.

Sam entered the kitchen dressed and all smiles. She leaned against Deb's back and slipped her arms around her waist. "You're incredible, you know," Sam said softly. "I just left you high and dry. I owe you."

"It's not about owing. And I definitely was not dry," Deb added. "There's plenty of time, isn't there?" She turned around to face Sam.

"I leave Monday to go back to Georgia for a few weeks," Sam replied with a small frown.

"Fuck," Deb said sharply. "Then let's make the most of the remainder?"

"Why don't you come by Mom's tomorrow after work? A bunch of the ol' softball girls hang out on the steps a couple of times a week. It's hang out time tomorrow. Bring a special beer if you want...and a koozie. I've seen them out there before, but the other night I was brave enough to sit with them."

"What's going on tonight?" Deb asked.

"I figured you might want a break. Don't want to assume anything."

"If *you* want one. I don't need one. I mean especially if you're going away for a few weeks!"

Sam was quiet for a moment. "Hey. Let's go to that rooftop bar downtown tonight—The Limit. I've heard it has incredible views of the river, the town, and beyond. Supposed to have the best sunset view in the city." Sam's animated excitement was hard to resist.

"I've been wanting to try it. Should we meet there, or..." Deb paused.

"I'll get a car service down. You can come to Mom's apartment building, and we'll go together from there." Sam suggested. "But you can't get so tipsy that you can't drive home from Mom's."

"When should I be there? Five-thirty?"

"Sounds perfect. Now, I'll get out of here so you can get to work." Sam pulled Deb close, and they leaned in to kiss. Deb melted as Sam pulled away, grabbed her coat and umbrella, and closed the door behind her.

Chapter Five

WORK WAS AS TO be expected. The day was overcast, breezy, but not too bad for biking. Deb half expected to see Sam when she made her rounds through the various lots, but no such luck. "Probably for the best, my friend," she said to herself and Angela, wherever she might be. "Need to keep my nose to the grindstone and out of trouble." She chuckled. She so missed conversations with her friend. Even after they decided they should no longer date, they'd remained close. Angela was the one with whom she could discuss anything. Ask anything. Say anything. Angela had felt the same way. They knew that, on some other plane, they'd known one another before they met as Deb and Angela. There was no reason to take a chance of losing their connection. Deb kept on talking, so Angela would know she was still there for her. "Got another date tonight. You probably know that already, though, don't you?"

She stopped the UTV at the meters near the beach wear store and hot dog place. Everybody had been so good today. No tickets so far. She didn't think she'd ever seen that happen. "And yes, I am paying attention!" *Am I though?* The shift had flown by, and because she hadn't written any tickets, she had driven around three times more than she usually would have. She headed back to the office and traded the UTV for her bike.

While she was locking her wheels and frame to the staircase underneath her house, she noticed a vase and bright colors on the top step, visible through the risers. She ran up to find an assortment of beautiful gerbera daisies. The handwritten note said simply, *See you this evening. S.* She smiled and shook her head as she opened her door, bringing the flowers inside and setting them on the kitchen table. "So sweet. So sweet...and *hot!*" She chuckled as she jumped in the shower.

The afternoon sun peeking from behind the clouds warmed the porch. Deb stretched out on the zero-gravity recliner for a nap. Before dozing, she stretched both arms above her head to help mobilize what looked to be mild lymphedema on her upper arms, just below her armpits. It had been two years since the surgery, so it was rare to have a collection of fluid now. Every few months, she saw something she suspected to be fluid, so she'd exercise, and the puffiness would subside. The sun's warmth soothed the mild exercise aches, and she drifted off smiling at Sam's gift.

The phone alarm sounded, and she busied herself changing. It could still be chilly in the breeze, even if it seemed to be a scorcher during the day. Layers were always a good idea. She wore almost a carbon copy of yesterday's outfit, except with long pants and a simple blazer. She wondered if she was too dressy for the bar. Downtown. Rooftop. Pretty classy. Business casual should be just fine. She checked herself out in the mirror again. No telltale evidence. Should she just tell Sam? "Argh. I don't want to lose this one!" She shouted and punched a fist into her other palm. "Crap." If they were going to be close, trust one another, shouldn't she talk with Sam? Get it off her chest? *Yeah, right. Good one, Martin. Shit. Get going.*

When she arrived at the address Sam had texted her, it looked as if she were in the right place. The two-story apartment building was simple and long, mostly brick. Sam had said to park in the first spots along the left when she pulled in. Deb texted her arrival. Within a couple of minutes, Sam tapped on the passenger window, waving. Deb motioned for Sam to enter, and Sam slipped into the white Tacoma's passenger seat.

"Hi." Sam's face reddened, as if she were embarrassed.

"Hiya yourself. How's your mom today?"

"Same. Feisty. Let me summon a driver, and they'll be here in a few minutes. Then we can talk."

"I've been thinking...I'll just drive us if that's okay with you. There's a deck adjacent to the hotel. First hour is free. It's an easy-peasy drive."

"Okay...if you want."

"Why not? I had enough adult beverages last night for an entire week." Deb shook her head. "You know? Then I'll run you back by here on my way home."

Sam nodded, and Deb headed downtown. "Your mom?" Deb asked again.

"Mom refused to eat anything but ice cream again today. She wanted a root beer float when she finally woke up at noon. Incorrigible, really. I didn't ask her, but I warmed the senior center meal and left it in front of her.

"She was eating the apple crisp when I left. She wasn't touching the meat or vegetables. Tom will probably have to give her more ice cream when he comes by with Sasha this evening. It's not doing her any favors, but who are we to judge? Right?"

"She's...what did you say? Eighty-seven, eighty-eight? She's earned the right to have what she wants. Hasn't she?"

"Don't encourage her." Sam looked out at the buildings they drove by. "Incorrigible."

"It's nice you care enough to spend so much time away from your home to be with her. That's a real gift. I would've done the same for my mom." Deb knew she shouldn't say anymore, because that would lead right to a discussion she wasn't ready to take on.

"A lot has changed down here." Deb pointed as they drove past yet another construction zone. "All this convention and railway building reno."

"Yeah. I notice every time I come, there's some new road. A big difference from when I left for college, lo, those many years ago." Sam laughed. "Hey, there's the parking garage entrance." She pointed.

Within five minutes, they were in the hotel and walking toward the elevator to the top. "I've tried to come here twice," Sam said. "Once they were closed. The other time the wait was forty-five minutes. Forget that!"

"We're here today, baby," Deb chuckled. They were alone in the elevator, and Sam leaned forward against Deb.

"Hi...again. I'm glad to see you," Sam whispered.

"Hey, I forgot to say how much I loved the flowers. That was such a nice treat when I came home." Deb leaned and kissed Sam just as the elevator dinged their arrival and the door opened. "Here we are."

"Y'all sit wherever you want. Someone will be right there," the perky bartender said. "The world is your oyster, as you can see." He waved his arm toward the mostly empty tables.

"Big difference," Sam whispered to Deb. "Let's look around."

"The battleship, obviously." Deb pointed to Battleship NC moored across the river, then swung her arm to the right, following Cape Fear River. "Memorial Bridge...the marina...and that is exactly where the sun should drop." She pointed to a spot between the battleship and a hotel.

"So that two-top right at the far edge of the roof there will be perfect, don't you think?"

"I have to say it...I'm going to say it."

"What?" Sam scrunched her face into a grimace.

"This view is fantastic, but it's even better than what everyone said." Deb wasn't looking around; she was looking right at Sam.

"Ha ha. Funny, but sweet." Sam flicked her finger toward the bartender. After answering a few questions, Deb ordered a local draft, and Sam a dirty vodka martini. They ordered the veggie rolls and onion fritters.

They chatted about old friends, sports, the university, Wilmington's movie business, and what an adventure it would be to live on a boat in the marina. They discussed how it seemed as though they had been friends a long time, with a level of comfort that didn't seem typical, based on previous relationships.

"I wonder if age, or maybe lived experiences, helps break down barriers," Sam offered after she scanned the horizon again. "Time flies, you know, and you realize there isn't going to be much left."

"I was just thinking that earlier." Deb nodded in agreement. "I mean, I'm not getting any younger. And you're the first date I've had in a year. Shit. Too fast?"

"I never would have slept with someone on a second date, years ago."

"Yeah, that was a different time too, though, wasn't it?" Deb thought back to group dates. Talking on the rotary telephone. She chuckled. "I wouldn't have either. I mean, could that have even presented itself back then? There'd always be a car full of us on those group dates."

"You're right. I had totally forgotten those. And then maybe it was all girlfriends, and you wouldn't have room if you spotted guys you liked."

"Same at softball games. We'd all go out together, but you'd have to be home at a certain time for work the next day. You didn't play sports, Sam?"

"Nah. I was babysitter while they were at work. Then bus driver when I got my license. I didn't do much of anything until I went to college. Even on my own, though. I really had to know someone, bring them home a few times before I'd have sex."

"We're way beyond that now, I guess, but I sure don't regret any of our time together, so far." She smiled as Sam shook her head. "Can I say something about last night?"

"Sure. It was effing hot," Sam said, audibly sighing.

Deb's squinting from the afternoon sun obscured her smile. "It seems so much harder to hold myself up now because of my knees, so I thought spooning would help my discomfort. I loved having you close that way."

"Wow. No problems from my perspective. Oh my God, I volunteer for any other ideas you have." Sam dropped her head backward and blew out a breath. After a moment, she slowly raised and cocked her head sideways. "I could so kiss you right now."

"Likewise." Deb reached across the table and touched Sam's hand lightly.

"You know I feel that somewhere other than my hand, right?" Sam teased.

"Mm-hm. Noted." Deb reached under the table and raked her fingertips on Sam's leg.

"Jeez. If there weren't people around," Sam sighed. She sucked in through her teeth as her chin slid off her hand. "Oh my God. I cannot believe that. I am on fire." She downed the remainder of her martini in a gulp.

"Yeah." Deb sat back in her chair with a slight smirk.

They settled up as the sun moved lower, its reflection painting oranges and reds in the sky. Deb noted the golden light and pale pink on the tips of the clouds as they stood. "Beautiful," she said softly and lightly brushed against Sam's side. "You. And the sky."

Sam sighed and Deb followed her to the elevator, where the presence of two other couples put their antics on hold.

When they slid into the Tacoma's seats, Sam pulled at Deb's arm. Deb quickly looked around and kissed her. Slipping her tongue in, she found Sam's.

"You are so fuckin' hot." Sam slowly slid her hand from Deb's thigh to her crotch. Deb whispered into Sam's mouth. "I have to have you soon." An approaching car that parked two spots down brought them back upright and into reality. "Fuck. I need to make love to you. I am on fire right now." A couple exited the other car and disappeared around the side of the garage.

Sam slipped her hand along Deb's shoulder and toward the front of her shirt. Deb grabbed Sam's wrist and pulled her closer. *Not yet. I'm not ready, but is that fair to her?* Deb wasn't sure this self-chat was helping to convince herself it was okay to wait.

"I want to feel you, Deb. You're driving me crazy, making me wait. Why don't we go back to your place for a while. I—"

"Hey now. I don't mean to be a spoilsport, but we gotta get out of here. Your mom's expecting you, right? And the next time we're together, I'd like us both to be all in. Deal?"

"Yeah, I guess she is. Okay. I'd love to…" A beat passed before Sam spoke. "Shit. Never mind. You're right."

There was silence almost the entire way back to Bea's apartment. She wondered if Sam was pissed or simply trying to shift from lover into daughter mode. Deb purposefully left the truck running, and a feeling of relief washed over her. A little more time would make it easier, right? "Here we are. What time is the get-together on the stairs tomorrow?"

"Jeez. You're really going to leave me in this state? Cold." Sam grinned. "I wish I could come there for a while, but you're right. I've got some mom chores before tomorrow."

"I know. And yes. I can be cold, but you know it's for the best tonight." She chuckled. "So, what time tomorrow?"

"Cold." Sam shook her head. "Oh my God. Cold...come around five. Four-thirty or five. You're never quite sure when they'll all make their ways here, but it's right there on those steps." She pointed at the top of the outdoor stairwell's stoop. "Text when you get here. I'll let you in. You can meet Mom, then we'll hang out with the girls on the steps. Okay?"

"Sure. Your lips are something else, you know?" Deb teased. "Can't wait till I taste you again."

"Stop. Really. Stop. I had a really nice time. I mean...fuck. Really nice. See you tomorrow." Sam gave a quick wave as Deb backed out of the spot and slowly drove toward the complex's entrance. Deb looked back before turning out onto the road and saw Sam still standing in the doorway. *Crap. You realize what you're getting yourself in for. You'd better brace yourself. But she isn't like the others...is she? Please, not like the others.* The churn of concern wrestled in her stomach, and she let out a deep, long sigh. *She's not like the others.*

Chapter Six

SAM COULD NOT BELIEVE it was another gorgeous day for riding. She left her mother's by seven to be on the road by eight, hoping some rush hour and school traffic had passed. If only she could ride right to Deb's door and make her late for work. *Nah, not cool, but she's definitely in places other than my head.* "Oh, yes you are," she said aloud. *Pretty sure you're in my heart too. Geez. Could this be true?* She knew it could be, but was she crazy? *What business does someone my age have to start a romance? Much less a sexual one. Crap, Avery. You can barely turn in bed without something cracking or popping. And you groan when you get out of the car. Shit. And you're considering upending your life for someone you've just met.*

Simply the thought of Deb holding her—shit, even looking at her—made Sam sigh...or more. Still, there was something off in Deb's seeming reluctance to allow Sam to pay her that same attention. Lovemaking was incredible. *But when do I get a chance? Those kisses. God, those kisses. Her hand. I want to make love to her.* Sam blew out a huge sigh. "Get on the bike! And pay attention, would ya?" She looked around to make sure no one heard her self-admonishment.

At the usual lot, she put the parking pass on her dash, checked her bike lights were on, and headed to the north end. That quick ride up and around the loop that faced Shell Island helped her verify that she had everything she needed and that everything was adjusted properly. As she approached her lot, she thought she saw someone at her car door. She pulled her key fob out of her back jersey pocket and hit the panic button. They scrambled away and into a car that pulled quickly out of the lot, tires squealing.

She turned in and looked through her window. Everything was how she'd left it. She always locked up, and there wasn't much to be seen in the 2003 vehicle. Others out riding or surfing might leave some sort of valuables in their car. Sam traveled as lightly as she could, and anything important would have been in her back bag or her pockets. She cursed herself for not doing a better job of identifying the car that sped away. Some nondescript black sedan, probably mid-2000s, maybe a Corolla or a Camry. She thought Toyota but couldn't be sure.

She noted a camera on a pole in the lot and jumped back on the bike, heading south. *Should I call the police, or Deb? You'll see her; just keep riding. Maybe, just maybe, they'll be able to check video.* If she didn't see Deb, she could always head to the police station after the ride. *What could they do, anyway? And does the camera even work?*

A light crosswind was blowing from the ocean onto land. When it gusted, she watched her speed drop a mile and a half per hour on her computer. She used that as her riding challenge today. Keep her speed at twelve. Regardless how many miles she rode—eight or twenty—she would feel that workout.

She loved the ocean, but she loved this island. Memories flooded her as she rode. Her great-aunt and uncle had lived on Lumina Avenue when she was a child. If their house was still standing, it had been remodeled in such a way it was no longer recognizable. *How many summers have I spent here? Too many to count.* One of her cousins, David, still lived there. It dawned on Sam that Deb might have known him and probably did know David's youngest daughter, Eleanor. *Didn't Deb say she knew most anyone who'd lived here for that long?* Eleanor and her husband kept up David's old place, renting both floors. Occasionally, Sam rode by there. The building was on a side street, and Sam wouldn't meet her speed challenge if she were looking at scenery.

The beach supply store used to be quite a place when Sam was young. Back then, it was called Newell's. Her great-aunt and grandmother had worked at the Atlantic Coastline Railroad. When Seaboard and Atlantic merged, operations moved to Jacksonville, Florida. Bea would take Sam and her siblings to the train station downtown, from time to time, to drop the women off on their journey back to Jacksonville. Beforehand, they would go to Newell's and buy bags of penny mints—white, soft mints rolled in foil-coated paper of various colors and wrapped with clear cellophane. Geez, she loved that candy. She remembered clearly, Grandma and Auntie waiting to board the train, and the kids handing a bag of mints to each of them to take with them. She still pictured Grandma crying as she waved goodbye through the train window. Auntie would wave and smile. A walk to that store with a dollar in her pocket was a mighty good feeling. Everybody who worked at the store knew them and knew who to call if there was any trouble. Though, of course, there was none.

Weren't times simpler then? All those walking trips from David's or Auntie's to Robert's or Newell's. Just a few short blocks gave such freedom. Her baggy shorts were styled much like painters' pants. Early cargo pants, with pockets full of penny—yes penny—prizes out of the gumball machines. She'd collected the little plastic doodads—seahorses, dogs, hamburgers. Occasionally, she got lucky with a Beatles photo on a button pin or a slingshot. Her pants almost slid off her, they were so heavy with swag. She chuckled. Dang, that was a wonderful time. What a contrast to now. She couldn't imagine letting Sasha have that much freedom. Time seemed heavy somehow. *And you want to start a friggin' love fest. Now? At your age?*

Sam was lost in those thoughts, when a black SUV pulled out from one of the parallel spots past Chadbourn. Just in time, she noted in the vehicle's side mirror that the woman driving was talking on her cell. Obviously, the woman did not notice Sam's flashing white light. Sam slowed abruptly and prepared to stop as she pressed her high-pitched, piercing horn. Red brake lights and a startled expression let Sam know the woman heard, then saw her. The woman waved her apologies.

Sam thought of the bumper sticker, *Shut Up and Drive*. She also realized that, had she not been lost in her thoughts, she may have better anticipated the woman's move. *Mental note. Pay attention. Remember?* When she turned left onto Waynick at the Blockade Runner, Sam identified what looked to be one of the parking UTVs approaching from behind. When she saw in her mirror that it was Deb, she pulled off the road. Deb stopped behind her.

"Out early. Beautiful," Deb said.

"It is beautiful. The gusts are puttin' a hurtin' on my speed, though, so I'm trying to outrun it. Grateful to have a little break." She tilted her head sideways, squinting as she looked back toward the sun.

"I didn't mean the day, although it is. I meant you, silly." Deb chuckled.

"You're sweet to say so. Thanks." Sam shook her head and blushed. She couldn't remember the last time she had received so many compliments. Mom's didn't count, of course. She always gave Sam some sort of compliment...usually about her dimple looking like her dad's, or her beautiful curls, when her hair had been long enough to curl. These felt different, no doubt. Butterflies in her stomach. Warmth elsewhere. Not just where her face or neck reddened.

"I gotta head on down to check those meters at the end. Maybe I'll see you there."

"Hey. I guess I can tell *you*. Tell me what to do. I saw someone casing my car down there. I was doubling back, after riding north around the circle. I happened to see them and was able to push the key's panic button. Looked like a guy that jumped in a black sedan and squealed out of the lot. Don't know if the camera works, but it was quarter to nine. Then, near Chadbourn Street, a chick in a black SUV almost pulled out into me. Maybe not my day to ride, eh?"

"Dang. Be careful. We've had a couple of reports of break-ins in the lots. Thanks, though. We're trying to build a good description. Just not enough intel yet. Hey, if I don't see you before, see you this afternoon. You really are hot in that Lycra, I gotta say." Deb walked back to the UTV and drove off. Sam just waved, glad to have a bicycle seat between her legs at that moment, to tamp down any reactions to Deb's flirtations.

* * * *

Sam showered, had fed her mom lunch, checked her mail, and helped her with a bath. She was folding two loads of her mom's laundry while telling her that Deb was coming over. A text pinged, and Sam looked at her phone. It was four-thirty, and Deb was in the lot.

"She's here now. I'm going to let her in."

"I'll keep folding," Bea said.

Sam opened the outside door. "Hey, welcome." Sam waved Deb in and led her to the apartment.

"Mom, I want you to meet my friend, Deb Martin. Deb, this is my mom, Bea Avery."

"Mrs. Avery, very nice to meet you. Sam tells me you were born here in Wilmington. And that she was too. You just don't meet too many native Wilmingtonians anymore," Deb extended her hand to Bea.

"Saw you eyeing those photographs on your way in." Bea pointed toward the shelf across the room. She stood, then quickly sat. "Oh Sam, you tell her who everybody is. My legs just aren't working right. What can you expect when you're almost ninety?"

"This is my baby brother, Tom, his daughter Sasha, and his wife, Sagal. Then this ol' guy is my brother, Jeff. He's the one that lives, most of the time, in the Philippines."

Deb picked up a black-and-white photo and turned it toward Bea. "And who are these cutie pies?"

"Aww. I love that photograph." Bea's face lit up.

"That's Dad there, giving Mom one of his wonderful hugs." Sam's dimple mirrored her dad's as she spoke.

"Oh, and I do miss those hugs...and that dimple. Sam told me you two have been going out. She said—and I can tell it too—that you used to have auburn hair. I can tell by the freckles. Just like her daddy. Blue eyes, red hair, but he was fair, like Sam. I always was amazed with fair skin that tans." She pointed to Deb's arm, then looked Deb in the eyes. "I hope she told you I'm partial to redheads." Sam cringed. Her mom made no bones chatting up Sam's dates. After all these years, she wasn't surprised, but still amazed. They didn't grow up in a time when homosexuality was accepted, yet her mom always acted as if it were the most normal thing in the world.

"She did tell me that." Deb smiled. "Here, let me help you fold." She sat down on the couch and began pulling towels out of the basket. The three of them sat folding, making neat stacks that Sam put away.

"Do you have any siblings, Deb?" Bea handed Deb a folded facecloth to add to the stack.

"No ma'am. Only child. Likely spoiled rotten, too. And my mom died pretty young. Late forties. Then I think Dad just kind of gave up. He died pretty young, too. Younger than I am now. That's pretty young, right?"

"Yes, it is. In case you haven't noticed, the older you get, the younger young folks look. Yeah, mid-fifties to seventy looks pretty young to me, too." Bea laughed and Deb joined her.

"Exactly."

"Mom, the two Barbs, Peg, and Ida all used to play softball. So did Deb. Deb thinks she may have played with Peg and one of the Barbs. We're going to join them out on the steps in a few minutes. Can I get you anything before we go outside?" Sam placed a glass of iced tea and a pill cup on the table in front of her mom. "Here's your afternoon Tylenol."

"Oh, thank you. No, I'm fine. That's all I need. That sounds like fun for you gals. Did I eat lunch?" Bea asked.

"You did," Sam replied. "A barbecue sandwich, slaw, and some baked beans. Then you had a piece of pie for dessert. And you took all your lunch pills." Sam took in a deep breath. It was so hard to see her mom's decline. Seemingly vital and alert one minute. Then confused and debilitated a few minutes later. Mostly the latter.

"I don't remember," Bea replied softly, shrugging.

Sam grabbed two beers out of the refrigerator, two foam can coolers from her mom's cabinet, and opened the door to head out.

"Mrs. Avery, it was nice to meet you. Maybe I'll see you again soon."

"I hope you do. Now y'all be sweet." Bea always smiled with her typical message to anyone who was departing. The apartment door closed behind them.

"She's a doll, Sam. I saw the photos of her and your dad on the wall. Your smile is just like your dad's. And the dimple." Deb pushed back against Sam's shoulder. Sam quickly checked the hallway was empty.

"See. You only touched me, and I am on fire for you now. And yeah, I definitely am his daughter." Sam just shook her head as she pushed open the fire door to the stairwell landing.

As soon as the door closed, it opened behind them, and Peg walked out. "I'll be damned! Deb Martin. What are *you* doing here?" She reached forward, and Peg and Deb gave one another a one-armed hug, each lightly slapping the other's back.

"Peg. It is so good to see you." Deb beamed as if she had seen a long lost friend. As Peg and Deb moved down a few steps, the door opened again. "Ida? Is that you?"

"Deb! *Shit*, girl. Where have you *been*?" Ida took her place at the top of the stairwell in the plastic lawn chair next to the smoking chimney.

The two Barbs, Barb and Toots, came up from the sidewalk. Toots squinted and tilted her head as if she was trying to place Deb. "Deb Martin! Dang. It is so good to see you." Everyone started asking Deb questions. "Where've you been? Have you retired?"

"Woah. Slow down, y'all. I met Sam here down at the beach. I work in the parking service down there."

"So, you retired from teaching?" Ida asked.

"Yes. The parking job is seasonal, so I have winter months off. And it's only part time, you know, just for a little extra."

"This reunion definitely deserves a toast," Peg said. Everyone popped open their cans—beer or soda—and toasted. "To friends, old and new," Toots exclaimed. "Hear, hear," rose up from the small group.

"Here goes..." Deb turned to Sam. "Barb, Toots, and Ida all played for Caldwell-Polk Mortuary, best team in the league, every single year we all played. Peg and I were on another solid team, the Cardinals, playing for the Third Street Pub. We might have won a game or two against them, but never could sew up the league title. Dang, they were good."

"We sure were." Ida chuckled, holding up a power fist. Everyone laughed and nodded.

"Deb. I haven't seen you since you had to have surgery. I had always hoped to see you at the games from time to time." Peg seemed genuinely concerned. Sam looked at Deb's face and tried not to give away her feelings.

"Yeah, it took a while to be able to move my arms the way I needed to. And my knee keeps me from running. I do some cycling now. And fishing, just like always, but I think team sports are history for me, even in the senior league. Especially with my knees. I had a replacement too. I'm good, though, Peg. Thanks for asking." Sam tried to read Deb's face but couldn't glean anything meaningful regarding a surgery other than her knee.

"How long has it been, Deb?" Toots asked.

"Two years. All good so far." Deb raised her can again. "To us, the oldies!" Everyone laughed and took slugs from their cans.

"Ida, I swear the last time I saw you, you were pregnant. Is that right?"

"Yeah, Deb. Bring that up. You always so skinny an' all." Ida laughed and pulled out her phone. "Here. That's, Dotty, my daughter, the one I was pregnant with, and her little girl, Nita. If I was pregnant, you see how long it's been."

"Dang. It really has been a long time. They're beautiful. Not that I would have expected anything less. And your husband left, I heard from Peg, maybe."

"We left him, you mean. Kicked the sucker out. Wouldn't work. Wouldn't lift a finger. Like the entitled asshole he always was. Then wouldn't send child support. Good riddance. I mean, I wouldn't change a thing about Dotty and Nita. Best things that ever happened to me. For that, I'm grateful to him, but after Dotty. Shit." The head shake was nothing but pure disgust. "Gotta have a man for something, I guess, but y'all always knew I could swing both ways."

"What ever happened with your ex, Toots?"

"Shit, Deb. You know she was five years younger. Once I hit fifty, she wanted the young ones. Started up a thing with one of the younger softball gals, a catcher."

"Sorry I brought it up." Deb flipped her hand at the wrist.

"No worries. I must admit I got some satisfaction in all that. Soon as she hit fifty, her little gal started up with the wanderin' eye herself. Left her high and dry." Toots laughed. "You know she had the nerve to call me up, like I was going to soothe her wounds. Shit."

"With all y'all living here, nobody's found any non-softball sistah friends?"

"Oh, yeah. There are a few," Barb answered.

"She's right. They're in the closet, though," Peg added. "Damn shame people still feel they gotta live that way. Surely, their kids gotta know."

The conversations settled down, and the Barbs and Ida excused themselves. Sam had learned more about her mom's neighbors in an hour than she had in the past ten years. Peg waited until the others were gone.

"I'm really glad to see you here, Deb. Now that Sam comes by fairly often, maybe we'll see you more. I missed you. I just had a hard time reaching out, you know?"

"Yeah, I do. I know, when your sister died, that was a rough time. You didn't need any more reminders. Totally get it, Peg. You were there when I needed it the most. That's what's important, right? It was really good to see you too." Deb stood and put her hand on Peg's shoulder. "Don't be a stranger anymore, okay?" Peg stood up, hugged Deb, and disappeared inside.

Sam looked up at Deb. "So…"

She was hurt somehow, but she shouldn't be. Sam knew if Deb wanted to discuss whatever surgery it was, she would…eventually. They hadn't been dating long enough to feel entitled, but it needled her nonetheless.

"So, I'm gonna scoot myself, Sam. I can't believe all those crazy ladies live right here. We had some good times back then." A beat passed. "I'm glad you asked me here. I really am. And I loved meeting your mom. Okay if I call you tomorrow?"

"I hope you do." Sam looked into Deb's eyes for something. It seemed as if Deb was looking at her lips. A smile broadened.

"There it is." Deb pointed at Sam's mouth. "You are…those lips…mmm. I gotta get out of here." Deb leaned and put her hand on Sam's upper arm, slowly moving it down to her elbow. "I could so—" She looked down, turned, and walked down the steps. At the bottom, she looked back up at Sam. "I'm not just going to call. I want to see you. Please keep your calendar clear."

Sam laughed loudly. "That'll be *real* tough." Sam gave a little wave as Deb pulled out. She leaned against the brick wall with her arms folded in front of her. *What was that all about?*

Chapter Seven

NO MATTER HOW SAM rolled things around, she could not quite figure out why Deb had left something so seemingly important out of their life discussions. Those odd comments Deb made about Sam changing her mind if they were intimate might be related. She thought of how Deb had left on most of her clothes when they made love. Worry was eating Sam up. It was after eleven, and she knew Deb would be asleep, but she knew sleep was not coming to her.

"Fuck it." Sam got up and pulled a pair of khakis on atop her sleep shorts and an Oxford shirt over her sleep tank. She slipped into her low-slung clogs. Bea, surprisingly, had turned in early, and Barry was crooning. Sam pushed the door open just enough to peek. Bea was in her typical sleep position, and Sam noted the rhythmic rise and fall of shoulders that indicated sleep. She couldn't just leave though, so she left a note for her mom.

I'll be at Deb's. Call my cell if you need anything.

Regardless of how brazen it might seem, she had to see Deb. Sam had so wanted the kiss that never materialized that afternoon. And she wanted to ask Deb what Peg meant. Deb had to know Sam was curious. She pulled in behind Deb's truck, making sure her car wasn't blocking anything. All Deb's lights were off. She texted Deb, *Downstairs. Can I come up?* After five minutes without a response, she got out of her car, closed the door carefully, and locked it. She slowly walked up the wooden steps. She texted again. *Wake up. I want to see you.* This time, the stairway light came on.

"Jesus, Sam! What are you doing?" It was clear Deb had been fast asleep, and a crease ran from her left cheek all the way across her forehead.

"I hate that I woke you, but I can't sleep. Can I please come in?" Sam pleaded.

"Get in here." Deb shut the door behind Sam. "What? Because you can't sleep, I don't get to either? Jeez. *What?*" she spewed, obviously irritated.

"Do you really not know?" Sam couldn't believe Deb wouldn't understand why she was there. "Please talk to me." Sam heaved something akin to a groan and stiffened her arms at her side.

Deb stepped forward and pulled Sam into her arms. Sam melted and thought she might slide to the floor with Deb's touch. Then, putting her hand on Deb's oversized tank, she said in whispered exasperation, "You don't wear things like this when I'm with you, Deb." Deb pulled Sam's wrist to keep her hand from brushing her chest.

"Stop, please." Deb leaned and kissed Sam. "I'm glad you're here," she whispered. "Come on. Will you come to bed with me?" Sam nodded, and she followed Deb to the bed. Sam pulled her shirt off and slid out of her khakis. "You planned for it, eh?" Deb smiled as Sam slid into the bed next to her.

"Not exactly, but I did come directly from my own bed." Deb pulled Sam close, and they kissed again.

"Whatever it is Deb, you have to trust me. You have to. I don't want to be in a relationship where we can't trust one another. Something big. Something. You keep clothes on. You wouldn't let me make love to you. Peg indicated you had some kind of surgery. What is it? Please tell me." It was time. Sam had her theory, but she wanted to know. She wanted Deb to trust her.

Deb pressed her lips on Sam's again, and Sam slid her tongue in to find Deb's. Deb moaned. Sam pressed harder, as their tongues explored. The moans and sighs were guttural, and instinctively Sam reached for Deb's breast. Deb once again held Sam's wrist.

"Wait a second, Sam," Deb whispered. She sat up and slid the tank off and dropped it on the floor. She pulled Sam in to kiss her. Sam kissed Deb and pushed her gently back onto the bed. She laid her head on Deb's shoulder.

"I want you to trust me Deb. Don't grab my arm to stop me, but I want you to feel safe." She kissed Deb again. "I so needed your lips, your arms. It feels so good to be with you." Sam gently traced the scar where the left breast had been. "Is the scar still tender?"

"Almost never anymore." Deb's voice was almost quivering. Sam very lightly traced the scar on the right side. "Your surgeon did a good job. You're lucky there isn't a lot of bunching." She traced the scar to the breastbone, and drew an invisible line up Deb's chest, neck, chin, and bottom lip. She tipped Deb's head toward her and lightly nibbled her lower lip. Deb moaned lightly, as they continued the kiss. Sam rested her head back on Deb's shoulder.

"I worked on a surgery floor. We got a lot of mastectomies. I'm sorry you had to go through it. Sometimes it's just what must be done. I can't begin to imagine how it would feel to enter the dating scene." Sam gently kissed Deb's chest. "Did you have to have radiation and chemo?" she asked softly.

She could feel Deb shaking her head. "No. My mom was forty-five when she was diagnosed. I mean, back then, we just didn't know quite as much. The cancer was fairly aggressive, but Dad and I begged her to get it all. If we hadn't, I think she would have maybe had the mastectomy and then just let the chips fall. But no, we had to beg and beg. She was so sick, Sam. The treatment ruined her life, then the cancer killed her. It was horrible to watch.

"Around three years ago, Peg's sister was diagnosed. Peg was a wreck watching her sister and best friend slip away. We used to talk quite a bit. She was the one who suggested the testing, because Mom had been diagnosed before fifty. Sure enough, it said I was positive for the BRCA2 mutation. I was just under sixty, so lucky, I guess. I just decided to go for it. Prevention. You know...prophylactic mastectomy." Deb sighed as Sam lightly stroked her chest.

"I was always a tit girl, you know? It was a hard decision because of that. I mean, I sure didn't want to get cancer, but how could I be a tit girl anymore? Stupid, I guess.

"After the second runaway date, I put my dating life in a box and packed it at the bottom of my storage closet. I never thought I would have the nerve to pull it back out," Deb said softly.

Sam gently ran her fingertips across Deb's chest and down her ribcage, around her navel, and down between Deb's legs.

"Oh God," Deb whispered as she sucked in between her teeth. Sam leaned and kissed Deb's cheek, surprised to find the saltiness of tears. Sam wiped the tears from Deb's cheeks, and gently kissed her, as she lightly sucked her bottom lip.

"May I please make love to you?" Sam whispered. Her tongue found Deb's in a deep hard kiss. Deb pulling Sam's bottom firmly into her wet, warm flesh was her answer. Sam did not neglect Deb's chest; nor did she lavish it. Deb was Deb, with or without breasts. She was still the most incredible lover Sam had ever known. After slow, intense, wet, athletic sex, both collapsed. Sam held Deb, who had backed into her arms. Deb pulled Sam's arm around to her chest, and Sam's leg was between Deb's.

"Sam, I'm sorry. I was so scared," Deb whispered.

"Now you know...you're safe with me." She kissed Deb's shoulder and ran her tongue along the bone, up the neck and to the ear. Deb sighed.

"I keep pinching myself. How did we find one another? You know?"

"Yeah," Sam said, as she turned to her back. "I think I could go another, but if you have to work today, you should probably get some sleep," she said softly.

"Off today. No alarm." Deb turned around to face Sam. "I have to keep this leg straight, but I want to feel you against me." She pressed her warm wetness against Sam, assuming the scissors position. They both sighed loudly.

"Me too." Sam moaned as she stretched her top leg straight out. They rocked and slipped in the warm wetness as they both came.

* * * *

At ten o'clock, Sam slid out of bed and ran to the bathroom. She heard "Me too," from Deb. After Deb returned, Sam rolled on top of her, rocking until she had wedged herself between Deb's legs. She pushed up on her arms to increase the pressure between Deb's legs. Deb moaned softly, "Kiss me."

Sam leaned down to oblige. Deb pulled Sam forward and took Sam's breast in her mouth, gently stroking the nipple with her tongue.

As Sam sighed and closed her eyes, she whimpered lightly. "You can't stop now," she whispered.

"I don't want to," Deb said, pulling Sam into her arms.

* * * *

"I've gotta go back to make sure Mom is up and dressed," Sam said when she was able to speak again. "But I'd prefer to stay right here, at least for a few more hours."

"Sam. Thank you for coming last night. I think..." Deb stopped.

"I'm glad you didn't call the cops or cuss me out." Sam laughed. Then, with a serious tone, she added, "I feel good with you."

"It isn't just the sex, though. Although that is incredible. I feel safe. First time in two years. That is a real gift. I'm really falling for you, Sam." Deb stared at her.

"Hey now. Don't look so scared. You just said you felt safe. Do you?" Sam asked.

"I don't want to scare you off by saying sweet nothings."

"You're fucking hot. And those sweet things are not nothings, I assure you. I think you have some sort of electrical current you're shooting at me when you say things like that. When you kiss me. When you touch me. I'm on the verge of coming all the time when I'm with you...even when I'm not with you. And then something else too. Not sure how to describe it. A pull of some kind...in my stomach. And pressure in my upper chest."

"If you don't think you're having a heart attack, then go see your mom. Come back later, okay? Can you? I promise I'll get up and shower. And change the sheets." Deb gave her an impish grin.

"Oh God. *See what I mean!*" Sam whined softly. When she kissed Deb again, she felt the strong pulsation of a gentle orgasm, and she moaned and fell into Deb's arms again. "Lemme go, so I can come back."

Sam started the car, but she had to sit there a moment. She had known Deb for only a week or so. Why did it seem she had known her for months? Her heart was full, and her stomach had butterflies. She was not a teenager anymore. She was fast approaching sixty-five, and she felt as if this was her first crush. *Am I too old for this?* She took a deep breath in, held it a second, and blew it out slowly before she backed out onto the street and pulled away.

Chapter Eight

THE REALITY OF SAM leaving in only a few days hit Deb like a ton of bricks. *How could she possibly just leave and go back home now? What about Bea? What about me?* Deb adjusted the temperature knob and let the hot shower loosen her stiff muscles. While the sex had been incredible, her bones ached. She soaped her cloth and ran it across her chest.

Sam had not recoiled when her fingers gently caressed the scars. Deb felt fear and grief mix with the salt in her eyes as the tears flowed. She threw the cloth into the corner and drew both hands to her face as she sobbed. Sam had made her feel desirable again, and she was leaving. Not like the others, but still, she was leaving.

"Fuck!" she cried out loud through a sob. She wished she could drop to her knees, but that would hurt. She leaned against the back of the shower, then slowly lowered herself into the tub. The water streamed across her and hid her sobs.

Several minutes passed. She squeezed out her facecloth and blew her nose. She rinsed it, then carefully placed it on the bar under the soap rack and stood. After turning the water off, she pulled her towel in and dried her face, her hair, her neck, then moved on to the rest of her body. She was exhausted. Tired. Pissed. And sad. Oh, so sad.

"Fuck. Why did I ask her to come back tonight?" she admonished herself. She needed time. Time to figure out how not to lash out at this woman who had done nothing but make her feel alive again. Why did she have to feel alive again? She wanted to go back to her routine. Not feeling. Not feeling ugly. Not feeling desirable. Not feeling excited. And for fuck's sake, not feeling in love. In love with someone who was fucking leaving. She knew Sam would sense something was wrong. She couldn't act as if there weren't. What was she going to do?

Trying to pretend that busying herself would help, she put clean sheets on the bed, freshened the water in the daisies, swept the porch, vacuumed inside, and dusted. "Not helping," she said aloud to herself. She slammed the porch door shut as she stepped out into the humid morning. "Not helping." She stood at the porch's edge, leaning against the rail, watching the clouds, and breathing in the saline air. "Maybe helping a little." She closed her heavy eyes, which stung from lack of sleep and crying.

A deep honk drew her out of her thoughts. She opened her eyes to the beautiful great blue heron standing on her bulkhead again.

"Hey! You came," she said softly. "You knew, didn't you? Help me figure this out, friend." The bird watched, but didn't move, except for the occasional primp. Deb considered the things Angela would ask if she could talk to her right now and what truthful answers would be. Deb's thoughts answered that no one ever knows what is to be. Answered that life is short and precious. She 'heard' Angela say, *Deb you deserve to have this experience of love like you haven't known before.* "Yeah. Okay," Deb said softly. With another honk, the bird spread its wings and flew north down the channel. "You always know. Best friend ever," she whispered as the bird disappeared. *Helped a lot.*

Deb sat on her lounger and let the back down. Relaxing in the sun's warmth, her joints didn't feel quite as stiff. She drifted off easily.

Deb dreamt that Sam was kissing her, softly. Full, luxurious kisses. She moaned.

"I wasn't sure you were awake. I can't see your eyes," Sam's voice whispered. Deb questioned whether her early evening stupor was a dream at all. She opened her eyes to find her porch screen rolled down, casting a muted shadow. Real or dream, Sam placed a glass of ice water on the table beside Deb's chair. "I don't know how long you've been out, and I wasn't sure if you had on any sunscreen, so I rolled the shade down. You must be thirsty. It's hot."

"Hiya. I was having the nicest, most incredible dream," Deb said. "But then it wasn't a dream. Still incredible though." She sat up and gulped half of the water without a pause. "Thank you."

Sam reached to lightly rest her hand on Deb's forearm. She gently stroked up and down. Deb raised the back of the chair, and they both sat looking north across the water, avoiding the fierce sunlight now streaming in between the shade's edge and the horizon. Deb felt such warmth inside, all grief and fear now a distant memory.

"Everything good at Bea's?" Deb asked softly.

"Yeah...you know." Sam shrugged, both gazing steadily forward.

"Can you stay this evening?" Deb hated asking, and she hoped she didn't sound needy.

"Yeah. I brought a toothbrush and some clothes this time."

"Good. Because I sure do get tired of seeing you in the same clothes you had on the day before."

"What*ever.*" Sam gently pinched Deb's arm, then resumed stroking.

"You know, I really am pretty bummed that you're leaving in a few days."

"I am going to miss you, but I miss my home, too. Sometimes, when I wake up in the night, I look around to figure out where I am. It's so disorienting."

"It's gotta be hard. I shouldn't even think about myself, but I really want you to stay."

"You *should* think of yourself." Sam continued to stroke Deb's arm. "You're important to me. I hope you know that. Do you get any vacations? Could you come for a visit? It'll only be a few weeks before I come back...maybe a month."

"I could get someone to cover, sure, but no work, no pay, you know. I'm part time. I have insurance through teachers' retirement, but this job is helping to repay my surgery costs. It was considered elective. I've got another year to go."

"I'd love you to come up and spend some time with me there. Will you? I mean, will you consider it?" Both continued to look forward.

"Yeah. I will. It wouldn't be too hard to get a long weekend or a week. In the summer, the kids pick up shifts all the time. They want the money, and they scope the scene. You'd be surprised how that job gives you access to all sorts of gorgeous people getting in and out of their cars in swimsuits...or Lycra."

Sam swatted Deb's arm. "I've noticed you excel in *that* part of your job description." A beat passed. "I'm serious Deb. Come see me. Or sometime when I go back, ride back with me. You can always fly home. You probably wouldn't want to drive on the roads up there anyway, being a flatlander."

"Sam," Deb waited for a response.

"Yeah." Sam didn't turn her head.

"What are you makin' for dinner tonight? I'm hungry."

Sam swatted Deb's arm again. "Me? Hmph. I'm going to walk up the street. You're welcome to join me."

"Hm. Maybe I will. Am I still in that dream where you kissed me?"

"Yes. And it's going to happen again, but don't moan this time. Your neighbors might hear you." With that, Sam stood from the rocker and pulled a stool next to Deb's chair. She kissed Deb firmly, slipping her tongue in to find Deb's. Deb gripped Sam's shoulder to bring her closer. "Oh shit. Oh shit!" Sam pulled away and sat up, grabbing at her lower back. "I can't do that. Crap." They both laughed as Deb stood and pulled Sam to her feet.

"Neither of us are getting any younger. We're really going to have to figure out this being older thing, but hey, let's go take a stroll down the street, and I'll pick back up on that dream later." Deb chuckled.

Chapter Nine

FOR HER FINAL WILMINGTON area ride this trip, Sam wanted a long one—forty miles, she hoped. She decided to ride from a park off the Carolina Beach Road down to the aquarium at Fort Fisher and back. Wade Park, one of the access points on the Cross City Trail, made parking easy and free, something it was not at Wrightsville Beach. No, she wouldn't have a chance of running into Deb, but she really wanted to increase her miles. Sure, she could ride for several hours on the trainer at home, but the scenery of the living room could get boring, even if she were watching recorded television programs or a movie. She needed time and changing scenery, and it was good training. Time amidst vehicles was essential to feeling comfortable on the road. That's just the way it is.

The sky was cloudless, and the wind was light. The high was slated to be seventy-five. So even if the roads warmed the air a little more, it sure seemed like it was the perfect day.

Sam had run by Bea's early after she left Deb's. She sighed a little when she thought of how sweet the night had been. They sat out on the porch and talked until ten, then turned in and went to sleep. Easy. Comfortable. Not even any sex. Just hanging out and being close. She was pretty sure Deb felt the same way. Her good morning kiss from Deb had almost led her astray, but Deb had a staff meeting. There was no time for hanky-panky. Sam chuckled as she thought it was a blessing and a curse.

After Bea's coffee was poured into her carafe, a peanut butter and jelly sandwich plated, a glass of milk poured, and both left in the refrigerator, Sam left a note on the counter.

Hi Mom. Your lunch is in the fridge. I'm doing a long ride down to the aquarium and back. Love you.

Bea was used to Sam's rides. She had been biking for almost thirty years, having participated in several summer weeks of the Bike Ride Across Georgia, a Cycle North Carolina, and a BikeFlorida. Bea had provided support by ferrying supplies and luggage on a few of those rides. What a great sport Bea had been, driving all over kingdom come, meeting Sam at rest stops, dropping her off at starting points, or picking her up at a ride's end. Bea would never be shocked to know Sam was off riding somewhere. "Best mom ever." She chuckled to herself as she pulled into the park's lot.

Sam's safety checklist was complete: lights on, car locked, plenty of water, and a couple of energy bars. She was off at ten a.m. sharp. The turn onto the busy Carolina Beach Road from one of the off streets was, luckily, at a stoplight. And the few more miles of bike lane heading south were a blessing. Business traffic was typical, not at all the beach pace Sam had been used to, so far, on this trip. The ride was good, though. No problems. She pulled into the aquarium parking lot an hour and a half later, and locked her bike, so she could run in and use one of the public toilets before heading back for the return ride.

Back outside, Sam was pulling her gloves on after unlocking her bike, when she felt someone standing a little too closely. She looked up to see what Bea would have called 'a rough looking character' staring at her. His hair was stringy and hanging out from under his beer logo ballcap. He was wearing some slogan T-shirt and jeans. Nondescript but giving off an odd vibe.

"You were riding on that bridge a while ago. I passed you in my truck." He smirked, beer heavy on the breath.

"Yeah, probably was me. Wouldn't ever be hard to pass *me*." Sam adjusted her gloves and checked the brakes and tires.

"Don't take this the wrong way, but your ass ain't small. Aren't you kinda heavy to be riding?"

"It sure helps to ride then. I'm just working off some calories." She adjusted her helmet and swung a leg across the top tube to clip into her pedal...hackles up.

"Why don't you come back to my truck with me? I'd like to see exactly what you feel like in those clothes." He grinned big and put his hand on her handlebars to hold the bike in place.

"Look. My mom is expecting me in a couple of hours. I have got to get back on the road. I have to make her lunch. She can't cook." Sam was coming up with some excuse she thought any person might be able to relate to. She was beginning to feel nervous, even though there were scores of people milling about. She put her hand in her back jersey pocket and double-checked her pepper spray was there. Her hand remained in the pocket, and she looked around to see if anyone was watching.

"So, you think you're too good, huh?" he challenged, giving a light shove on the handlebars.

"Look. I don't want any trouble, okay? Just let me get back to my ride." Sam tried to seem confident. She felt anything but.

"You sound like a lesbo. Look like one too. No wonder you don't want to come with me." He flipped her the bird, hmphed, and walked away, murmuring.

Sam looked around to see if anyone else had seen the exchange. No one appeared to be paying attention. She was somewhat uncomfortable, but nothing had happened, so she clipped in and slowly pulled out of the lot and onto the road. "Situation averted," she said softly to herself. "Whew."

She was riding along, considering the weathered-looking trees of this maritime forest—mostly wax myrtles and live oaks. She had always marveled how dense stands of trees in this area looked as if the wind had sheared off the tops, or just blew steadily with such frequency that the trees looked to be permanently windblown.

She noticed, in her mirror, a truck coming quickly from behind. Nothing unusual on a long ride. As it went by, she felt a strong, painful pop between her shoulder blades. The force of the hit knocked her off balance. She and the bike slid into the sand off the side of the road. Not having enough warning to clip out of her pedals, her thigh landed on the top tube, right at the groin. The truck sped up as it passed. and the horn blared.

"Fuckin' asshole," she yelled when she hit the ground, bike on top of her.

A car traveling in the opposite direction quickly pulled off. A young man jumped out and yelled to see if she was okay. She thought for a minute. Her back was on fire. Tears were streaming down her face. Her groin and leg were killing her. She managed to clip out of her pedals, move all her fingers and toes, her neck, legs and arms. She slowly stood. She nodded.

"I think so."

The young man sprinted across the road and was now holding her bike upright. He was checking the brakes, handlebars, spokes, and spinning each tire. He adjusted the lights that had twisted sideways.

"The bike checks out okay. I ride this route all the time. I've never seen anyone do something like that. I've got a vehicle description, but unfortunately not the plate. The guy had on a ball cap. That's the best I could do. Are you sure you're okay?" The Samaritan was wearing shorts and a T-shirt, ankle socks with a pair of running shoes, and sporting what could be called a military haircut.

"Thanks for stopping," Sam said softly, wiping her eyes with the terry cloth thumb of her glove. "I've had friends hit by cars, but I've been pretty lucky I guess."

"Hey look." He walked back several feet and reached to pick up a dented beer can. "It's still cold and half full. Let me grab a plastic bag out of my car. If it's okay with you, I'm going to empty the beer out, put the can in the bag, and go report this to the police down here. If you'll report it, I'll be your witness. My name is Todd. Todd Yancey."

"Sam Avery. Thanks again for stopping, Todd." She shook his hand. "He harassed me back at the aquarium. Asked me to come back to his truck so he could have his way with me, I guess. I could easily give a pretty good description. He said he was driving a truck. He was wearing a ball cap, you're right. It had a beer logo on it. That's all pretty circumstantial, right? They probably aren't going to run DNA, but if there are fingerprints on the can, he's probably in some kind of database. They may be able to give him a warning, right?"

"Who knows. Maybe more, but worth a shot."

"I'll stop when I make it to town and see if they'll take a report," Sam agreed. "I'll give them the can. Thanks."

"I'm going to head that way now. If you want, I can throw your bike on my rack and give you a lift. If you're able to ride, you can head back on your way. If not, I'm happy to give you a ride or wait with you until someone can come get you. Not everyone is like that guy, you know." Todd seemed genuinely concerned. "And they probably have a first aid kit at the station. Your knee has a nasty patch of road rash. Elbow too."

"I'd really appreciate it. I fell on the top tube. Hit in a not so fun spot. And between my shoulder blade is on fire where the can hit me. Man, it hurts! If I can get back on the bike, I'm going to give it a try after the station. So yeah, a ride there would be great."

"Don't blame you. You'll be sore tomorrow, you know. And maybe worse the next day."

"Yeah. Thanks for the cheery encouragement there, Todd."

He chuckled. "Yeah, I know, but we've all been down at least once, right?" When traffic was clear, he rolled the bike to his trunk rack. She hobbled across the road, trying to feel what was starting to get stiff. She knew she'd never finish the ride if she waited too long. She'd hit hard, and she would probably have that whiplash feeling that comes with a fall. *Swell.*

Todd drove straight to the Kure Beach Police Department. Luckily, one of the officers took the information, the can, and even had one of the female officers come in and take a couple of photos of her back and scrapes. She also offered Sam some first aid supplies. Both officers encouraged her to get checked out at a clinic and have all of her injuries photographed there. The male officer wasn't hopeful, but he seemed earnest and gave Sam and Todd his card. He said to expect to hear from him soon, and gave her a case number. Todd unloaded her bike, held it up one last time and turned the pedal to ensure the gears shifted properly. "I'd take it in and have it checked as soon as you can," Todd advised. "Glad you're basically okay."

"I can't thank you enough for your time, Todd. Good Samaritan Award for sure." She shook his hand again.

"Semper fi, Sam."

"And thanks for your service! My dad was a marine. He would have done exactly the same thing you did. Did it often as I recall from my mom's stories. Even stopped on their wedding night to help at an accident scene. Thanks again, Todd." Sam gingerly threw her leg across her top tube, groaned, and clicked her right foot into the pedal. He walked to his car, cringing in sympathy, and drove away.

A few minutes of riding did seem to help loosen her up a little, but she was not comfortable. "What a way to end a trip. Shit." Somehow, she made it the fifteen miles back to her car. Bike put away on the back of the Element, she groaned as she sat in the driver's seat, hooked her belt, and drove back to Bea's.

Bea voiced concern about Sam's scrapes and bandages but was happy Sam had reported the incident. It was not surprising to Bea that a marine had helped her out. "What a nice young man. That's just like something your dad would have done."

"Exactly what I told him, too." Sam forced a smile.

"Are you going out again, or just resting?"

"I don't feel I can do anything, really, but I haven't talked with Deb."

"Tell her to come here. You're injured. She should come take care of you."

"I'll make sure to tell her you said that." Sam nodded and suddenly felt sad. This was really her last night to spend with Deb. Her brother, sister-in-law, and niece were all coming to Bea's tomorrow for a ta-ta-for-now pizza dinner. Deb might agree to join the "fun," but Sam really didn't know for sure. *No hanky-panky tonight either.* She decided to take a shower before calling Deb. "Not how I wanted things to be tonight. Not at all." As she undressed, she looked at her back in the bathroom mirror. "Ooh. That's going to be a bad one." Her daily aspirin made her more susceptible to bruising, and she could tell it looked red and swollen. "Nice hematoma there, Avery." She wished she could feel how swollen.

Indurated. She thought that was a perfect word for the swelling that occurred with an injury. It sounds painful, even if it isn't. Hers was. If she moved her shoulder or back in a certain way, even the shirt brushing against it would smart. "Ooof." She shuddered at the thought of having to towel dry her back.

The shower was nice, and she felt maybe it would prevent some of the stiffening. She was able to bear the shirt. The bra wasn't a problem, thank goodness, since the can hit just above the strap. She picked up her phone and texted Deb. *Whatcha doin?*

The phone buzzed with a reply text. *Missed you today. Ride?*

Since it was too complicated for a text, she just punched Deb's number to call her. "Hiya," Deb answered.

"Hey. I went for a longer ride today. Out from a park off the Carolina Beach Road to Fort Fisher and back. Just finished my shower."

"That's a long ride. Good? It was a beautiful day."

"It *was* beautiful. Shit, Deb. Some asshole threw a beer can at my back. I fell off the bike, and I am S-O-R-E. Ooh wee. Sore. Big ol' bruise between my shoulder blades—"

"What? Are you okay? Really okay?" Deb's concern was almost palpable.

"The bruise on my back is one thing. I landed on my top tube, right at my groin and top of my thigh. Oh, jeez it hurts! And road rash. And I am gonna be stiff as a board tomorrow."

"Oh no, Sam. I am so sorry. Did you go to a doctor? Is your bike okay?"

"Bike seems fine. This nice marine dude stopped. He was going in the opposite direction, but he pulled off the roadside to check on me. He rides, and he checked the bike's safety—tires, spokes, handlebars, et cetera. Once we left the police station, I rode back to my car. So, I'm alive, and the bike is at least rideable." There was silence for a few seconds.

"Shit. I'm so sorry," Deb said a little too softly. "You probably don't want—"

"I *do* want, Deb. I want to see you," Sam said. "My mood's okay, but I know how sore and stiff I'm going to be. And my back and you-know-what will probably be off limits for a while. Bummer that it is...oh yeah! Mom said you should come *here*. That I'm hurt, and that you need to come take care of me. So there."

"That Bea. She doesn't miss a thing. But you know, I can take much better care of you here."

Sam could hear the warmth in Deb's voice. "Mm-hm. I'm sure you could. I'm so sorry this happened. I had big plans for what I wanted to do with you tonight."

"Me too." Deb sighed. "I had big plans for what you were going to do to me too." She almost sounded sad as she said it.

"Sorry. And tomorrow is family pizza night. My last night here. Would you come have dinner with us?" Sam sounded pitiful enough, but she hoped she didn't sound desperate.

"Hm. If I tell you a proper good-bye tonight, I don't know how I'll feel tomorrow. You know?" Deb said softly.

"I do know. I know exactly. And I'm going to miss you. Now I can't even give you a proper good-bye." There were another few seconds of silence. "Deb?"

"Yeah." A few more seconds.

"I'm really going to miss you," Sam said with a deep sigh.

"So, get your ass here then," Deb teased, trying to lighten the mood. "I've got some mentholatum ointment I can use to give you a good rubdown."

"You're real funny," Sam snarked back. "I'll take a partial rubdown though. Mm. That doesn't seem half bad."

"We'll order in. I'm not sharing you this evening. You're all mine." Deb ended the call. Sam wasn't sure, but she thought Deb was being funny. She hoped so. She sure didn't need any more harassment today.

After redressing her scrapes, she warmed Bea's dinner and poured another glass of milk. "Tom's coming by, right?" Sam asked.

"I don't know. I think so. You're going out though?" Bea was perceptive. "She'd better be nice to you. You're one of my million-dollar babies. And you're hurt." Sam leaned to hug Bea and kissed her cheek. "Now you be sweet," Bea said as Sam walked out the door.

It was hard for Sam to walk down the steps. She realized she must have twisted her right knee in the fall. "Great. Just great," she thought to herself. "Ice and elevation at Deb's. Oh yeah. I'm going to be a lot of fun tonight!"

Chapter Ten

BY THE TIME SHE arrived at Deb's, Sam realized exactly how sore she was. It was a struggle to walk up the stairs, but she used "up with the good" appropriately. It was painful to try to pull hard on the handrail for assistance, and her groin was uncomfortable in the process. "I hate this," Sam said in frustration.

Deb was at the top of the stairs, "Oh no, babe. I'm so sorry. Look at that road rash. How bad is it under the dressings?" She lightly touched a place on Sam's arm where there wasn't scrapes.

"It could be worse. You know what it's like. After a few days, that'll be the stuff hurting. The big purple, pink, and blue blobs on my back and groin will just look bad...maybe a little sore, but the road rash. Ugh. I absolutely *hate* road rash." The concerned frown said it all. "I need to ice my knee. I realized coming down Mom's stairs that I probably twisted it. It happened so fast; I didn't have time to unclip from my pedals."

Deb brought the zero-gravity recliner from the porch into the living room and motioned for Sam to sit. She raised the lower part to elevate Sam's legs and placed a covered ice pack on Sam's knee. The position was not uncomfortable, and Sam smiled. "If I just sit here, I can't even tell I'm hurt. If I'm not moving, it feels okay."

"It's a nice vantage point for me." Deb pulled a chair closer to Sam's head. She leaned and gently pressed her lips to Sam's. "Hiya." She smiled and kissed Sam again.

"Oh God. That feels so good. My lips don't hurt at all." Sam considered the idea that kissing Deb all night long would not be a bad recovery strategy. "Don't stop now. This is the best I've felt all day." She smiled, looking into Deb's eyes. "Although, that's how my day started, isn't it?" she whispered. "Come here and kiss me again."

Sam melted as their lips came together. There was something raw in the kiss this time, and she moaned as Deb found her tongue. The fact that Deb wasn't touching her anywhere else was somehow even more exciting. Sam tried to raise her arms, but she winced at the pressure between her shoulders. If she tried to turn her hips, she felt bruises from the fall. Why not just enjoy the feeling of those soft lips making love to hers? That tongue. Sam's moan became guttural. Deb was ravishing her mouth, and it was more than amazing. It was stupefying.

When Deb began unbuttoning Sam's shirt, she stiffened for a second. Deb gently sucked Sam's bottom lip and then her top lip. She melted again. Deb opened Sam's shirt and stroked her nipples with her fingers, lips never leaving lips. When Deb leaned down and slid her tongue inside Sam's bra cup and enveloped the erect nipple and surrounding flesh, Sam came, moaning loudly through heavy, short breaths. As the pulsing slowed, Sam could only breathe. She pushed out slow, deep breaths peppered with low, guttural sounds. Sam was 100 percent relaxed. She was not moving except to breathe. She was not in pain. Her eyes opened long enough to see Deb looking at her. Sam wasn't sure if she even had any thoughts. She closed her eyes and drifted off to sleep.

* * * *

Deb sat up and removed the ice pack, which she returned to the freezer. She called for some Thai take-out to be delivered and opened a bottle of pinot noir. She poured the wine into a tumbler and inserted a flexible, paper straw. She poured some into a stemmed, red-wine glass for herself. Swirling, then taking in the rich scent, she sipped. *Delicious. Just like Sam. Delicious.*

How am I going to console myself when she leaves? Can I even do that? She looked at Sam's face. Sam was so calm when Deb woke from her nap the other afternoon. Sam instinctively knew what she needed. She thought of how sweet it was to be next to Sam and have Sam stroke her gently. How funny Sam was. And God how she ached with desire when she even thought of her. *Lust generally becomes a smolder at some point; I know that.* She was pretty sure she had moved beyond pure lust. Quickly even. Sure, there was plenty of lust still there, but there was something else also. *Have I already fallen in love?*

At the moment, all that mattered was making Sam feel better. Deb was pretty sure she'd succeeded. She chuckled to herself.

The delivery car brought her back to reality. She hurried downstairs to meet the driver.

After plating the food and setting places, she leaned and touched Sam's lips with her fingers. Sam's lips responded with a kiss, but her eyes did not open. Deb kissed her. "I'm going to tip your chair up, so you can swallow without choking," Deb whispered.

Sam whimpered. "I feel so good right now. I'm scared to move."

"I know, but you know you need to move." Sam's closed eyes and slowly nodding head verified she was ready, if reluctant, to move.

"Can you just please kiss me one more time before you move me?" Deb leaned in, and they resumed the kissing of earlier. Sam moaned again. "You are the most outstanding kisser I have ever known. Your mouth is amazing. What the fuck am I supposed to do when I go home?"

"I have pondered that 'til I'm sick of it. I've freaked out with worry. I can't seem to shake off this sadness," Deb said softly.

"Okay. Push the chair up." Sam winced as the chair forced her chest forward and pelvis back. "Ow. Ugh. Shit. My back...oh...dang that hurts." A tear rolled down her cheek.

"You need to eat. You decide if you can drink. You really need to take some anti-inflammatories, you know. And drink some water," Deb said with concern as she wiped the tear away. She placed a tall glass of water, with another flexible straw, next to the wine tumbler.

"You're absolutely right. If I can eat and drink without triggering trapezius movement, I think I can do it." There was sincere trepidation in her voice as she raised the water glass. After a few deep straw sucks, she groaned. "My neck's beginning to feel that whiplash-type pain. Do you think I should go to a clinic or something? There's a sports-medicine clinic two blocks from Mom's. I hate to do it. I have to pay out of pocket. And they'll want to do a bunch of X-rays."

Deb sympathized with her, glad to have good health insurance for herself. "Just take some ibuprofen or naproxen or something. See how you feel tomorrow." Sam groaned again. She pulled a few large swigs of wine through the straw.

"Yeah. That's another problem," Sam said, sadly. "My stomach burns when I take them, sometimes. Non-steroidal anti-inflammatories are off the table, as a general rule, but...I know that a day or two of them should be okay. After I've eaten though, because of my princess stomach.

"I have to admit, this bike fall has thrown me...literally." Sam actually made an attempt at a chuckle, then groaned. "Don't make me laugh."

Deb leaned and kissed her cheek. "I'm so glad you're not injured any worse than you are." Deb stroked her cheek, then handed her a plate of food. Sam managed to eat quite a bit.

"Ibuprofen, please. Four."

"Comin' right up."

"I'll switch to my trusty acetaminophen in a couple of days. Don't you think a little more wine is okay since my stomach is full?"

"You're the expert, right? I don't know. Doesn't seem to be a good combo, but I guess a little's not a bad thing."

"Deb...thank you for taking care of me. It's sweet. It really feels nice. I'm sorry—"

"Uh uh," Deb interrupted. "We've been around long enough to know this kind of shit happens, but none of this was your fault. You feel secure? I mean...that guy? That shit's scary."

"I guess so. Maybe if I find out nothing happens to him, I'll feel a little more uneasy. What if the investigation ends up with him knowing my name, or worse, name and location. Shit. It's enough just to deal with the physical aspects. I wanted to be with you tonight...really with you, you know?"

"Sure, it would have been nice to have a marathon night of sex or something, but shit. I'm just glad you're here with me and alive." Her hand rested on Sam's arm. "So glad you're here," she said softly.

"Where do we go from here?" Sam asked.

"I know I want you in my life, but we've both lived on our own for so long, you know? We both love where we live. We're used to our routines. We don't answer to anyone. I don't know, Sam." Deb looked down and sighed deeply. She lightly caressed Sam's arm.

"I agree with everything you just said. I've thought of those exact things so many times, but I'm pretty sure I have fallen in love with you, Deb."

Deb was not shocked that Sam said those words aloud and hoped Sam wasn't shocked they came out. Deb leaned and softly kissed her.

"It's weird, though, isn't it?" Deb watched Sam's face for any reaction. "I'm sixty-two, Sam. Did *you* expect to fall in love again? I told myself today that I knew I had fallen in love with you, too. Where *do* we go from here?"

Even after an hour of serious, heavy discussion concerning what it meant to be in a new relationship in their sixties, nothing was solved.

"Except for today, right now, I feel I'm in my thirties....in my mind, anyway," Deb confessed.

"Yeah, me too. My body wants certain things, but I can't always do them anymore."

"I know. It's like the drought of being alone has made me an expert on pleasuring myself. And I guess made me more sensitive to understanding what you might need."

"You're sure a success at that." Sam blew out a breath. "How could we have possibly dredged up that intense libido again?"

"I don't know, but I'm diggin' it." Deb smiled and winked. She willed her face not to betray her sad feelings. Sam would be leaving the day after tomorrow. This was their last night together for who knew how many weeks or months. If Sam's prediction that Tom and Sasha would stay for one of Sasha's summer vacation months was correct, it might be four to six weeks before Sam returned. The heavy sadness pulled her back onto her sofa.

"I guess we just have to see how things go, right?" Sam slowly blew out another breath.

"Suppose we do, yeah. You seem as sad as I feel right now."

"I am, I'm sure." Sam turned her head toward the window.

"Come on. Let's go to bed. I go to work tomorrow, and you need rest and sleep. Your body needs to heal." Deb stood by as Sam figured out how to stand. She slowly pulled herself to one side and motioned for Deb's arm. She lifted herself up, pulling against Deb's arm.

"Oh...this is not good. It's searing pain between my shoulders." As she stood, she began crying and leaned into Deb's body for comfort. Deb carefully placed her hands where she thought they would cause the least pain. She knew Sam's tears were not just from physical pain. She slowly turned Sam and led her to the bathroom to ready for bed. She helped Sam work her clothes off, then slowly helped her under the covers. As she slipped into the other side, she heard Sam groan as she turned to her side.

"Can I hold you tonight?" Sam whispered.

"Yeah. That'd be nice." Deb was glad her back was to Sam. Grateful Sam couldn't see the tears rolling down her face.

* * * *

The next morning, Sam struggled to get out of bed alone, but she managed. Deb was in the shower and getting ready for work. Sam dressed herself and was determined not to seem too debilitated. She understood that the body took a little more to heal from an injury as one aged. She moved her joints. Her knee was surprisingly better. She found her groin moved a little freer than it had yesterday evening., but where the can hit her was still as sore as it could be. Searing pain. At least eight on the zero to ten scale she'd used in healthcare.

Sam waited for the bathroom door to open. Deb stepped out of the shower with a towel across her shoulder. Sam walked up next to her and pressed against her. She melted as Deb put her arms around her, ever so gently. "Hiya. You're getting wet."

"You have that effect on me, if you haven't figured that out," Sam whispered.

"I wasn't talking about that, but you know that already." Deb's grin spread across her face. "You must be feeling better. You feel pretty good to me."

"There you go with sweet nothings again," Sam said sheepishly. "I do." She laced her fingers with Deb's, and they stood together, arms down. Just holding hands. "Deb, I meant what I said last night. And I'm serious. Please see if you can come visit me. I'm not trying to convince you to move up to Nowheresville with me, although I could sure see it. I just want to see you, you know. Share some of my life there with you. Have you meet my friends there. Please come see me at my place sometime." She hoped she didn't sound pathetic.

"Hope to. I'm going to see if I can make it work out sometime in the next few weeks. Just make sure I know when you're coming back. It would be a tragic tale for me to schedule time off to travel when you're planning to come back here."

"It would," Sam agreed. She leaned her head up, grimacing as the invisible knife tore through the flesh between her shoulder blades. They kissed, and Sam lost all track of pain for a moment. She moaned into Deb's mouth, and it was not a moan of discomfort. When Deb slipped her tongue in to find Sam's, she was glad Deb had not dressed. She was sure Deb would be wet and not from her shower.

"I do not want this to stop, but I have to dry off and get ready for work," Deb said softly. She kissed Sam. "God, I'm going to miss you. Call me soon. Okay?"

Sam gathered up her things and pulled the door behind her. She heard the click of the latch and faced certain sadness. She didn't allow herself any tears. No small feat.

Chapter Eleven

SHE COULDN'T DECIDE IF she really had stiffened up and was hurting more than when she walked down Deb's steps, or if she was simply sad. Either way, she felt worse. She worked her way out of her car and stood looking at the outside steps that led to the door into the building. Would it be easier to take the short route up the steps and be at her mom's door? Or would it be better to walk half the length of the building to the main entrance, take the elevator up, then walk that same length back to her mom's door? She dreaded either, but it just made sense to take the shortest route. Stairs. When she started her trek up, the building door opened. Peg.

"Girl! You look like crap. Deb called me yesterday and told me what happened to you. You really should go get yourself checked out at a clinic or something."

"I'm thinking about it. I really don't want to walk back out to the car and drive right now, though. I thought I felt better, but I don't." Sam grimaced.

"I know I don't know you well, Sam, but all I have ever seen is Little Miz Positive from you. Just like Bea. Always roses and blue skies. I'm not seeing that now. Let me drive you to that sports-med clinic. It's a short ride. Let them take a look. If they say soft tissue, great, but if they think you need some X-rays, then let them do it. Come on. Let me take you. I'll tell Deb, and then she'll feel better too."

"Oh, okay. You're right." Sam reluctantly turned around and headed back down the stairs to the parking lot. Peg pointed out her 2005 Corolla. She opened the door, and Sam worked her way in, groaning as she sat. "That place on my back hurts like a mother," she admitted.

In five minutes, they were in the lot down the street. The staff were just opening up, and no one else was waiting. *A miracle.* The receptionist took Sam's information and photocopied her insurance card. "I have to pay any visits out of pocket until I reach $7,900, so I need to know the cost of a back X-ray and the office visit up front. I want your cash price." She had learned to be savvy and ask. The young woman handed her a price list; they must have seen that enough to be prepared. Sam studied the price list, Peg looking over her shoulder. In just a few minutes, she was back in the clinical area, getting weighed, having her blood pressure checked, and giving a quick medical history. The young med tech led her to an exam room and told her the physician's assistant would be in shortly. She pulled off everything but her panties and socks and put on the provided gown, as instructed.

When the door opened, she was surprised to see a beautiful young woman, maybe thirty-two, walk in confidently. "Hi, Ms. Avery. Janice Robeson. I'm the PA here, working under Dr. Davie." She extended her arm. Sam grimaced from the simple contact.

"Whoa. A handshake doesn't warrant that kind of pain. Bike accident, huh?" Janice asked, as she adjusted the height of the stool and sat down at eye level with Sam.

"Not exactly an accident," Sam said slowly. "A guy threw a beer can at my back. It knocked me clear off the road. Didn't have time to unclip. Twisted my knee. Have all this fucking road rash. Oh, shit, sorry. Oh, crap. I'm sorry. And my top tube tried to castrate me," she blurted pointing at the groin.

Janice was laughing, but her face had quite a sympathetic grimace. "It's okay. I would have said much worse. What an asshole! The guy, not you."

Sam smiled. "This was after he tried to get me to his truck in the aquarium parking lot for God only knows what. I was lucky to have a witness to my wreck. He had a description and found the can, and he took me to the police station. They took some pictures, but I think the bruising has increased quite a bit, naturally. The officer there said if I went for medical care to have you guys take the appropriate pictures. He said you can use my phone. I'll send them to him."

"Sure. We don't usually do that, but since it's on your phone and unofficial, I don't mind." Her voice was soothing and kind, and Sam relaxed. "I'll need to look at that place on your back. You okay with that? I mean, alone in the room?"

"Yeah. Sure. I need to know why it hurts. I know you're going to ask, so I would describe it as a searing pain. Seven right now, eight often, on a zero to ten scale. And whenever the trapezius moves, I imagine a heated knife blade tearing my skin between my shoulder blades. It feels better only when I don't move that part of my back. Not even sure that eight hundred of ibuprofen helped."

"You were ready for that, weren't you?" she chuckled.

"I'm a retired RN. I sure know the drill."

"Now, let me pull the gown back...oh crap, that makes *me* hurt! I think I'm going to have to get an X-ray. I'm not sure you don't have a little break or something. I really need to palpate, but I'll try to be gentle."

"If you have to, but I wish you wouldn't. Just know, it hurts like a mother. I'll try not to curse." After a beat, she added, "Or cry." She held her breath, as Janice gently pressed.

"I'm going to start on the edges and go in. I can tell you have a big hematoma, but I want to feel if it's only a soft tissue injury. Okay?" she asked softly.

"Okay." Sam took another deep breath in and held it.

"It's better to breathe, Ms. Avery. Try to relax." Sam nodded at the request.

As Janice neared the center between her blades, Sam let out a high-pitched howl of some kind. She had never heard herself make such a noise. "That really hurts," she said, tears welling up in her eyes.

"Yeah. I need to get an X-ray, Samantha. Okay to call you by your first name?" Janice asked, softly putting her hand on Sam's shoulder.

"Sure, but call me Sam, okay? Samantha is what my mom says when she's mad at me."

Janice chuckled. "Deal. Let me have your phone, and I'll get a couple of shots of that. Now what about that groin injury?"

"Can I defer on that? It feels better than it did yesterday, so I think that'll resolve. I can deal with pain, but not that from my back right now. I iced my knee and elevated. It helped the twist and the road burn. I have knee stuff all the time, so I'm used to dealing with it."

"Sure, but if you want me to take a picture, I'll need to document some sort of information regarding the incident. I hate to ask you, but I think I should examine your groin. The police may really want to charge this guy with battery. Painful looking photos go a long way to help. Your call though." Janice was matter of fact, providing information needed to make a good decision. Sam appreciated that.

"Okay. God, you know when you're a kid, and your mom tells you not to wear underwear with holes, because you might be in an accident?"

Janice chuckled. "I sure do. Always good advice. Do you have holes in your underwear?"

"No. But I haven't showered since yesterday. I'm afraid—"

"Sam. Don't worry. If it makes you feel any better, my allergies are crazy. I can't even taste my food right now. I sure won't be able to smell anything. So there."

"Oh no you didn't!" Sam laughed out loud, then groaned. "Don't make me laugh. I think I have whiplash of the body. It hurts to laugh."

"You do have something like that." Janice nodded, and the grimace showed her sympathy. "Let's look at that bruise."

Sam pulled up her gown and pulled away the crotch of her panties so Janice could see the bruise. It looked worse than it had yesterday.

"Sam. That's pretty bad. I know you don't want a picture of that, but you should send one in. I am so sorry. I know it hurts. I'm not going to touch you, but you push in on your pelvic bone and let me know where it hurts. If you know your anatomy, you know what the ramus, the femoral head, and all those good things are. I want to make sure we don't suspect a small break. I know you want to avoid any additional X-rays. Sorry." Sam pressed at various locations until she found the spot where it hurt the most.

"I don't think the bone area feels particularly sore. It just feels like a big ol' bruise. Maybe the diameter of a quarter? If it gets worse, I can come back, right?"

"Of course. Watching where you pressed, you're probably correct. If it does get any worse, though, I really do want you to come back in, okay? I mean, it's going to look a whole lot worse, right? And it's probably going to travel dependently into your labia and down your thigh. You're describing a nice hematoma. That blood's gotta go somewhere, you know."

"On the bright side, I won't be seeing my lady friend for who knows how many weeks, so there's that," Sam said sadly.

Janice laughed out loud. "Okay then. Let's get the camera show finished, okay?" After she took a picture, she handed Sam the phone. "Now, let's go down the hall here and get that back X-ray. I'm going to have the doc check it out with me. The tech will bring you back to this room. I'll be in shortly after." She held her arm out so that Sam could step down from the table. "Right this way." A young woman in scrubs popped in and led Sam down the hallway to radiology.

When Janice returned to the exam room, she slid the film into the light box on the wall. "See this little spot right here? It's a small crack. That's T4, at the thoracic spinous process. That little crack is what's causing your pain. It's small, but it's no joke. It's going to hurt. It's irritating all the other little nerves around. Luckily, there's no visible displacement. That's great news, but we don't want you to lift your arms above your shoulders for a few weeks. Nothing too strenuous. No lifting heavy objects. You don't want that to move out of place. Pain will be your guide to what you can do, likely. Let's redo the film in a month, unless you begin to hurt more, or you notice numbness or tingling. Sound okay? You don't have any tingling or numbness in your hands or around your torso now, right?"

"None. I have to drive seven...eight hours tomorrow. Can I?" Sam asked. "I'm leaving to go home for a few weeks."

"Oh. I wish you wouldn't. Wait a day or two, at least. I'm giving you some pain meds. No driving if you're still having to take them. You'd probably be okay, unless you had to brake or twist hard. I'm advising you not to drive for at least a day or two, and I'm putting that in my notes." After a beat she added, "But listen, Sam. If something happens on the road, you have got to go to a doctor and be seen. Likely, your spinal cord is not in danger, but you want that bone to heal in place. Can you come back in a month?"

"Yeah, sure. I come at least once a month to care for my mom. We take turns—my brothers and I. Hey, thanks for your advice...and laughter. Best medicine and all," Sam said.

"Here's a script for five pain pills. That'll get you through a few nights if you need it. I know you want to avoid the NSAIDs, and if acetaminophen gets you through, then great, but you might have some discomfort trying to sleep. Get dressed and get out of here. I'll see you in a month." Janice gave her a big smile and a wink as she closed the door behind her.

When Sam returned to the waiting room, Peg stood up and they walked to the car.

"My advice," Sam said. "If you ever need care, go there. That PA. Mm-hm. Gorgeous. And funny."

"Yeah, that's all hunky-dory, but what'd she say? Did they do X-rays?"

"They did. I have a slight break of one of the bones of my spine."

"You should've led with that." Peg's curt response indicated she was peeved.

"I know. I'll call Deb and let her know. I can't leave for a few days...or as long as I'm on prescription pain meds."

"I have to say...the thought of that beautiful woman at the clinic touching you is wiping out any frustration I have with you right now." Peg chuckled.

"Haha," Sam said. "Let's hope the pictures don't go up online." They both laughed. "Oof. Laughing is not my friend."

"I bet."

"You know, Peg. I really appreciate your support here. And the push to go be seen. It really is taking a load off my shoulders...so to speak."

"I love your friend. I don't want her to ever have to suffer another moment....and I know she would be worrying. You're kind of growing on me too." She chuckled again.

Sam reached and gave Peg a light tap on the arm. "Oof. Guess that'll teach me."

Chapter Twelve

SAM FELT LIKE CRAP, but she opted to continue with the family pizza-night plan. On previous visits, they had been used to her cooking every night. She'd been MIA most nights of this trip, since meeting Deb. She ordered the usual, two large pizzas from the nearby joint. One vegetarian, and one with meat for Sasha and her mom. Sagal had come to the United States from Nigeria more than twenty years before Tom met her. Once they felt emotionally and economically prepared, they planned for Sasha. Sam was Sasha's godparent and had taken her on trips to Maine and New York City. Last year, Sasha had come to stay a week at Sam's house in the mountains. Sam truly loved having these small, family get-togethers at least once during her stays at Bea's.

"Hey, Tom, do you mind picking up the pizzas?" Sam asked. "I just don't think I'm ready for another outing today. This is plenty of activity."

"Sure thing, boss. Back in a few."

"They're already paid for and ready."

"Just fire up MSNBC, so I can catch the latest scoop when I get back."

Bea had gone to bingo, but they all knew she'd be back soon. It was good to hang out. The family had always been close. Sasha was used to climbing all over Sam, even though she was heading toward her ninth birthday. She seemed frustrated that she couldn't use Sam as her personal mattress, but when Sam showed them her back, they all gasped.

"Are you going to die, Sam?" Sasha seemed worried. "That bruise looks really bad."

"Nah. It's just a little broken bone. It'll heal up if I follow the doctor's orders."

"Okay."

"You're a sweet child." Sagal hugged her daughter and pulled her close. "How do you think your mom is doing, Sam?"

"She's declining. You see it. We all see it, but as long as she's safe being here, I can't see moving her."

"It's stressful for Tom. He's so tense when he comes back from getting her settled for the night. He told me that he and Sasha are going to spend June here, so you can have a real break."

"He offered that—"

"Yay! You sure you won't miss me, Mama?"

"I'll miss you, but maybe I'll get some sleep while you're visiting Grandma." Sagal laughed as Sasha play-slapped her arm. "It's a good time for you to get to visit with Grandma, and help your dad help her."

"Okay." Sasha immediately picked up her tablet, already tired of the discussion.

"I'd really like Deb to come visit me for a week or so."

"Mm-hm, I bet you would." Sagal raised her eyebrows in a tease.

"C'mon now. You can't even imagine what it's like to have found someone who gives me the time of day, much less seems to find me attractive at this age."

"You are attractive, Sam." Sagal drew a shapely body through the air with her hands.

"You're a babe," Sasha added, not looking up from her tablet. Sagal and Sam laughed.

Tom pushed through the door with pizza boxes in hand. "Okay, large box is veggie; small is meat. Dig in." He picked up a paper plate and served himself before parking in a chair at the table facing the television.

After the group left, Sam washed a few dishes. She knew as the oldest, and the woman to boot, most of the housework fell to her. Just as it had since Bea taught her how to wash dishes. She figured they all had their strengths, though. Female personal care stuff, cooking, cleaning—her duty. The woman and the nurse. No-brainer according to the guys. Tom was more of a hands-on-worker type. Trash, plumbing issues, heavy moving. Jeff was the organizer. Sorting through and thinning Bea's magazines, photographs, her VHS collection. He'd organized important papers for Sam. *We're really a good team.* Still, she was glad they'd used paper plates.

She had a little buzz from the wine Sagal brought. They had all been trying to make her feel better and knew her affinity for wine with dinner. It wasn't half bad.

Bea returned from bingo, deposited her mail at her place on the table, and started reading her *Guidepost.* Barry Manilow was already crooning from the bedroom speaker down the hall. Sam figured she should take one of the pain pills and head to bed. It was only eight o'clock, but she felt pretty wiped out.

When she retired to her room, she started organizing her various items into neat stacks for packing up. Bea called to her, which was unusual. Sam walked into the living room, and Bea looked her straight in the eyes. "Deb didn't come for dinner tonight."

"No. We said good-bye last night. I expect I'll get a call a little later."

"But you were in so much pain last night. You need to go see her or call her or something. She'll want to be sure you're okay." Bea's seriousness seemed earnest and heartfelt. She always had motherly words of wisdom. One thing her mom always said was to never go to bed without setting straight any issues, especially after fights. Tonight was no different, though there certainly had been no fight.

"Samantha. I have not seen you so crazy for someone since your early days with you-know-who in Maine. Now go and tell her good night. You know I'm all right. You don't leave at the crack of dawn anymore, so you have time to come by in the morning and get packed up if you're still leaving tomorrow. Now go on." She was so insistent. Sam walked around the table and leaned the best she could, giving her mom a hug.

She grabbed her purse and keys and headed out the door. She was halfway down the steps when she remembered she had been in pain. *That's weird. It's not too bad right now.* She slid into the driver's seat and headed to the beach. She felt odd; everything seemed foggy. She pulled into Deb's, but the stairway light was on. She couldn't see any of the usual inside lights, but the truck was there. Maybe she had walked to her hangout. She pulled out her phone and texted, *U home?*

A few minutes later, a text returned. *No. Having a drink.*

Later then, Sam texted back. She became a little irritated that she had driven all that way. "Shit, I'm not gonna wait around here." It hit her then, as she swayed and held on to the Element's door. "Oh crap. I'm high." She started chuckling. "Then I'll just go find her."

She walked down Deb's street and turned onto the sidewalk heading toward Bull's. She had to think hard to figure out if she was to walk on green or red. Then she saw the little, white, walking man light up. "Oh yeah."

When she arrived at Bull's, Sam opened the door to the bar and stepped in. She looked around and spotted Deb on one of the stools at the bar. Deb was watching a basketball game and had not looked when the door opened. Sam came up behind her and put her arms around Deb's waist, resting her chin on Deb's back. "I'm high."

Deb turned her head and looked around at Sam, puzzled and concerned. "What are you doing here? I thought you had family night?"

"Hiya," Sam said. She started laughing. Deb shook her head.

"I hope you didn't drive down here."

"Um. I don't think I did. Buy me a drink."

"No. Nope. No way. You are drunk." Deb tried to steady Sam by holding her shoulders. "Come on. Let's get you back home."

"Mm. Okay. My mom told me to come give you a proper good-bye," Sam said, smiling.

"She did, did she?" Deb took a few bills from her wallet and settled up her tab. She shook her head to the bartender and led Sam outside. "Where's your car?"

"You walked, silly. We don't have a car here." Sam was holding Deb's arm.

"Look, Sam. You have to pay attention, okay?" Deb said sternly. She whispered firmly, "It's not that I keep my life totally private, but I don't typically associate with drunks."

"Ooh. Sorry," Sam whispered. She laughed sheepishly.

"Look, the beach is too small for that kind of reputation. I'm as steady as a rock in most people's opinion. I want it to stay that way. Why the hell are you drunk? What happened to feeling so bad?"

"Shh. Someone might hear you," Sam whispered again. Then she laughed out loud.

"Jesus, girl." Deb shook her head as she gently guided Sam with her hand. Sam managed to walk with Deb's hand on her lower back. As they walked past the Element under the stairs, Deb checked to make sure it was locked. "Come on. Let's go up the stairs. Do you need help?" Deb offered.

"Yeah. Walk behind me….right behind me so I can feel you. That's the kind of help I need right now. At least until we get upstairs." Sam chuckled. Deb shook her head and continued guiding Sam up the stairs.

"So your leg doesn't hurt? Your back doesn't hurt anymore?"

"Oh, not now. I took one of those pain pills that Janice gave me right before I came here. And Sagal brought me some wine that we had for dinner. I feel pretty good. Only my back still hurts some. It still stings if I move my arm or back, but that's all. I'm almost as good as gold." Sam laughed again. "You know what that means, don't you? Mom saying to give you a proper good-bye."

"Uh, yeah. I know. Pain pill, huh? I think that might be helping your pain. Sure. Who is Janice, and why did she give you a pain pill?"

"Peg took me to that clinic near Mom's. Janice is a beautiful PA who had to have been a princess in another life. She said I have a broken bone on my spine, and I can't lift my arms or do anything too strenuous. I told her that was okay, because I wasn't going to see my lady friend for weeks. She laughed. She also looked at this place." Sam pushed on her groin. "She didn't touch me there, though, but if hurts more, I have to go to a doctor."

"Uh huh. I didn't know any of this because *my* lady friend didn't bother to let me know she had such a bad injury," Deb said through her teeth, clearly frustrated. "And why the hell would you take a pain pill with alcohol and think you could drive?"

"Don't be mad. I really didn't realize it until I parked the car." Sam frowned. "I'm sorry. I wanted to do something nice. Surprise you."

"Sam. I'm sorry if I seem angry. I'm more worried than angry. Do you have any kind of paperwork from the clinic in your purse that I can read? I need to know if you're really okay. I mean, are you even supposed to be out of bed? Why didn't you call if it was bad?"

"I forgot, I guess. Here." Sam handed Deb her purse. "I don't remember. I told Peg I would. But it got busy, and Sagal and Sasha came. And Tom got pizza. But you are so sweet to care for me that way," Sam smiled at Deb. "You're hot, too." She walked up to Deb and raised her arms to Deb's neck. Deb took her arms and lowered them to Sam's side.

"Until I read your paperwork, keep your arms down. You just told me you're not supposed to raise them." Deb unfolded the yellow discharge paperwork. "Fracture of spinous process at T4. Do not raise arms above chest level. No lifting more than five pounds. Minimize any twisting or turning. Your pain will guide your activity. Take pain medication at night to help you sleep if you need it. Continue ibuprofen for two days. Then switch to extra strength acetaminophen as needed within daily maximum. Return to the nearest urgent care if pain not relieved with pain medication or if pain worsens with activity. Return to clinic in one month for radiology follow-up." Deb sighed and sat on the arm of the couch. "Look, Sam. This is not something to sneeze at."

"No, it is not. I can't imagine how I would feel if I sneezed. I think it might kill me." Sam looked confused.

Deb shook her head in frustration. She slid onto the couch next to Sam. "You'd better be glad I love you," she said softly. "And that you're still so damn hot."

"Now you're talking my kind of language." Sam pulled at Deb. Deb leaned with Sam's pull.

"Don't do that. Did you see the X-ray, Sam?"

"Oh, yes. That Janice showed me right after she showed the doctor. She said it was not displaced. The main thing is not to displace it. She said if the pain gets worse, that probably means it has been displaced. She didn't want that to happen. She sort of gave me a talkin' to about driving tomorrow. She said twisting is bad, but I pretty much said that I was going to anyway. I am. I have got to spend a night in my bed. I want to sit on my porch."

"I know. It really sucks, Sam. It does. Can't you postpone a few days until your back feels a little better? You're definitely not with the program right now."

"I know that when you kissed me last night, I never even knew I had a back. If that's what people call being kissed senseless, then that's what you did. I'll be real still tonight if you want me to."

"I think you need to drink a glass of water, take some ibuprofen, and go to sleep. That's why you took that pain pill, remember?" she whispered, "Like you even remember."

"I'll do all those things if you'll kiss me the way you did last night." Sam leaned back against the sofa cushion with her arm to her forehead. Deb reached and gently pulled the arm down.

"How 'bout this? If you promise to mind Janice, at least for the next five days. I'll kiss you all night long. I'll kiss whatever you want, and I promise I won't fuss at you. Is that a deal?"

"Maybe…"

"There are worse ways for me to spend my night…or nights." A few beats passed. "I'm waiting for your answer," Deb reminded.

"Of course. I thought I answered you. I did in my head." She started laughing. "I wondered why you weren't kissing me yet. I'm high as a kite, Deb. That is not what my mom wanted me to do."

"Come on in here, and let's get your teeth brushed and face washed, okay? Then I'll undress you and get you in that bed next to me. That sounds good, right? Then I'll kiss you. Oh yeah…I'll kiss you." Sam had stood up and was leaning into Deb.

"Am I taking advantage of you?" Deb asked softly.

"Nah," Sam replied. "I love how you feel," Sam softly pressed herself into Deb's arm, which was guiding her into the bathroom. After finishing up, Deb led Sam into the bedroom. "I think you're going to have to help me remove my shirt and bra," Sam teased.

"Nope. Not taking advantage at all," Deb laughed. She slowly unbuttoned Sam's shirt and slid it off her shoulders and arms. She winced, even though Sam did not. "It really looks painful." Sam poked her arm. "Okay, okay." Deb chuckled. She reached down and unfastened the bra between Sam's breasts. She slid the straps off Sam's shoulders, and the bra fell to the floor. Sam had closed her eyes, and she sighed. Deb reached to the front of Sam's jeans. With her left hand holding the top button, she ran her fingers down the fly. Sam sighed deeply. Deb slipped the jeans off Sam's waist and slid them to the floor. She slid her hand into Sam's panties, wet from her arousal. Sam sucked in through her teeth. After sliding the panties to the floor, Deb guided Sam onto the bed and helped her settle into a comfortable position.

Deb slowly removed her own shirt and jeans, and her usual tank top and boy shorts. She slid into the bed beside Sam. Sam started raising her arm to pull Deb, but Deb took her arm and gently placed it down. "Uh uh. Remember, no kisses unless you follow Janice's directions."

"Kiss me then. My neck and mouth. Oh shit, I don't care where. Just kiss me," Sam whispered. When Deb leaned and kissed Sam, it was as raw as it had been the night before. Sam moaned into Deb's mouth and begged her to continue. Deb kissed down Sam's torso. She kissed carefully in the groin area, avoiding the injured side. When Sam came, Deb slid back up and kissed her mouth again. "That mouth." Sam pushed her breasts against Deb's chest. "Oh. That hurts...my back."

"Settle down then. Just feel." Deb took Sam's nipple into her mouth and made love to it with her tongue and lips. Sam whimpered and sighed as Deb moved to the other breast.

Sam reached her fingers between Deb's legs. Deb was moist and warm. As Deb made love to her breasts, Sam stroked her. Sam could feel Deb's pulsing in climax. Deb held herself firmly alongside Sam. "That's a little better good-bye for you than I gave you last night," Sam whispered.

"It's a really nice good-bye, Sam...I'm glad you're here." Deb stroked Sam's head, pulling her hair softly through her fingers, and very gently stroking her forehead. Sam held her arm gently. She heard Deb whisper her name, but was asleep before she could respond.

Chapter Thirteen

ONCE AGAIN, IT WAS Deb's alarm that woke them both. Deb rolled and saw Sam looking at her, head resting on the far edge of Deb's pillow. "Hiya," Deb said softly. "I love seeing your face in the morning. Such a sweet thing to wake up to."

Sam smiled. "I'm glad you think so...my mouth..." she said, smacking her lips. "Yucky. I must look like hell."

"How do you *feel*? I think you *look* just fine," Deb said.

"I'm okay...I think. But I haven't tried to move yet. My head's a little...I don't know. Maybe I'm dehydrated?"

"Look. I gotta get ready for work, and I want to shower. If you want to get in there first so you can head out, now's your chance. I'm going to start the coffee and put a bagel in the toaster. You want anything? You can get it when you're done in the bathroom."

"Sure. I'll pee and wash my face. I'll take a bagel in a paper towel and get out of your hair. I have to make coffee for Mom, so I'll have a cup there while I'm packing up."

"Take one of the water bottles up there where the glasses are," Deb suggested. "Use the filtered water in the refrigerator. Drink that on your way home. You need at least one bottle full."

"You're the sweetest. You know that, I hope," Sam ran her hand down Deb's arm.

"Your suitcases, though? You can't carry those down the stairs and load them," Deb asked with genuine concern.

"No. Tom's coming at nine to help me load up. I decided to drive halfway today. I'll rest in South Carolina overnight, then drive the rest tomorrow."

"Wow! That's a much more sensible Sam than I met last night." Deb smiled, her voice reflecting her mild frustration.

"Jesus. I'm such an idiot, Deb. I know. I know driving here was a stupid thing to do. I just wasn't thinking straight." She paused, smiled, and added very softly, "Not one hint of a straight thought in my mind last night."

Deb lightly pushed Sam's shoulder. "You're a mess...go pee." She leaned and kissed Sam. "And brush your teeth." Sam play-slapped Deb's arm before she began the arduous process of working her way out of the bed. Deb watched for a minute, then went to make coffee and busy herself in the kitchen with her morning routine.

"I'll let you know when I'm headed back. I know it'll be a month; I do have to come for my follow-up. Keep in touch, okay?" Sam tried to lean, but Deb gently pulled her in close.

"Don't lean and twist, remember?" She enveloped Sam with her arms, and they kissed again. She could feel a rock growing in her stomach...the sadness. "Be careful, please. Wait until your follow-up before you ride again? And will you text me this evening when you get to your stopping place? And then again when you get to your place?"

"Sure. That's a good excuse." Sam added in a whisper, "I'll miss you." Deb nodded and released her hug. She watched Sam descend the stairs and drive away.

"I wish you could stay." Sam couldn't have heard Deb's quiet plea, eyes filled with tears as the car turned left onto Lumina Avenue.

Chapter Fourteen

WHEN SAM PULLED IN at home, she noticed a neat stack of twigs and limbs next to her narrow gravel drive. The leaves had been neatly piled and bagged into large paper sacks. *Monty, of course.* How could anyone be so lucky to have such friends? Could her heart burst from the love, the relief, she felt at this moment? The day after her bike accident, she had emailed Liz and Monty to say she was headed back and to give a brief account of her temporary disability. Monty replied she would gladly come right down, as soon as Sam was ready to unload. What a blessing it was to have help when you needed it.

Sam pushed open the front door, fully expecting the musty odor of a cool, dank house. What greeted her instead was the lovely scent of rosemary; several long sprigs arose from a small cobalt vase on her table. The hum of the dehumidifier caught her attention. *Liz.* Her eyes welled as she felt the love of her good friends and relished the comfort of being home. She put her daypack, which she had carried from the top handle, on the floor. She was tired and achy from driving that final leg of the trip, body necessarily moving with multiple turns of the steering wheel around the mountain bends.

Sometimes, when she returned home after so many weeks gone, she appreciated anew her cute, 455-square-foot cabin, simple and rustic. When she bought it, she'd added to the porch so that it wrapped around nicely, increasing her living space in at least two seasons. Well, Monty had added to the porch. Monty copied Liz's hog-wire design to replace balusters. Sam had added a metal roof, and Monty had done extensive repairs to the inside. The insulation had been replaced and upgraded. New, double-paned windows were installed, along with new kitchen fixtures and hardware. A deep breath filled her with the rich scent of the wide-planked, solid wood lining the walls and floors. Floors Monty had varnished.

Sam walked into her bedroom and looked around as if to reacquaint herself—double bed with a simple metal frame. She touched the stitching of little blue birds and lavender flowers against the white background of the April Cornell quilt. The matching shams were soothing and homey. There was no dust on the small, Mission style, cherry end table, or its thin, tapered legs. The matching chest of drawers, handcrafted by Chilton of Maine, held most of her clothes. She ran her fingers along the foot of her bed before stepping to the bathroom.

The room was nice and clean, just the way she'd left it. Liz, she assumed, had put a small vase with some lilies of the valley on the back of the toilet. In the living room area, she rested her hand on the back of the cushioned recliner next to the woodstove and sighed.

The knock on the door startled her, but she motioned for Monty to come in. She quickly stepped to open it when she realized Monty was carrying several items from her car.

"Welcome home!" Monty pushed through the door and set the bags on the floor. Reaching to give Sam a kiss on the cheek, she lightly rested an arm on each of Sam's shoulders. "Are you really okay?"

"I'm glad I stopped halfway," Sam admitted. "But yeah. Y'all are so sweet. I love the flowers, and thank you for starting the dehumidifier. I was so expecting the usual dank inside."

"That was Liz's idea. It was a good one, wasn't it?"

"It was. Monty—"

"Hey, let me go grab the rest of your things. Liz really wants to help you unpack. She said you may want to nap first, though."

Sam gingerly plopped down onto her recliner and watched as Monty made two more trips with her belongings. Monty's sleeves were rolled up, even with the spring chill. Sam chuckled to herself when she noticed Monty's ribbed tank under the green-plaid, flannel shirt. Liz had told her many stories of their early days together. Sam herself had been witness to Monty's thin, but chiseled and muscular frame when she worked on the porch or yard. She couldn't fault Liz's attraction to Monty. Especially the tousled, short, blond hair. *Mm. Very easy on the eyes, with a heart of gold. Liz was no chopped liver either. Mm, mm curvy. And just as sweet as Monty. Oh, God. These two were tailor-made for some kind of romance novel.* Monty put Sam's backpack on the sofa and turned to Sam, bringing her back from her thoughts.

"I've put your bags where you can get to them without having to bend, twist, or lift. Just give us a ring, and we'll run back down. Like I said, Liz wants to help you."

"What would I do without y'all? And the yard! Monty, it's so nice that you cleaned up." Sam's eyes welled up with tears again. Monty stepped close and lightly hugged her. "I'm scared I'm going to hurt you."

"You won't." Sam wiped her eyes on her own sleeve. "I'm so glad to be home, but I think Liz is right. A nap is in my very near future."

"Liz is making pasta *puttanesca* for dinner, but look, we know you may want to be alone or be in your house. Liz said, if you want to eat here, she can either bring down your servings, or she'll bring everything down, and we'll eat with you. No pressure, babe. We really mean that."

"I'd love it if y'all would come here," Sam said. "I hate to ask you to do that though."

"You kidding me? We want to hear all about this hot chick you've been dating!" Monty kissed Sam on the cheek again. "Not kidding."

Sam nodded her head. "I need to email her and let her know I'm home safe and sound."

"Email? Call. She's probably worried sick." Monty seemed concerned. "I've never seen you that smitten. I can tell by that look on your face," she said, beaming. "Can't wait to hear more about her, but you absolutely *have* to wait for Liz. I'll get out of your hair. And please, call us when you're ready to put things away. Or we can do it when we bring dinner."

With Monty gone, Sam turned to retrieve the phone. "Ugh. No twisting, Avery." She nestled into the seat and lowered the back, raising her feet. Sam had thought that it was a crazy luxury to pay the extra for a chair with electronic controls. "See. I'm a forward thinker. Smarter than I look," she said aloud.

She looked on her cell to get Deb's number and programmed it into the cordless, glad she had done the same with her cell already. *Deb will be off work by now. God how I miss her.* When Sam had texted from her motel room in South Carolina, Deb's return text was short. Sam had said she was so tired she was heading straight to bed, but that she was safely in the room. Deb had sent a heart emoji. *Why am I so hesitant to call and talk to Deb? Monty's right, though. Deb probably is worried.*

On the third ring, Sam became a little anxious that Deb didn't want to talk with her. Then she heard the click. "Hiya," Deb said softly. Sam melted as she had done almost every time Deb spoke to her. "You're home I see. How ya feeling?"

"Better, now that I hear your voice," Sam replied. "I'm okay, I think...Deb, I miss you."

"Yeah. Me too. I know it's only been two days, but I tell you, I'm having a little bit of a hard time...missing you." Deb stopped.

"I'm not trying to change the subject, but I can't dwell on how much I miss you. It's like a hole in my gut or something. Deb, I'm almost sixty-five. How can I have such a schoolgirl's obsession?" Sam shook her head.

"It's weird, isn't it?" Deb replied. "Were you able to unpack okay? You still stiff?"

"I only took my daypack with a clean pair of socks and undies and my toothbrush into the motel, but when I got here, oh my gosh. Deb, Monty unpacked the car for me. Put everything up where I could reach it. Liz left little flowers on the table, and they ran the dehumidifier so the house wouldn't smell musty. Monty had tidied the yard. It was so sweet. I love it here. I really do."

"I know you do."

"Liz is making supper at their place, and we're having dinner here. Liz'll unpack my things for me."

"That's super nice; you have a great support system there."

"Monty said they're dying to hear more on that hot chick I'm dating."

Sam imagined Deb's smile. "I'd like to date you right now," Deb spat out between her laughs.

"Me too. Your voice does that to me."

Deb chuckled. "Gotta agree with you." After a beat, Deb said, "You know, that's how Peg was when I had surgery and had to go to the lymphedema clinic. I can't believe that we drifted apart."

"That must've been tough...I mean, it almost sounds as if she deserted you."

"She was with a pretty jealous partner, and Peg had a hard time convincing her that I was her best friend. Peg's partner wore her down. Once I was able to drive again, she backed off and her calls slowly decreased to nothing. I asked Peg about her distance, but she said it was because she couldn't deal with how much it reminded her of what she went through with her sister. Probably the combination."

"Yeah. Maybe so...I'm sorry that happened. It seems you're working on rebuilding your friendship, though."

"Hope so. You know, I suspected the real reason, and it was disappointing, but I've lived through enough to understand we do what we need to do to get through things."

"Yep. That's exactly what we do."

"Since I didn't want to hang out at the ball field, I just didn't see them anymore."

"If I were there right now—" Sam started.

"Oh yeah? What would you do?" Deb teased.

"Lie down with my head on your shoulder. Kiss you. Lightly run my fingers across your chest. That's what." Sam's arousal was evident in her answer.

"You gotta stop talking that way to me right now. I'm in the grocery, standing to the side. I gotta drive back home. I'm glad you called though." Deb sounded somewhat forlorn.

"Okay. Okay. I get the picture," Sam said. "Miss you. Maybe we can talk in a few days?"

"Yeah," Deb said softly. "And Sam?"

"Yeah?" Sam whispered.

"I'd like that too. What you said...your head on my shoulder and all."

"Yeah. And all," Sam whispered again. "Bye."

"Bye," Deb said softly as she ended the call.

Sam sighed heavily and pressed the recline button until she was almost flat. She was sore from the activity. She raised back up, grabbed some acetaminophen from the medicine cabinet and filled a small glass with tap water. Heaving a big sigh, she leaned back in her chair again and drifted off into a deep nap.

* * * *

Liz's knock was gentle, partly because she saw Sam asleep in the chair when they walked past the front-porch window. Monty set the salad bowl and wine down on the table by the door and knocked a little harder. When Sam did not stir, she opened the unlocked door, and they carried in the basket, bowl, and wine. Monty pulled some plates and silverware out of the cabinets. Liz leaned and kissed Sam on the top of her head, lightly putting her hand on Sam's shoulder.

"Holy crap, y'all! What time is it?" Sam blinked her eyes and squinted. After the recliner pushed her back into a sitting position, she rubbed her eyes, then turned to smile at Liz. "Sorry. Hey, Liz. Gosh. I was so tired."

"It's six, Rip Van Winkle," Monty teased. "Hope you're hungry. I am, so I'm going ahead and setting up dinner." Monty was not known for patience in the eating department. She had spent several years fending for herself. It had been years, but her mealtime habits hadn't changed much.

"I wanted to be sure you were okay," Liz said. "I was afraid you had had an embolus or something, being in that car two days for so many hours and all that bedrest...your having been so active just prior to the injury. Speaking of which, let me look at your back."

Liz had also been a nurse before her retirement. She was as down to earth as anyone, regardless of her wealth. Sam had had quite a crush on her when Liz first moved up the mountain. Beautiful tan, dark hair, and the bluest eyes Sam had ever seen. Anyone who heard Liz or Monty talk of the other, though, knew they were deeply in love. Sam wouldn't have wanted to break up anything between them. She loved them both, and she certainly couldn't have asked for better neighbors.

Sam pulled off her long-sleeve, button-front shirt, and Liz pulled up her undershirt to look. Monty ran to look and grimaced with a curse. Liz wore a more guarded expression. "Okay if I check the swelling by lightly touching around it?" she asked softly. When Sam nodded, Liz began a very light exploration around the edges, working slowly inward, the same way Janice had.

Liz described as she examined. "Still some swelling. The bruising makes for an interesting color pattern, similar to a burst. The center's much redder with specks of purple. There's a drift of color coming from the center down the back an inch or so, showing the settling of the blood into the dependent position whenever you're upright, but you're doing what you need to do, right?" Liz quizzed. Sam nodded. "I think it might help if you put some cold on it periodically—a cool pack or something, if there's pain. I can help you with that if you need it. Or heat. Whichever feels best."

"Y'all are way too good to me." Sam tucked in her undershirt.

"Let's eat, ladies," Monty said, having set the table, poured wine and water, and plated the food. They sat in their usual places.

"You know, Liz, we're lucky to have you around. Sometimes I wish you'd open a restaurant. There isn't anything you can't do—baked goods, sauces, cocktails. And the both of you. Parties at y'all's place are always the best gatherings."

Some time passed; they had finished eating and were sitting there catching up on neighborhood news. "Okay. Enough waiting, Sam. Spill. We want to know about this new flame," Monty's smile morphed into one of her adorable grins.

It was hard not to stare at Monty as she spoke. She really was gorgeous, and her eyes were as green as Liz's were blue. Sam lowered her head and eyes and couldn't stop her widening smile. Her cheeks reddened.

"Uh, huh. We definitely want details," Monty teased.

"I was literally swept away, y'all," Sam started. "I'm almost sixty-five. I honestly feel like a schoolgirl, though. She is taller than I am, thin, but with wide shoulders. Her hair is gray also, short, and her eyes are blue. She is so tanned, but she has freckles mainly across her nose and arms. And when she speaks to me or holds me, I melt." Her eyes welled with tears. "I can't believe I feel this way. I miss her."

"Wow." Liz rested her hand on Sam's arm. "That's so nice, Sam. You deserve that kind of relationship. Assuming she feels the same?"

"Pretty sure she does," Sam said softly. "Y'all. She is amazing. So sweet to me. Oh my God! I acted a fool that night. I had some wine that Sagal brought. They left, and I was tired, but my back was killing me. I wasn't even thinking and popped one of my pain pills. Then Mom started saying I should go tell Deb good-bye. That was sweet and exactly what I needed to convince me. I wasn't thinking. By the time I drove up to Deb's house, I was high as a friggin' kite!"

Monty and Liz were chuckling, but they looked horrified. "You drove?" Monty asked, incredulous. Sam nodded sheepishly.

"I also walked several blocks from her house to find her at her local hangout. Then I proceeded to make a spectacle of myself by hanging on her. I mean, she works down there where she lives. It's not as small as here, but people know one another. She walked me back, practically had to carry me up her steps, and took such good care of me. And she was still speaking to me the next morning." Sam sipped some water.

"I'll bet she was doing more than speaking to you," Monty teased, and Liz popped her hand.

"She had to go to work, and I had to get back to Mom's and pack up." Sam frowned. "I wasted that night. Friggin' wasted a chance to...shit, never mind." Sam blushed and looked down. "I can't wait for y'all to meet her." They talked some more about Deb's house, the beach, and Deb's job. Sam told them stories of Deb's softball days and how Deb knew several of her mom's building mates.

Monty and Liz cleaned up, leaving the kitchen as it had been when they arrived. Sam delivered her appreciation with effusive thank-yous. Liz reminded Sam to try a cold pack or heating pad as she unpacked and put away the few items Sam could not lift. Then she and Monty gathered up their belongings and headed out. Sam locked the door, turned off the lights, stripped to her boy shorts and tank, and slipped into her bed. Her bed. She loved the feeling of being in her own bed. She was asleep almost as soon as her head touched the pillow.

Chapter Fifteen

OF COURSE, SAM COULD not open the lid of the strawberry jam she pulled off the shelf. She tried, but there was an instant twinge between her shoulder blades. "Argh." She wouldn't dare ask Monty or Liz to come down just for that, even though she knew either one of them would have run down to help, no matter how small the task. She started a list instead. Jam. Open windows.

She would make them a loaf of bread. *Kneading might not be comfortable.* A test of trying the motion with a towel wasn't painful, but she felt tight. Maybe a muscle pulling. The hook on the artisan mixer should work just fine.

She wondered if she would need some sort of rehab services when she was released. At minimum, she thought a few choice exercises to get back to keeping her muscles flexible were in order. "Shit." She added to the list. *Remove mixer from cabinet.*

Liz would probably have already made bread. Sam struck bread off the list, frowned, and pushed the list and pen off the table.

She sat down, dejected, and attempted to rest her head in her hands, elbows on the table. That hurt too. Tears welled in her eyes; she was tired of pretending to be peppy.

"Hi, beautiful. Need a strong woman to come down and give you some relief?" Monty teased as she answered the phone.

"More than you know," Sam answered, trying not to sound pitiful. "I have a list, so there'll be no time for hanky-panky." This sounded, at least a little, more upbeat.

"Down in a couple, ma'am," Monty said, as she hung up.

Before Monty could knock, Sam waved her in the door and pointed at the list on the floor.

"Oh, Monty. Sorry...I was frustrated, but thank you. I so hate—"

"Piece of cake, babe. You don't have to keep thanking me, you know. I'm happy to help you." Monty chuckled as she looked at the two items on the list.

"I know. I didn't even get far on the list before I gave up...seems I need help with everything."

"Liz and I were talking the other day about having our own cohousing kind of place. I mean, as we get older, we may find ourselves needing just this kind of help. We read a cool article. I think we should consider it at some point." Sam nodded in agreement.

"I have talked with some of my other friends about that exact thing. We had discussed buying a place in Maine." She considered the definite pros of having a few people such as Liz and Monty, twenty or so years younger.

Sam was almost taken aback when her phone rang. She motioned a pause with her hand and cleared her throat, recognizing Deb's number. "Hiya," Sam said in as soft a voice as she could muster, lovingly mocking Deb. Monty popped her head around the door of the bedroom, eyes wide open. She slipped into the bathroom, peeking around the doorway, with her hands on her ears. Sam smiled at her.

"Hiya to you too. How can any one woman have such control of my body?" Deb asked.

"She likes that about herself. And I'm pretty sure she feels the same way you feel," Sam replied in that same low voice. She sat in her recliner and lowered herself back. Monty, having finished her list, pecked Sam on the cheek, gave her two thumbs up, and slipped out the front door, beaming back at Sam as she walked away.

"You're killing me here. I'm glad I'm home this time." Deb chuckled. "Guess what!" She exclaimed more than asked. "Peg and I are going up to Maine to look at some land. We've been talking cohousing or a snowbird kind of arrangement. I think I might be ready for nice temps year-round—"

"Monty and I were just discussing that exact topic! You and I seem to be on the same wavelength regarding a few things." Sam waited to hear Deb's response.

"Really...I guess yes on a *few* things then, but *really*? You were just talking about it? Are you pulling my leg?"

"We really were. I was literally thinking of it when you called. I mean, literally. Monty was here being my personal attendant. We had just spoken before she started ticking off the things I need. Can you believe it? I had to make her a list...then I threw it off the table, so then the list had to be in my head. Ugh.."

"I am so glad you have help. Is Monty still there?"

"She ducked out when I started with the sexy talk." Sam chuckled. "So...when is *your* trip?" Sam no longer sounded particularly happy.

"Now, now, Miss Pitiful. Don't sound all sad, thinking I don't have time to come see you. We're not planning on going until September. After the Labor Day rush. So, months away."

"But your time off..."

"Listen to you, would ya'? You must know I can't believe you're being so...so pitiful. I was hoping to fly up to Atlanta a week before you come for your follow-up appointment. If you can get me from the airport, somehow, I'll spend a few days with you, then drive you back. That way you don't have to stop. I can drive the entire distance or part of the way, whatever you feel comfortable with. That sound okay?"

"Oh, Deb. Better than okay...lovely. Liz and Monty should be around too, so you can meet them. I'll be glad to see you." Seconds of silence passed.

"You still here, Sam?"

"Yeah. Just overwhelmed. You're so sweet to me. Everyone is being sweet to me." She sniffled as tears welled up in her eyes.

"I would hold you right now if I could...I will be happy to be with you. I would fly to China if I needed to."

"Sweet talkin' me again," Sam whispered. "Keep it up, and I'll have to muffle my moans with a pillow." She heard Deb chuckle. "I'm serious. I am burning for you."

"Yeah. I know the feeling." Deb blew a breath.

"How are you getting so much time off? Not that it's any of my business."

"That's another exciting thing I want to tell you. I met with my financial person yesterday, after work. I can retire and still be okay. She advised me to go ahead and plan it. I have my teacher pension, and I have an annuity from some money I put away years ago. I had forgotten it, which was good. When I started pulling together papers I would need, there it was. I have a little from jobs prior to my teacher retirement, but enough to draw the small bit of social security at sixty-six...maybe not until seventy. I don't need it yet.

"Anyway, maybe I'll take a week off to go to Maine and then work another month. It's such a relief."

"That's great news. And congratulations. I'll be glad when we can really celebrate...together." Sam hoped Deb could hear her sincerity.

"Me too...really," Deb said softly. "So, it's okay if I make a one-way flight on the third?"

"Perfect. We'll talk later about the specifics of taking MARTA out to the North Springs Station. I'll pick you up there. It's two hours to my place, so make your flight as early as you can stand it. Okay?"

"Sure. The more time I have with you, the better. Talk soon?"

"Yeah. Soon. Late at night, I hope. Some time when you can talk dirty to me." Sam hoped her grin was audible. "Bye-ya."

"Bye." Deb's almost whisper elicited a shudder as Sam ended the call.

I miss that woman. I can't believe this has happened. Sam couldn't wait. She wanted to see Liz and Monty and share the news that Deb would be coming. She thought of nothing else. If she couldn't get the news out, she was sure she would burst. She walked tentatively up their steep driveway. Liz was sitting in the swing. "She walks!" Liz stood and walked to the edge of the porch to greet Sam. "How're you feeling? Must be better. That grin is something else. Monty told me you two were practically having sex on the phone."

"She has no earthly idea, Liz. None. Don't get me started about how she makes me feel." Sam blushed. "Don't tell Monty I said that!"

"Don't tell Monty what?" Monty popped out the screen door. "I heard you say something about feelings and don't tell Monty."

"Busted, but I'm glad you're out here too." Sam sat on one of the porch rockers while they stood in front of her. "Deb's coming on the third! I want to squeal, but maybe that's too much."

"Are you telling us that speaking with her on the phone makes you squeal?" Monty teased.

"As I said to Liz, you have no idea." Sam's face reddened as she beamed. "I only came to tell you she's coming for a visit. That *really* is the only reason I came. Silly, huh?" Sam blushed, but her smile did not diminish. "I don't think I'll be able to sleep the next few weeks."

Sam stood to leave. Liz and Monty both gave their nods of approval. "Sam. I can't wait. It's nice to see you this way. I know it's been a while since you've had this." Liz lightly touched Sam's arm.

"I have *never* felt this way. I've been in love and in lust more times than I care to admit. This is something way beyond any of that. I don't even want to describe it...or try to. It's incredible. And when she speaks to me, or says hello, or touches me...I think I'm going to pop or evaporate or something. She is so hot, y'all."

Liz and Monty smiled. "I know how you feel, Sam. I still feel that way." Monty pointed her thumb toward Liz.

"Aww." Liz pulled Monty's arm so that she fell into Liz's hug. "I hope you can feel even half of what we feel, Sam. Let us know if you need anything, okay?" Liz pecked Sam on the cheek, then gave her a hug.

Sam blushed and felt she could skip back to her house. She knew better, though. A nice stroll would suffice. A nice stroll with the biggest grin she had ever sported.

* * * *

The cabin looked incredibly sweet. Sam wondered why she had not thought to make these touches before. Monty lined the odd little driveway with some of the stones found scattered in the yard. She filled the holes with dirt, then covered the drive itself with a layer of gravel mixed with sand. The top layer was pea gravel, which she raked as smoothly as she could. Liz and Monty put a few flower boxes along the porch rails after Monty had washed off the thick pollen layer. Sam had washed and ironed the curtains before having Monty rehang them for her. The sheets had been changed, and Sam slept on top of the made bed. She wanted everything perfect when Deb came in. Liz refreshed the herbs and flowers inside. The result was gorgeous.

Deb had emailed from the Wilmington airport that everything looked to be on schedule. Sam checked the flight number and agreed with the assessment. Deb's one-hour flight was to arrive in Atlanta at eleven-thirty that morning. That flight had a good on-time record, and Sam was trying to time her arrival at the station close to the time Deb's train would arrive. Once Sam left the high-mountain valley, she'd be able to send and receive texts. Deb would text when she landed and still have a forty-five-minute, rapid-transit ride from the airport to the northernmost station.

She pictured greeting Deb at the kiss-and-ride lot. *You better believe it.* She'd have a hard time avoiding an R-rated greeting.

Sam had risen early from nervous energy. She opted for something to wow Deb, but she wasn't a girly girl. Neither was Deb. Falling back on her rooftop-date outfit, Sam wore her light, stone-washed skirt, soft and fitted, and her black shirt with the mandarin collar, unbuttoned to easily reveal the black lace bra if she turned even slightly. Microfiber always draped nicely and was temptingly soft. *Yeah. Temptingly soft.* Her simple silver hoops complemented the outfit. With her product-spiked hair, even *she* thought she looked pretty hot. Deb wouldn't even care what she was wearing, she knew that, but she still wanted to be ravished when they arrived at the cabin. Just thinking of Deb sliding against her was enough. She warned herself to calm down. Even after they hit the road home, it was almost a two-hour drive. And part of that was on some of the most twisty, tightest mountain roads in Georgia.

As soon as she pulled in and parked next to the kiss-and-ride lot at the station, Sam pulled out her cell. *Heading north*, the text read. A check of the time showed Deb would arrive in twenty minutes. Sam couldn't wait at the car; she had to be where she'd see Deb as soon as she made her way past the turnstiles. Sam checked her hair, again, in the vanity mirror and popped a breath mint. As she walked through to the waiting area, she was able to check herself in a full-length reflection. *Yep. Still hot.* She laughed to herself and texted Deb. *I'll be to your left when you come through the turnstiles.*

Twenty minutes flew by. She would have known that smile anywhere, and Sam gave a wave. Deb lightly placed her arms around Sam's shoulders as Sam threaded hers around Deb's waist.

"Hiya," Deb said softly before kissing Sam. Sam moaned and pressed herself against Deb, who laughed as she slid her hands down Sam's arms.

"You look fantastic," Deb said softly.

"You have no idea how happy I am to see you." Sam tilted her head, taking in the vision of Deb before her. Deb's blue jeans, white Oxford shirt, white tank, and natural color linen jacket looked just like her. Sam pulled her into another hug. She loved Deb's rolled up sleeves, revealing her muscular forearms. "Geez." Sam blushed, running her hands over Deb's arms.

"I think I might. I know that tell," Deb said, winking at Sam.

"Come on. Car's this way." Sam motioned. "I wish I could carry something. Still not quite right, but at least I can drive."

Once loaded up and in the car, Deb leaned across the console and pulled Sam's face toward hers. "Hiya," Deb whispered. They kissed, and Deb slipped her tongue and found Sam's. Sam moaned again, and Deb ran her fingertips along Sam's thigh.

"I have to be able to drive," Sam whispered, breathing her words out through a sigh.

Deb pulled Sam's shirt placket forward with her index finger. "Best view in the house." Leaning toward Sam's chest, Deb's warm breath fell lightly through her cleavage.

"Really. Should we stay here...find a hotel?" Her ragged sigh thwarted attempts at complete sentences. "Can't drive...and don't want you to stop." She held Deb's wrist.

"I'll behave for now, I suppose," Deb slipped her hand into Sam's bra and ran her finger across the nipple. "But you feel so damn good." Sam sucked in through her teeth, and her head fell back against the headrest. Deb leaned back and fastened her seatbelt. "Really, I'll behave, but I hope we're going to be alone when we get to your place."

"Oh yeah." The whisper barely made it out of Sam's lips. She felt she had melted and dripped off the seat and onto the floorboard, but a smoldering fire still burned between her legs.

Sam said very little for the next hour and fifteen minutes. Deb talked a little about the flight, but mainly she looked at Sam. Sam had thought of all kinds of things she wanted to remember to tell Deb on the ride back, but now she couldn't think of a thing but Deb's touch.

Before they started on the most serpentine of the roads, Sam pulled into one of the many areas that allow traffic to pass slower drivers. She reached and pulled Deb's hand onto her breast. She guided it down her torso, under her skirt, and between her legs. She leaned back against the headrest again. "If you didn't touch me, I knew that would be all I thought of. The rest of this drive is slow and winding, even though it feels fast. I must pay attention, but right now all I can picture is how you make love to me. I just—"

Deb kissed Sam firmly, their tongues touching. Her hand reached inside Sam's bra, and her face dropped to Sam's breast. She gently nibbled and caressed the nipple with her tongue. Sam moaned and pulled Deb's hand lower. Deb lightly raked her fingers up Sam's thigh. Then she lightly slid her hand back up across Sam's breast to her face. She kissed Sam again and leaned back in her seat. "Now. Let's get to that cabin to finish this."

Sam heaved out a large sigh and combed her hands through her hair. She pulled down and straightened her shirt and skirt. "Holy shit!" The whisper escaped as she pulled back onto the road.

Chapter Sixteen

"YOU WEREN'T KIDDING ABOUT these curvy roads," Deb admitted as Sam turned off the main road onto the roughly paved loop. "And you're right that it would take me a while to get used to them." She took in the unusual, rustic subdivision covering a very small area in the middle of nowhere. Sam pointed out the access to the Appalachian Trail. As the Element slowed and Sam pulled into the small driveway, Deb turned to her. "Wow. It *is* small, but adorable, Samantha." Such a different setting than Deb's waterfront home, but she understood its sweet appeal.

"I love it," Sam replied. "Everything. The look of the light, coffee colored, wooden siding and the lighter shade on the metal roof. The bright blue of the door."

"It's definitely special."

"Monty fixed up the driveway for me. A few weeks ago, she built the flower boxes and put them in. Liz added the flowers two days ago. It's lovely. That's their place up the hill." She pointed. "We'll have dinner with them tomorrow night, at their place," Sam informed her. "They don't expect to hear from me until then." She tilted her head to the side, watching Deb pull out her suitcase and messenger bag. "Come on in. I'll give you the grand tour."

They stepped in and Deb nodded as she looked around. "It's *tiny*. Is it considered a tiny house?"

"I think, technically, tiny houses are classified as four-hundred feet or smaller. This has an extra fifty, so I don't think it is."

"But it's damn close, I'd say. I love the use of wood. Everything looks, and smells, sweet."

"Thanks. I know I've said it only a million times already, but I love it."

"I might need to wear my fleece. I'm glad you warned me the temp is cooler. You're right." She smiled at Sam. "Makes it good for cuddling, though."

"Yes, it does."

After the six-step proper tour, Sam poured a glass of water for each of them. Deb drank half of hers in a few swallows. "You hungry?" Sam asked. Deb stepped behind her and pulled her close.

"In a different way." She kissed Sam's neck, breathing softly into Sam's ear, and ran her tongue along the lobe before lightly sucking. Sam melted into her embrace and turned her head to offer easier access to her neck. How Deb had missed Sam's body. And what it did to her. She reached around and unfastened Sam's blouse, opening it at the neckline. She turned Sam toward her and ran her tongue to Sam's collarbone and onto her chest. Sam sighed as Deb slowly moved her tongue to the edge of the silky bra.

She led Sam to the bed, and when Sam was safely in place, she slid across her. Deb's mouth found the inside of that bra, pulling it with her teeth. She pressed her mouth against Sam's breast, kissing and lightly sucking as her tongue caressed the nipple. Hearing Sam's moan stirred something deep inside. Deb moved to the other breast as Sam began pulling at the button above her fly. Sam's blouse and bra discarded, she dragged the soft skirt up Sam's thighs and exposed her center. Sam was wet, and Deb's fingers slid easily against heated flesh. She moaned her pleasure. Sam began undressing Deb, working her skirt off. Deb sat up to give access to her shirts.

As Sam exposed her chest, kisses and her warm tongue outlined Deb's scars. She moaned and leaned backward onto her arms for support. Sam drew a long J down her torso with her tongue, curving up just before her jeans. Sam unzipped her fly and helped remove and toss aside the jeans. Deb's boy shorts were wet, and Sam pulled them down and off. Her tongue resumed its journey down Deb's mons and lower. She sat back and opened her legs, breathing quick bursts as Sam slid her tongue deep into her wetness. She bucked and uttered something unintelligible through a sigh.

Sam eased herself up, kissing Deb's mouth with the same fervor she had used below. Deb sensed Sam's arousal mounting as she pushed her legs apart and straddled her, so that they could slide against one another, slipping together in their warmth as they both came.

She kissed Sam softly. She turned onto her back and pulled Sam to her chest. Sam kissed her scars and softly sucked the flesh, then lightly stroked her chest. Deb wiped the tears from her eyes, hoping Sam wouldn't sense her emotion. How had she found Sam? Someone so accepting of her body as it was. She pulled the covers across them. She heard Sam's breathing and guessed she had fallen asleep. She relaxed into Sam's arms and did the same.

* * * *

When Sam awoke, she could feel Deb against her back. The sun was low enough to be behind the mountain, so Sam was pretty sure it was after four. She whispered Deb's name to see if she stirred. She pulled Sam close. "You think we can just stay in bed for a few days?" Deb asked softly, obviously teasing.

"I can live with that." Sam turned so she could stroke Deb's chest.

"Do you have any idea how much you mean to me? How much it means to me that you have, or seem to have, no qualms about doing what you're doing right now?"

"It seems the most natural thing in the world to me." Sam seemed puzzled. "I haven't found a part of you that I'm not in love with," she whispered. "Although, come to think of it, I don't think I've explored the bottoms of your feet." Deb teasingly slapped Sam's arm.

"I'm starving." Deb sat up in the bed. "I haven't eaten since five this morning."

"Yeah, me too. We have some pasta puttanesca that Liz put in the refrigerator. Monty made a salad. They wanted everything to be nice for you. And Liz is an incredible cook."

"Well, what are we waiting for?" Deb jumped across Sam, quickly pulling on her clothes. Sam still couldn't move that quickly, not as much because she was experiencing pain, but more because she was *afraid* of it. Deb was already pulling things out of the refrigerator. "Oh my God. They even grated some cheese?"

"Everything but opening the wine and setting the table for me. They're some nice folks." Sam stood and watched Deb for a minute. "Let's warm it in the pan instead of the microwave."

"Agree. It won't be chewy." After two cabinets, Deb found and pulled out a pan.

"Rioja?" After Deb nodded, Sam uncorked and poured, allowing the wine to breathe in the glasses while they were busy in the kitchen.

"It's definitely a one butt kitchen," Sam said.

"It sure is, but I'm glad it's yours in here with me." Deb smiled at Sam.

"Some people can't tolerate having such limited space. I've always thought it would just be me. It suits me."

"Yeah. Easy to clean, maintain, navigate... Peg and I thought about that when we were discussing using shipping containers for our old folks' compound in Maine. Wonder if we should rethink that idea."

"You should talk with Monty. She'd probably be thrilled to help build some out for you. She's discussed container homes several times. Given her building experience, she could do most anything that was needed.

"Knowing her, she would research materials best suited for that climate, and if she couldn't find what she needed, she'd call someone she'd found during her research. I mean, the woman's fearless."

"One of the things we've considered," Deb said, as she stirred the food, "is each person having their own smaller container. Then we'd have a larger container with the shared living space. That way, each person has their privacy with bed, bath, and sitting area, but cooking would be centralized."

"Gosh, y'all really have thought this through." Sam wondered where she fit into this scheme. *Is she considering me...my friends? Sounds as if we need to circle back around to this sometime.*

As the sauce and pasta warmed, they took their wine out onto the porch. "To good friends," they toasted together, raising their glasses and clinking. Deb stood close enough to press her arm into Sam's. "I'm so glad you have them here. I mean, this place really is sort of remote."

Sam chuckled. "Tell me about it." They sipped as they looked around at the multitude of wildflowers coming up in the yard—mostly foam flower and wild geranium. Sam left a part of the yard relatively wild. Trillium, bloodroot, and even trout lily flourished in the soil there.

The sound of the timer ringing through the screen door brought them inside, and they dove in after plating their pasta. Deb sounded as if someone was ravishing her. She moaned, appreciating Liz's sauce. "Told you." Sam smiled. "The wine's nice also, I think."

"God yes. Wonder what we're having tomorrow? I can hardly wait," Deb said, wide-eyed.

"It'll probably involve some freshly baked bread with butter."

Deb moaned again. "You had me at bread. Oh yeah, and at butter."

Sam enjoyed watching Deb's expressions. She was still learning Deb, but she felt comfortable with her. Sam loved her life in the mountains, and she could easily see Deb there. The incongruous part, though, was that she could easily see Deb at the beach. When she was honest with herself, she could picture herself at Deb's. She wondered if that was odd, but she wasn't ready to float those thoughts aloud quite yet. And the Maine idea? The two of them hadn't even discussed future living plans to any sort of resolution. Not even a suggestion.

"Now that I think I've tamped down those evil passion needs, what's the plan for the evening?"

"I don't know. Walk around the circle, maybe just talk?"

"I think a quiet night in reading or talking suits me. I know we talk on the phone, but big discussions or items, not so much."

"You know, Deb. I've been considering something you mentioned earlier. I don't know if it's the right time to discuss it, but I'm wondering. When you mention your plans with Peg...the Maine thing...do you see me in those plans? I mean, I know we both have our own separate lives right now..." Her voice trailed as she contemplated how to say things.

"Honestly, when we began those discussions, I wasn't sure how...what...we were." She pointed between Sam and herself. "I certainly can see you as part of those plans. I've wondered how we go from here even with the properties we have now." She shrugged. "This is definitely a big discussion."

"And my friends. They're younger. Yeah, great to have younger folks involved, but they may not want that. I just can't see losing touch. They're such a huge part of my life...my family of choice, you know."

"Yeah. I do know. I've been alone. I mean, you know how Peg and I had lost touch, but it's been long enough that I had lost any hope of anything but alone. Just seeing her again is huge for me. Finding you even more so, really. I don't know what to think, but we need to figure some of this out, at least sometime soon. Yeah?"

Sam nodded. "Yeah. Maybe one of us will come up with some brilliant way to figure this out."

"Maybe together, it'll go even more smoothly." A beat passed. "You know, even with that long nap, I'm exhausted. All this heavy stuff."

"Ditto," Sam agreed. "Do you think it's odd that we feel so comfortable just hanging out, even if we have heavy discussions?"

"Maybe not so odd. It feels natural being with you. Honestly, I relish being close, being held. It's peaceful, internally. And if that leads to flames from any of the ashes from our earlier blaze, so be it. I love being with you, Sam."

"It feels good to me too."

Sam loved how cozy it felt sitting in a chair close to Deb. She watched Deb thumb through a local field guide book to find the wildflowers Sam had pointed out in the yard. She caught Deb sneaking looks at her, watching her. She felt warm, watching Deb unconsciously run her thumbnail across her bottom lip as she read. Deb's lips were full, and her eyes danced back and forth with the lines she read.

Sam stole glances at Deb for an hour. Her yawns signaled that she needed some sleep. When Sam stood, she held an arm out as invitation. Deb took her hand and stood. She kissed Sam good night. "I'll be right behind you," Deb whispered. "It's nice, you know, being here with you. I know I can picture that in the future." Sam lightly brushed a finger across Deb's lips and left the room to prepare for bed.

The smell of coffee woke Sam the next morning. She felt behind her and verified that Deb was no longer in the bed. She found her at the kitchen table looking at her phone. Slipping her arms around Deb from behind the chair, Sam kissed her neck and rested her face there. Deb rested a hand on Sam's arm. "Good morning," Sam said softly. "You sleep okay?"

"Hiya," Deb whispered. "I woke up a couple of times. You know, different bed and all, but yeah. You?"

"Deb, thanks for coming. It means so much to me." Sam straightened up and stretched backward. She raised her shoulders and rolled her head, preparing to face the day. "Coffee smells good." She poured a cup and joined Deb at the table.

"I have some homemade muesli and milk, or I can make toast and eggs," Sam offered.

"Muesli sounds good. Lighter is better if we're having some fancy dinner tonight. Hey, can we go for a light hike, or walk, or something?" Deb seemed excited for an activity.

Sam suggested a couple of things. Deb could take one of the kayaks out on the lake while Sam walked around the lake. Sam had not been cleared for activities that required her arms to be raised quite so high with that type of intensity. They could both walk around the lake and campground, then drive a few miles to Sosebee Cove to see wildflowers. The third idea was a hike on the AT. Sam had several ideas for both short and longer hikes. They could also drive the thirty minutes to Brasstown Bald, where there were a couple of options. They could fish, but Deb would have to cast for both.

"Who would have thought there would be so many options in this little ol' place?" Deb teased.

"If none of these are to your liking, we can always find an inside exercise right here."

Deb laughed and reached for Sam's hand. Sam stood and walked to Deb, who pulled her into her lap as if she were a child. Deb put her arms around Sam's waist, and Sam leaned up to kiss her. "It's a good thing you haven't made the bed." Deb tried to stand while holding Sam, but relented quickly and led her to the bed. "And you're going to owe me a chiropractic visit after that!" They both laughed, and Sam pulled Deb down. "Be careful," Deb cautioned.

"Spoilsport," Sam whispered, Deb's lips only inches away. "We are not both dressed, though," Sam pulled at the front of Deb's collar to bring her closer.

"Yeah, and you keep trying to make me miss meals. I didn't even finish my coffee." Deb kissed her hard, and Sam released a guttural moan when Deb found her tongue. She gripped Deb's shirt, holding her in position. This earned her another rough kiss, although she felt Deb controlling the pressure and intensity.

"You remember that kiss in the car on the road up here?" Sam whispered. "*I sure do.*"

Deb pulled at her wrist. "I think you may be violating your exercise restrictions with that grip, so let me make this easier for you." With that, she opened Sam's robe and pulled her close. Deb continued roughly kissing her while firmly holding her face. The kisses were raw, and their tongues firmly explored each other's mouth. Sam moaned again, pulling Deb's hips into her and rocking her pelvis up.

Deb's breath was hot against Sam's ear. "Now. I'm going to pour myself another cup of coffee and eat some cereal. When you're ready, come join me. You now know what to look forward to later..." Deb left the room.

"Oh no," Sam sighed through ragged breaths. "Remind me not to make you mad!" she shouted. "I knew you were hungry, but *shoot.*" She shook her head and brought her hands to her face. *How am I supposed to function?* How could Deb make her lose her mind so totally? Ravish her in seconds? She couldn't decide if she was a little pissed or totally motivated to make it through until later rolled around.

"What was that?" Sam asked as she made her way to the kitchen area. She grabbed a bowl of cereal and milk, and sat across from Deb, who was smiling at her and eating her cereal.

"Let's go to the lake. Can we take a picnic and stay for the day?" Deb suggested taking the kayak and the fishing poles. Sam laughed at Deb's avoidance of her question. To have a day where they could enjoy themselves was so appealing that Sam let her prior exploration slide. She knew that when later rolled around, she wouldn't care anymore.

Chapter Seventeen

SAM SAT ON THE boat launch with her arms wrapped around her knees, watching Deb paddle across to the far side of the lake. The position was somewhat uncomfortable, so she stood. After a few minutes, she set up the outdoor rockers and small camping table on a grassy spot in the shade, along the path to the beach. She waved and pointed to the spot when Deb turned her way. Deb's return wave signaled she'd seen her. Sam grabbed her binoculars and headed along the path around the lake. It was good to exercise, even if it was only walking.

As she walked, she wondered about the future—one future in particular. One with Deb. How would it work? How much time would it take before she—before they—figured it out? These were the same things she had wondered on multiple occasions since they began dating. Would others call this a committed relationship? Did they? She could only assume that they would. Going out, having sex, talking on the phone. Yep. Dating behavior. But now they were *staying* with one another, at least as much of the time as they could. She assumed, when she went back to the coast to see her mom, she would be staying with Deb, but they hadn't finalized anything. Deb had said the L word to her, though, and she to Deb. There was no reason, if that was what they were feeling, that it wouldn't or shouldn't be shared. They each recognized the fleeting nature of life, especially since they were sixty-somethings. They were much too wise not to recognize the emotion. And there was no reason to avoid saying it, but translating it into a future wasn't a certainty.

When Sam arrived back to the chairs, Deb was still out on the lake. She wasn't paddling but had her head back and was holding the paddle across the boat in front of her, seeming to soak in the warm rays. Sam drank some water and started reading. Her eyes grew heavy and tired of squinting, so she stretched out across the picnic blanket.

* * * *

Deb watched Sam stretch out on the blanket. The sun was warm, and the cool breeze barely rippled the surface of the water. Occasionally, a fish jumped. Deb contemplated the contrast of the peaceful surroundings with the unrest within her. She recognized the emotion as joy when she thought of Sam and knew she loved Sam. Deb felt enormous gratitude to have Sam in her life. But how would they proceed? Would they eventually live together? Where? She knew they should talk; she was sure Sam shared the same concerns. She paddled back, wishing in that moment that she could make love to Sam, right there on the shore. She ached for it.

Having easily carried the kayak to the picnic spot, Deb lay next to Sam on the blanket. She lightly brushed Sam's arm with her hand. "I almost regret having left the house. It is beautiful here...peaceful. But I ache for you right now."

Sam sighed and blew out a heavy breath. "There are a lot fewer folks than when we were at that rooftop bar. Pretty sure you could do quite a bit toward that end if you're creative."

"Hmm. You're right. Well, I certainly know what I'm going to be thinking. I'm going to give it a try...without talking."

"Oh, but I love it so when you talk to me that way." Sam whimpered in disappointment.

"Come on now. We always have that *later*."

Sam closed her eyes, as if in resignation.

"You okay, Samantha?"

Sam didn't answer or turn, but her hands moved to her eyes again. Deb lightly touched Sam's back; she could feel Sam was sobbing. "I'm going to load up the car. Let's go back, okay?" Deb said softly. After everything but the blanket was packed into the car, she sat down next to Sam. "I love you. I hope you know that. I want to hold you, but I don't want to get shot, and I don't want a cross burning in your yard. Let's go back." Deb stood. "I mean, you know. This isn't the most liberal area of the country. It's a little rural for me to feel comfortable."

Sam nodded. She slowly got up and pulled the blanket with her, shaking it as she walked up the hill to the car. Deb followed, and neither spoke. Deb drove the five minutes to the cabin. They left everything in the car and went inside. Sam began sobbing again and walked to her bed, sitting on the edge. Deb sat facing Sam's side, half straddling her. Sam relaxed into her arms but continued sobbing.

"I wish you would tell me what you're feeling, Sam," Deb said softly. "If you're not in love with me, I need to know. If it's something else, I want to know. God, I'm so crazy for you. Please talk to me."

"It's just...I don't know what's happening to me. It's intense. Maybe thinking about our conversation last night." Sam leaned up and kissed Deb. "I love you. That's what's the matter. I mean, we don't know where we're heading. It scares me."

"I want to continue this conversation, but we're headed to Liz and Monty's in a couple of hours. I know how you feel when your face is all puffy...folks wonder why you've been crying. Then you know they'll ask." Deb retrieved a cool, damp facecloth from the bathroom.

"See? You're so kind. And you're hotter than fuckin' hell. I come when you haven't even touched me. I mean, you're incredible. Why am I so scared of losing you? How do I just accept that we love one another? And what the fuck does it mean?"

"Let's talk about that, but not for the next few hours. Okay? Let's relax, go spend some time with those nice friends, and see what happens." Deb hoped that no answer meant that Sam agreed. "If you want to talk all night, I'll be right here with you. And if you want to do something else all night, I'm all in for that too."

Sam looked up. "You're so fuckin' hot...so hot. Deal."

Sam's seeming unrest was needling Deb. *I know we love one another, but why so worried?* She continued analyzing until she decided that, without discussion, it was wasted effort.

* * * *

After her shower, Sam felt infinitely better. Dressing up seemed to help her already lightened mood. Deb brought her another facecloth she had cooled in the freezer to help the still-swollen eye area. Twenty minutes more, and Liz and Monty might not have any idea Sam had been crying. Sam could even fudge by saying her allergies were bothering her, or that she had napped, which was technically true.

Deb wore the nicest outfit she had brought her jeans, the white Oxford shirt, a tank, and her natural linen jacket. Her hair was still wet, but she had it parted down the center and pulled behind her ears, as usual for this length.

"Okay?" Deb asked as she looked at herself in the mirror.

"I know you're not really expecting that I would say anything other than you look great. If I knew they weren't deliberately chaining themselves to the cabin to keep from coming down here, I'd cancel. Oh, wait. I'd feel the same way if you came out with nothing on at all." Sam smiled and reached for Deb's hand.

"I'm a lucky woman to be so admired." Deb locked their gazes, and Sam squirmed with the intensity.

"You really gotta stop that. I won't to be able to function when we arrive. I am what they call 'turned on' right now. Would you be willing to share your mouth for a minute or so before we head out?" Sam pulled Deb's arm down toward her. The kiss was rough, and Sam moaned. "We really gotta go. Don't let me make a fool of myself this evening, okay?"

"Okay, silly. Let's go." Deb gently pulled Sam's arm. They strolled up the road, Sam holding the bottle of Sinskey Vin Gris Pinot Noir for the appetizers in one hand and a small bag with a headlight, a flashlight, and pepper spray in the other hand, for their stroll home.

Monty was waiting on the porch, leaning against the rail on her hands, beaming her usual gorgeous smile. "Ladies!" Monty cheered. "You emerge!" She chuckled as they came up the drive. Deb took the bag from Sam's hand as Liz walked out smiling.

"Oh wow," Deb whispered. "You can feel the love and warmth, can't you?" Sam nodded as they topped the stairs to the porch.

Sam introduced Deb, and Monty shook her hand. Liz put her hands on Deb's arms. "Welcome to our home, Deb. We're glad to meet you."

"Likewise. I'm grateful Samantha has such good friends," Deb said. "She told me how sweet you had been to her since her return. I really appreciate you two looking after her." Sam felt Deb's warm gaze much lower than her blushing cheeks.

"Samantha, huh?" Monty teased, looking at Sam's reddening face.

Sam handed Monty the wine, and she immediately went inside with the bottle and returned with a tray of four filled glasses. They each took one and toasted to Sam's health.

"Sam showed me the work you've done at her place," Deb said.

"Monty, you should show Deb the work you did to add the room here." Liz pointed inside.

"Sure. Come on in, Deb." Monty and Deb disappeared into the house, giving Liz and Sam a chance to talk.

"How's it going, Sam?" Liz looked directly into Sam's eyes.

"You know I've been crying, but it's all good, Liz. Really, it is."

"Okay. You're right though. I know you too well for you to hide that puffiness."

"I know. Deb was a trooper, trying to help me hide it. She's so sweet." Her eyes welled with tears again. "It's been so intense. Don't know if that's a love thing, an age thing, or what. We've used the L word several times already."

"Well, then. That speaks volumes right there, doesn't it? And just think. Wasn't it just the holiday get-together, when Lee never showed? And you thought your love life was finished for good?" Liz smiled. "Here they come. We'll table that."

"Table what?" Monty asked as she and Deb returned.

"Just girl talk, that's all," Liz answered sheepishly.

"Hmm." Monty turned toward Deb. "What are we?" She shrugged, and Deb followed suit.

They sat and chatted as they sipped their wine and noshed on cheese, crackers, olives, and fruit. Sam stood to pick up an apple slice. As she was eating it, Deb stood and sidled up behind her, threading her arms around her waist. Pulled back against Deb, Sam melted. Sam's reaction was not lost on Liz nor Monty. Deb began swaying with the beat of the tune playing on the portable speaker. Sam's eyes closed.

"So Deb, tell us about you met and your first date," Monty suggested.

"Do you want the R-rated version or the—" Deb started.

"Not R or X, please." Sam blushed and play-slapped Deb's arm.

Monty and Liz both laughed, but Sam looked up at Deb in anticipation.

"I don't know what Samantha has told you, but I am one of the part-time parking czars at a beach near where her mom lives. I was in the lot where she parks, and of course, I was doing my duty writing a ticket. This chick walks up and says, 'Hey. I was getting my pass when you walked to my car.' And I say, 'Oh, this is your car? I didn't see you.' The chick answers, rather snarkily, I might add, 'Yeah, well I walked right past you while you were telling that guy the parking season dates.' Of course, she had me at Lycra." The others laughed loudly, and Monty almost spit out her wine, which made them laugh even harder.

"Yeah, but the date!" Monty blurted after she could speak.

"Officially, we met up at one of my local hangouts, a small pub-type place, classic beach watering hole—"

"But this was only *after* she literally undressed me with her eyes while she was blocking my exit at the parking lot the second morning," Sam interrupted. They all laughed again.

"Yeah. I did, didn't I? And you didn't seem to mind at all, did you?" Deb said softly, looking down at Sam. "Back to the date, though. She had a little too much to drink to feel safe driving, so we walked to my place just to add some time until she could drive—"

"Sure. Uh huh, as if we believe that!" Monty interrupted.

"We did kiss, as I recall," Deb said. "And then I walked her back to her car, and she went back to her mom's. Just that simple." Deb smiled.

"Yeah. Just that simple," Sam said rather softly. "Then she *called* me. I was dying there, you know. On fire, I must admit."

"Dang!" Monty teased. "Look Deb, if you ever feel that—"

"Uh uh, no, Monty. Forget it!" Sam interrupted, waving Monty away. "She is all mine." She leaned backward into Deb's arms again. Deb gave her a squeeze, rolled her eyes, then looked back at Monty, shrugging.

Liz shot Sam a grin, clearly noting her blush. Sam leaned a little more firmly into Deb, who squeezed her arm lightly. Liz interrupted the noticeable silence, "Monty, can you help me bring dinner out?"

"Can I help?" Deb asked.

"No. You two lovebirds stay out here." As soon as the door shut behind them, Sam turned around and looked at Deb.

"I...that was...if..." Sam struggled to express herself.

Deb leaned and kissed her softly, interrupting the clearly tortuous communication attempt. "I love you. You don't have to explain why you said what you said."

Something in Deb's response caught her as if a floodgate opened, letting out whatever she had been keeping inside. The thing she had wrestled with earlier in the day. The thing she felt, even more profoundly than usual, when she melted yet again as Deb held her. There was that L word again, but something was different. Sam felt it this time, really felt it. They belonged together. Tears welled in her eyes, and Deb wiped the falling drops from her face.

"It's okay," Deb said softly as she squeezed Sam in a hug.

Monty burst through the door, hands full of bowls. "Okay y'all. Enough with the goo-goo eyes. Let's eat!" Monty was always so upbeat and funny; it was back to happy-family time as they sat. They raised their glasses, and simultaneously, without prompting, toasted, "We made it through another day!"

The evening was fun, and the company warm and loving. Monty and Deb discussed tiny house living and containers. Monty was as interested in Deb's cohousing idea as Deb was. They talked about all going up at the same time to look at Maine property. Liz was all in for any talk of going to or living part of a year in Maine. They talked cycling and how Deb should meet their friend Val, who had cycled from Maine to Key West. Sam had met Val at a holiday gathering the previous winter, and they confessed the unsuccessful attempts at fixing Sam up with Val's friend, Lee. They described their favorite beaches and small towns. Two hours passed without a break.

Liz attempted to railroad the cleanup, but Sam and Deb did their fair share. It took only a few minutes for the kitchen to be as pristine as it had been before Liz and Monty started cooking. Hugs and see yous all around, Deb and Sam strolled back, flashlights and pepper spray in hand.

It was the time of year when bears were making their appearances around the neighborhood, and while bears might be easily scared off, no one wanted to take that chance. "I can't believe you really have to consider bear encounters. That's so weird for me," Deb said. "I guess it's no worse than worrying about drunks, though." They both chuckled.

Chapter Eighteen

BACK INSIDE SAM'S CABIN, Deb joined her in closing the curtains and windows and turning on the lamps for cozy night lighting. There was little talking. The moment at Liz and Monty's weighed on Sam's mind. She truly felt there was some sort of connection that was not there previously. Something beneath the surface that she had kept stuffed inside her until it started seeping out at the lake. Then this evening, a simple tease released nearly everything. She was scared, apprehensive. She wasn't just in lust. She was almost sixty-five, and she wanted to share her life with this woman.

"I sure would like to know what you're thinking right now, but I'm afraid a penny might not cover it." Deb smiled and motioned for Sam. "Come with me." She led Sam back to the bedroom and pulled the covers down. Sam shivered when she allowed Deb to slip the shirt from her shoulders. When Deb unfastened her bra, she sighed, but when Deb unfastened her jeans, she moaned, and Deb had to help hold her upright. Deb guided her to the edge of the bed, then slipped her panties down her legs and eased her under the bed covers. Sam watched Deb remove her own clothes.

Sam's overwhelming desire was eclipsed by wanting to linger in each kiss. She savored feeling Deb's body touching hers, intoxicated by Deb's embrace. She allowed herself a moment of presence to see if Deb was feeling the same. Deb lightly gripped Sam's wrist and whispered, "Not yet."

"Let's…oh babe…I want to feel you…take this in with you. I love you." Sam sighed. Her eyes welled with tears. She found intense comfort in their synchronicity. Every wonderful, beautiful, full, erotic feeling. She smiled and pulled her head back to look at Deb's face, and her lips softly took Deb's again.

Their lovemaking continued for another hour or so. Their climaxes provided both satiety and pleasure of another sort—a comfort that would have been difficult for Sam to explain. It was steamy but sweet, calming while stirring. Sam rested her head on Deb's shoulder. Deb stroked Sam's shoulder with her fingertips.

"This is one of my favorite places in the world, I've decided." Sam tilted her head to see Deb's face.

"We need to talk, Samantha," Deb said softly.

"I know, Deb. We do. By the way, hearing Samantha instead of Sam...it's nice. I've never thought of that before. I've been Sam since I decided that Samantha was too girly. College, I think."

"You're beautifully womanly to me. I love your name. Sam is fun, but you're Samantha to me...

"I guess I'll start," Deb continued. "I love you. I never thought I would be feeling this. I certainly never thought I'd say it. I had given up. It's incredible with you. For the first time since...I never...you make me feel that I'm attractive. That I'm special."

Sam could feel that Deb had begun to stifle a sob. "Deb, please. You are *striking*. And yes, you're attractive. There is nothing about you that doesn't make me ache for you." She wiped Deb's eyes. "Tonight...there is something, Deb. Something I can't even describe. I could die right now and have lived the happiest life I have ever lived. I love you. There is nothing else I can compare this to. Deb, I want to be with you, live with you. I mean it—*live* with you."

"I feel the same. I do, but I cannot see myself *not* at the beach, at least most of the year. That's me, my life. As we've said before, we have our own lives and places. We have friends and places we go and things we do. I can't see giving up my place, but I love you, and your place is incredible, rich with beauty, not the least of which is you."

Sam pinched Deb's arm and chuckled. "I could never expect you to leave your home there. What were you going to do if you found a place in Maine, though?"

"I don't really know. I'm not thinking past the snowbird phase. If Maine is anything close to what Peg says it is, I'm there...even if it's only a few months a year." Deb seemed more animated, but Sam didn't want to move from the comfort of their embrace.

"Maine is beautiful," Sam said. "Ask Liz. She's been there, but I lived there. I have good friends there. Lifelong friends, like family. I don't know that I want to give up my place here, but I could rent it. There are a few times I'd want to be here, though. We have a huge Thanksgiving up here with our friend group." Sam didn't want to foist herself on Deb. "I want you to feel a part of that family of choice. Then again at our Tween Week holiday gathering, the one Liz and Monty described at dinner."

"You would *consider* snowbirding?" Deb asked softly.

"I would. I want to have a Southern connection to remain a part of Sasha's life. To know that I would see my brothers and family and that family of choice, you know? I've had my share of long winters in Maine.

I'm not sure I could go back to those, but nine months there would be fine. Are you *really* saying you want us to live together?"

"We have no reason not to try it. It's not as if we have thirty years of active living left, right? We love the way we feel together. Shit. We're having hot sex! I feel I could make love to you this way forever. And I never thought anyone would *ever* find me attractive after my surgery. Samantha, I felt I was a *freak*. I suppressed feeling anything, even with myself."

Sam looked up at Deb and waited for her to look down. She whispered softly as she reached for Deb's lips. "You are so smokin' hot." They kissed again, and Deb flipped Sam onto her back.

Deb used her knee to part Sam's legs. After they had brought one another to a point of no return, they came together, almost collapsing with exhaustion, then snuggled together to sleep.

* * * *

It was after ten when they stirred the next morning. Deb kissed Sam and pulled on some jeans and a T-shirt to head into the kitchen for coffee. She jumped in the shower as it was brewing. Towel drying her hair, she walked back into the bedroom to see Sam stretched out, sheet barely covering her, and looking up at her. She held her hand up, and Deb leaned to kiss her. "Come on. Time to get up. I've gotta move around. I'm a little stiff this morning." Deb shook her head. "Most mornings, I suppose."

"Moving around is what I had in mind."

"Mm-hm. I just bet you did." Deb shook her head again. "Come have some coffee with me."

"Spoilsport," Sam teased. "I'll be there in a second." Sam showered, then met Deb in the kitchen. "I'm a little stiff too," she admitted. "The warmth of the water helped to loosen some of my muscles." Deb poured her coffee.

Sam took the cup from her hand and placed it carefully on the table. She slid her arms around Deb's waist and pulled her close. Deb wrapped her arms around Sam's shoulders.

"I love your being here," Sam whispered.

"It's really nice to spend time with you here." A couple of seconds passed. "I guess we haven't settled our conundrum, though, have we?"

Sam slipped out of the hug and sat at the table, her hands wrapping around her cup. Deb took the seat across the table. "I don't think we have," Sam replied.

"So, we love one another and want to be together, but we both have separate homes."

"Same old, same old. Maine, here, there. I guess neither of us has the perfect answer. As long as Mom is living and needing care, I'll be visiting frequently. I love the beach, especially late fall through mid-spring. I could rent this place during the summer and live in Maine."

"Likely, neither of us could afford the same lifestyle in Maine that we have currently, if we attempted it alone. Why shouldn't we live together there? I don't want you to feel as if you're giving up your life, though. I would love you to stay with me when you come to Bea's, if you feel that's safe for her. It would be so nice to wake up with you every day. Are there any of your things you would want to bring to my place that would help make it yours?" Sam looked across the table and sipped her coffee.

"I don't think so. I don't know. Maybe. I feel terrified on some level. Don't you?" Sam asked. Deb nodded. "Though I know nothing feels better than having you hold me. How can I be terrified then?"

"There is an unknown...almost turmoil, isn't there? I know that for the first time since my surgery, I feel whole. And when you touch me, I forget. It doesn't even matter that there's nothing there, it feels like they're still there...that electrical current that shoots. You know what I mean?" Deb wiped her wet eyes with her napkin.

"I know *exactly* what you mean. It's that same current I feel whenever you touch me...look at me...whisper in my ear...moan in my mouth. Yeah. I know." Sam moved to the chair next to Deb and pulled it close. She raked her nails across Deb's thighs as she kissed her. "That one?"

Deb sighed and slipped her tongue to find Sam's in the next kiss, this one much firmer. "Yeah. That's the one," Deb whispered. They laughed and hugged and kissed again.

After breakfast, they strolled around the circle and out to the highway and then back around to complete the circle. They waved at Liz and Monty, who were drinking coffee on the porch.

"Hey, y'all wanna go to the lake?" Monty stood and shouted.

"Sure. We're game. It's a great day for the lake."

Deb nodded.

"Great, I'll pick you up at your place in an hour." Liz clapped her hands.

Chapter Nineteen

MONTY AND DEB WERE kayaking while Liz and Sam took advantage of the path around the lake and campgrounds for a quiet walk.

"Deb and I discussed living together."

"Oh, Sam. That's big. But you'll keep your places? I mean, it's early, wouldn't you say?"

"Yeah...well, maybe early. We're not getting any younger." Sam chuckled. "We are seasoned enough to know what we've had and what we want now, you know?"

"I get that. Monty and I are a little different. At different stages, in some ways, but now we know one another well enough to be able to talk out differences. Have you had any big blow-ups?"

"Not big ones. Mainly when I was drunk and acting a fool." Sam shook her head as Liz laughed. "But no, we haven't. Maybe that's why I'm still nervous. We've looked at the pros, mostly." After a beat, she added, "So we haven't examined the cons...or lack of them. I guess we feel, at this point, there aren't any real cons."

"Well, the biggest pro to me is that you both want to be together."

"Exactly. At our ages, waiting a year just doesn't seem to be an option. If it turns out we aren't compatible—and I hope that's not the case—we have our own places."

"Do you think Deb and Monty will talk about this?"

"I'm not sure. I doubt Deb would bring it up. Not sure if Monty would."

"Ha! Are you joking? Monty has no filters and no secrets. You know darn well she would pump Deb for information."

"You're right, she would. Maybe I'll ask Deb if she brought it up."

"I'll keep this confidential if you don't want me to talk to Monty."

"Nah. If we can't speak about this, what kind of friends are we?"

They had walked the entire perimeter and the discussion waned as they returned to the kayak input. Deb and Monty pulled the boats out of the water and onto the grass next to the picnic table. Deb walked up behind Sam and put her arms around her waist. "Hiya," she said softly into Sam's ear. Sam leaned backward into her.

"Um. I think we agreed PDA out here wasn't a good idea." Sam frowned.

"Shoot!" Monty teased. "I was hoping for some R-rated action." They all laughed.

"*Shoot* is what I'm afraid of," Sam said. "I would be hesitant even at *her* beach. Especially after having a beer can thrown at me, but I don't want to steer the convo into homophobia if it's okay with y'all." The faces said it all. Total agreement.

Deb and Monty both grabbed some chips. Sam watched them stuff their mouths. Monty started laughing, which made Deb laugh, and chip pieces flew everywhere. They all started laughing, seemingly punch drunk. Sam stroked the front of Deb's shirt, gently, pretending to brush off the chips. Her hand lingered a little longer than necessary, and she ran her palm back down the front. Sam could have devoured Deb if they had been alone.

"That's what *I'm* talking about!" Monty spewed more chips, triggering more laughter. Sam and Deb just stood gazing at one another, breathing raggedly. "Do Liz and I need to take a walk?" Monty asked with some sincerity. Sam sat down on the bench. "Come on, Liz, let's load these boats up, okay?" Liz nodded, and the two of them hauled the boats up the hill to the car, giving Sam and Deb some time.

"What's going on?" Deb asked, sitting next to Sam, pressing against her arm.

"Just overcome with feelings again. Liz and I discussed the moving in thing."

"Makes sense why you'd want to sound it out to your friend."

"Is it okay if Monty knows?"

"Of course, if she doesn't already." She waited a beat. "She hinted around out there when we were close enough. I just didn't take the bait."

"I'm surprised she didn't force it out of you," Sam said, chuckling.

"Think I'm more worried about sharing the news with Peg and Bea before they hear it from someone else we might leak it to."

"We should make time to talk with them before sharing it with others. I agree." Sam looked around and kissed Deb's cheek. Deb smiled at her. Sam felt it was crazy they were already leaving the next day. "It'll be soon enough."

When Liz and Monty returned, Sam motioned for them to sit. The sandwiches were prepared, and beverages and napkins set in places at the table. "Okay, y'all. We're done with serious chatting for now. Sorry," Sam said resolutely.

"What are you worried about?" Monty said with a smile. "I thought it was hot the way you were looking at one another. I mean...whew." A smirk accompanied Liz's light slap of Monty's arm.

Sam looked at Monty. "We wanted y'all to know that we plan to start living together as soon as we can figure out how best to care for Bea. I might have to stay with her, but it might be okay to stay with Deb. I just don't know yet. Then at some point, I think we'll consider that place in Maine." Monty looked a little sad. "We'll keep this place too, so for Thanksgivings and our other special holidays we can be together, but we'll stay at the beach during the winter."

Monty stood and walked around the table to Sam and Deb. She patted Deb on the back and gave her a little sideways hug. She kissed Sam on the cheek.

"That is so cool, y'all. I hope you're half as happy as I am with Liz." Liz's nod punctuated Monty's sincere demeanor. When Monty sat, Liz squeezed her hand.

"It's a big deal. Sounds like you guys have thought and talked this through. You've done the hard work. You have options, and you love one another. We love you both. If you ever need anything, you know to call us, right?" Liz's warm sincerity elicited Sam's thanks. She held Deb's hand as they talked, albeit under the tabletop in case anyone happened upon them.

"You guys have been so sweet to me since I arrived," Deb said softly. "And how many nice things you've done for Samantha is amazing. I don't know if she has said anything regarding my situation, but she has made me feel not only special, but alive again. I had a radical—" Deb cleared her throat with a choke and wiped her eyes. Sam squeezed her hand tightly. "A radical mastectomy. I thought I was dead on the inside. I had two dates with women who either looked at me like I was a freak or..." She stopped again and cleared her throat. Monty came and sat next to her and put her arm around Deb's shoulder. "Anyway, I feel lucky to have met Samantha. And I think you know I love her. She is something special." Sam wiped tears from her eyes, and Deb squeezed her hand.

They sat in silence for several minutes. Deb took some deep breaths to gather herself, and Monty remained sitting with her head on Deb's shoulder. Liz came around to the other side of Sam, so all four of them were seated on one side. "I know that was heavy," Deb said, breaking the silence. "I just felt the need to share it with you. And for you to know one of the reasons why Samantha is so special to me."

"Deb…I can't even imagine. We sure appreciate your trust. That's some deeply personal stuff to be sharing. And we agree with you. Sam *is* special. We never doubted that for a minute, did we?" Liz looked at Monty for confirmation.

"Not ever," Monty chimed in.

"I think we're still figuring things out…but it's clear that we want to navigate that together," Deb said.

"Deb, do you mind sharing what kind of follow-up you have? Do you have to be tested every year or whatever?" Monty shrugged and added, "My mom died before I was a teenager…also breast cancer."

"My surgeon reviews all the latest research with me at my six-month follow-ups. I'm two years out, but since I'm BRCA2 positive, she likes to keep a close eye. She's understanding, though, and she listens when I say I don't want a barrage of treatments that will make me sick."

"That's why she kept working even though she had retired from the school system—to help cover her out of pocket for the surgery and for increased testing that her policy wouldn't cover," Sam explained.

"Argh. Our country's costs are so high, it's truly depressing," Liz said.

"On a lighter note, does anyone want to try fishing off the pier for a while?" Deb asked.

"Yeah," Monty said, raising her hand. "Me, me," she added as she jumped up.

"I'm in." Sam looked at Deb. "Just pass me your pole if we see anyone looking all official, since you don't have a Georgia license."

"Or to me. I'd like a cast or two myself. Been a long time, but Monty and I even bought trout stamps this year." Liz proudly brushed her fingertips on her chest beneath her raised chin.

"Yay. Let's go." Monty beamed.

They bundled up all the picnic supplies, returned them to the car and retrieved fishing poles, a bucket, stringer, and the tackle box and worms. Monty was the first to catch one—a nice, keeper-size trout, then a couple more of similar size. Deb caught another, also large enough to keep. Liz and Sam both caught smaller breams that they threw back. Monty cleaned the fish on the dock and put them on the ice they had thrown in the bucket.

"I think some fish tacos are in order. There's enough for a taco or so each, and I'll grill the fish," Monty offered.

"I'm on tortilla griddle duty," Deb said.

"We'll make the pico," Liz offered.

"And grate the cheese," followed Sam.

After dropping gear, Liz, and Sam back at their respective homes, Monty and Deb drove to Goober's, the small store down at the town's corner, for an assortment of beer. They returned, put the beer on ice at Sam's, and Monty returned home to shower and get ready.

The remainder of the day passed quickly, with the afternoon prep and the cooking that followed. As usual, lively and probing discussions complemented the couples' activities.

In the process of learning each other, Liz and Monty shared their stories.

"I don't know what Sam has told you about us," Liz said. Sam shook her head and zipped her mouth with her fingers.

"I'm one of those million-dollar lottery winners—"

"What? I know you're kidding me, right?" Deb looked astounded.

"No, I'm not, but you are sworn to an oath of secrecy...please, please, please."

"Of course."

"And I spent a year in a women's prison for fraud," Monty said. "And this crazy gal took me in anyway."

Deb looked around as if searching for something on the ceiling or rafters. "Okay. Where are the cameras? This must be one of those shows."

"It's all true." Liz smiled. "Truth really is stranger than fiction."

"You're not shitting me." Deb kept blinking as if trying to figure out if she were in a dream. "Sometime, I want to hear the long version of this story."

"Next time, maybe," Liz said, and Monty lightly slapped Deb's back.

"It's a lot to take in...even for us, right Liz?" Monty asked.

"Yes, it is. And it seems so long ago now." Liz and Monty nodded.

After dinner, they sat around the firepit. By the end of the night, everyone had told most of their biggest deep-dark secrets. It was more truth than truth-or-dare. Everyone took their turns discussing old girlfriends or boyfriends, family issues, jobs, and even a few bucket list items.

As with the night before, cleanup was quick with the four of them. Before Liz and Monty headed back to their place, they exchanged contact information with Deb.

"And I hope y'all are in for a road trip to the beach sometime soon," Deb offered.

"Drive carefully, y'all. We'll look out for your place, Sam. You know, don't worry about anything. We got this."

"Thanks, Liz. And Monty, you too. Love y'all." Sam walked the two out and up the driveway, waving as they headed toward their cabin.

Alone again, Sam seemed sullen.

"What's goin' on? That was so lovely." Deb's face indicated her concern.

"It was lovely. I try not to do this, but I feel heavy...you know, going back to Mom's. It isn't that I resent it. I just hate seeing her become more and more debilitated, especially mentally."

"I know that's gotta be tough." Deb put her arm around Sam. "I wish I could do something."

"Your support is what's getting me through even thinking about it."

"I can come and relieve you, you know."

"Don't think I won't take you up on that. I'm also going to miss your bed. Oof. That bed at Mom's." She rolled her eyes. "But I know you'll be glad to get back to yours."

"Especially if you're in it," Deb teased lightly. Sam smiled.

"At the park..." Sam started slowly, trying to find the right words. "I'm sorry...I sort of lost it. I felt your electric shock when I touched you. In those next few seconds, I was on the verge of...I mean I almost..."

"Yeah. Me too. I know," Deb said softly.

"How do you do that?" Sam decided, since everyone was telling heavy stories, she might as well try to find out Deb's secret to the electric-ray-gun mind zap that yielded an orgasm in zero to sixty, almost without a touch.

"It just happened. That first night when we kissed, for me too. Sometimes I think we've been so starved for it, it just happens."

"Maybe."

Sam pulled on Deb's shirt collar and kissed her. Deb's arms wrapped around her, pulling her forward, hard. "I love your friends," Deb whispered. "But I have been waiting for this all afternoon. We're going to have to postpone packing, I hope you know that." Her mouth found Sam's lips as she heaved out a moan.

In contrast to the slow, exploratory, tender lovemaking previously, this was raw and rough, rougher than they had been on other occasions. This was the desperate lovemaking that elicits deep and audible sighs and gasps, guttural moans, bites, thrusts, and begging. When they came, the release was primal. They were loud, and they did nothing to stifle or muffle it.

Rather than burning out in a fiery crash, Sam rolled onto Deb with her full weight, pressing firmly against her, kissing her hard, and biting her lower lip. Deb wasn't giving in, and she rolled Sam onto her back, giving her what had been given. Deb licked Sam's nipple hard—hard enough to hear her gasp loudly. Sam's grind against Deb continued. Deb took the cue and held Sam's arms down as she buried her face in Sam's neck. Her stiffened tongue raked across Sam's midline until she reached the top of her thighs. She inserted her tongue roughly and sucked until Sam came again with a loud moan, her hips and abdomen bucking.

"Oh God. That was crazy...crazy nice," Sam whispered. She sighed again and pulled at Deb to kiss her.

It was as if something triggered a fierce need, and yet both were all in. Was it exasperation released from pent-up anxiety of how relationships were supposed to work? Was it an acknowledgment that neither would give up their independence? Or was it simply years of sexual energy finally released in a safe haven?

Chapter Twenty

TWO HOURS BEHIND SCHEDULE, their lovemaking having delayed an early start to their travel, Sam needed to attend to online banking, mail hold, answer a few emails, and simply sort out her head. She knew she could pack dirty clothes, but she also needed to replace the sheets, shower, and prepare the house for her being gone for as long as three weeks. Coffee helped.

Something was nagging in her gut. She had loved last night's sex. It was sex; it wasn't just lovemaking. She had needed Deb to make her come. She didn't want to *imagine* sex. She wanted Deb to take her, to make her beg. And she did. Sam had never wanted something on such a visceral level. What was that all about? She wanted it still. She'd breathed in Deb's scent on waking, and when she kissed Deb good morning, she'd smelled herself. It was tantalizing, and she wanted more. Was it some sort of 'you can't have it, so you want it more' thing? They had not been anything close to celibate—far from it. What did she want more of then? She wondered if this is what newlyweds experienced. Those newlyweds who had never had sex and were saving themselves. But they were both experienced, and they had not saved themselves.

She still felt incredible when Deb held her. She thought that straddling Deb with her head on Deb's shoulder was the absolute most wonderful place in the world. Stroking Deb's chest, watching Deb shiver when she stroked her scars, or licked them, or sucked as if her breasts were still there. Deb clearly wanted that, maybe even needed it. They were excellent at communicating sex needs. Not just communicating them, but translating them into fulfillment.

* * * *

By the time Sam dropped Deb off at her place, it was beginning to get dark. The days were still long, and it was only eight o'clock.

"I think I'll stay at Mom's tonight. I need to." Sam knew Deb would understand.

"You know where I am. I have a couple more days off. I can hang out there if you want."

"I'll call you tomorrow. I already miss you." Sam smiled, knowing how silly that would sound.

"Yeah, I know. Me too. Tell Bea hello for me." Deb walked Sam to the edge of her porch. "When is your follow-up?"

"I'm supposed to go by tomorrow afternoon for the X-ray."

"It's surprising how much discoloration there still is, but at least you don't have the swelling. Mainly though, I'll be glad you're able to carry your own weight again. I was really getting tired of doing everything for you." Deb teased. Sam play-slapped at Deb's arm.

"I tell you what I look forward to. It's putting my arms around your neck when I kiss you," Sam grew warm between her legs as she looked at Deb.

"Get out of here before... I could so easily try to keep you here," Deb said softly. "Call me later, okay?" Sam nodded, ran her hand down Deb's arm, and left.

Bea was slumped in the seat of her walker at the table. Sam unloaded her luggage easily and without pain. Even carrying it up the outside stairs didn't cause discomfort. Coming in and going out two more times did not disturb Bea. Sam busied herself tidying up the kitchen.

"Hey," Bea said with a smile when she woke. She curled her index finger with a come-here gesture. Sam hugged her mother, who felt ever frailer. She remembered the size-twenty woman who'd once enveloped her children when she hugged them. Now a size twelve, Bea was a mere wisp of her former self. "Where's Deb?" she asked.

Sam smiled as she answered. "I took her to her house at the beach, Mom. She'd been gone for almost a week and wanted to get settled in. She'll come here sometime, maybe tomorrow. She's off work two more days this week."

"Oh, that's nice. When are you heading back to her place?" Bea asked.

"Not tonight. I wanna be able to spend some time with you. And she wants to settle back in, you know?"

"Well good, then. But when you love someone, you should stay together if you can. It's one thing if it's a long way away. But I sleep late. You don't have to stay here at night."

"Maybe tomorrow night, then," Sam said.

"I know when your dad and I were courting, we couldn't bear to be apart. And then when we were married, and he went to Korea..." Bea's voice trailed. "Well, when he came back, there wasn't anything keeping us apart. And I mean for years."

"Okay, Mom. Okay. I don't need to hear any more. I get a king-size picture. It's not necessarily one I want of my parents."

"Don't be so silly. Now, how long are you staying?" Bea looked down at the calendar that served as her placemat. She looked puzzled because Sam had not yet written down when she was leaving. "It just says, *Sam here*. It doesn't say when you leave."

"It's on the next month, Mom. The plan is that I'll be here for two and a half weeks. So that ends next month."

"Oh! How *nice*!" she said enthusiastically. "I'll bet you'll be coming more and staying longer now that you and Deb are together." Bea was perceptive, even if she didn't know what day it was or what she needed to do to get dressed in the morning. "And Deb is coming tonight?"

"Tomorrow, probably. I'm going to the doctor tomorrow. They're going to x-ray my back again."

"What's the matter with your back? Nobody tells me anything." Bea seemed irritated.

"You remember how the guy threw the beer can at my back and knocked me off my bicycle, Mom?" Sam said, trying to jog Bea's memory.

"Oh yes. You were scraped up, and Tom had to help you with your luggage. Did he come today? Or is your luggage still in the car?"

"I'm better now. I don't have any pain loading or unloading luggage anymore. I just can't raise my arms above my head until they say it's okay," Sam explained. Bea nodded, but Sam wasn't sure she understood.

The visit was nice and Sam showed her mom photos of the fish everyone caught.

"Oh, I love fish. You know Dad was an expert fisherman," Bea reminisced.

"I remember Granddad coming back with a mess, when we were at their house. Here are some pictures of my neighbor friends. The four of us went to the lake near our house. That's Deb and Monty out on the lake, and this is Liz looking out at the lake. She's so pretty, but I'm not sure she knows it."

"They look to be nice friends, and it looks like y'all had a great time." Her mom may not have followed everything, but she always seemed to enjoy hearing stories or hearing people talk, even if she didn't process the conversations. Later, Sam encouraged her mom to get ready for bed, and she started Bea's Barry Manilow CD as she did every night she was there.

* * * *

Sam knew she might have a wait when she returned to the sports-medicine clinic. The assistant eventually called her back and took her vital signs.

"Sorry for the wait," Janice said when she opened the exam room door. "How've you been feeling?"

"Pretty good, actually. I was able to carry my luggage up a flight of steps without any discomfort."

"Any remaining problem areas, though?" Janice was speaking from behind her, examining her back. "Swelling's all but gone, but a few color splashes remain. Let's get that X-ray." Janice walked Sam back to the radiology area, and the technician guided her into the correct position. After the X-ray, Sam found herself waiting again.

This time, Janice and Dr. Davie both came in. "Good news, Ms. Avery. The break looks great. Nicely mending." Dr. Davie crossed his arms over his chest. "Given that you're not having pain, it's well on its way to completely fusing. If it doesn't hurt to lift your arms, I don't see any need for restrictions. Let pain guide your activity, just as you've been doing." Before he turned to open the door to leave, he tipped an imaginary hat.

"I've thought about you a lot, Sam. Wondered how you were doing." Janice smiled as she looked into Sam's eyes. "Now that it seems our professional relationship is ending, would you have a drink sometime?"

Sam was a little shocked, but she smiled. Janice was probably twenty years younger, had long sandy hair pulled back in a clip, and welcoming brown eyes. She was captivating, Sam had to admit. She must have waited too long to answer.

"Sorry. I didn't mean to put you on the spot." Janice rested a hand on Sam's forearm. "I loved your sense of humor. And I'd be lying if I said I didn't find you attractive, but I don't want you to feel uncomfortable."

"I was surprised, of course. That's all," Sam replied. "I'm actually seeing someone...regularly, I mean, but I'm flattered to say the least. If I weren't, your offer would have been quite lovely."

"Well, it never hurts to ask." Janice slapped the paper chart on the desk, still smiling. "Take care of yourself. You know where we are if you find a beer can in your back again, God forbid." They shook hands and parted.

It was hot and humid when she left the clinic. The air conditioning had let her forget the state of the steam room that was Wilmington.

Why did I say I would come here for two weeks again? This is why I live in Suches. It dawned on her that she had not yet gone in the ocean this season. It was almost Memorial Day, but the water would still be cooler than the air, even if warm in the shallows. She drove to the beach and stopped at the supply store. She found a one-piece and a pair of cute nylon shorts that didn't make her look too fat. She would be thrilled if she could get this extra fifteen pounds off, but it was hard unless she could keep a routine. She grabbed sunscreen, flip flops, and the cheapest, thinnest towel they had.

When she arrived at Deb's, she was glad the truck and bike were there. Deb was probably at home. She hadn't called, but she intended to walk to the beach regardless, so it didn't really matter. She needed to remove the tags, so she walked up in hopes of changing and then heading to the strip of beach near the pier.

Deb was in the lounge chair on the porch, wearing her boy shorts, sunning or staying cool. The ceiling fan was on high. "Hiya. I heard footsteps coming up, but I didn't know it was you." Deb seemed surprised to see her.

"Don't get up." Sam leaned and kissed Deb. "I want to go swimming, even for a few minutes. It's so damn hot here. Can I change?"

"Of course," Deb said. "Your appointment?"

"Or maybe I'll just strip and stretch out on top of you. Damn you look hot in those shorts. Mm. Come to the ocean with me."

"All those options sound okay with me." Deb cleared her throat. "Your *appointment*?" Sam stretched an arm out toward Deb's hand. Sam pulled lightly for Deb to stand, and when she did, pressed herself firmly against Deb and slid her arms around her neck.

"Now kiss me, and make it a good one," Sam whispered. Deb obliged, and Sam sighed audibly, pulling against Deb's shoulders. "Oh my God, this feels nice. I hope we can do this in the water. I'm going to go in and change."

Deb gasped when Sam came out in her new attire. Sam rubbed against her again, and Deb ran her hand along the Lycra swimsuit and down Sam's back onto her ass. "One-piece Lycra with ample-access leg openings? What's not to love?" Deb grabbed a towel and slid into her flip flops. Towels across their shoulders, they headed the few blocks to the ocean.

There were a few people scattered around and under the pier, but in two weeks it would be wall to wall people. They removed shoes and used them to hold down their towels in the wind. Deb ran out to the water and dove under. Sam walked slowly, jumping as waves threatened to break on her. She knew the water would feel cold only at first, but she couldn't bring herself to dive under a wave. Deb surfaced and began splashing her. Sam squealed for her to stop. The only way Deb wasn't going to win that battle was for Sam to dive in, which she did. Once in, she no longer felt so cold. She wondered why she always delayed the action. It's not like she hadn't known since she was a child that it was the easiest way to acclimate.

There wasn't much wind. Just enough to blow lightweight cloth towels into balls of sand. They felt confident their towels would be safely under their shoes when they came back out of the surf, so they concentrated on enjoying jumping in the swells. Deb swam under and between Sam's legs, running her hands under the shorts. She gently raked her fingers between Sam's legs. Sam pulled on her to stop. Deb's head popped back out as she stood. She shook her head, slinging water from her hair before combing it back with her fingers. Sam nearly swooned as she took in the wet clothes clinging to Deb's body. "Oh yeah!"

Sam dove under the water again, coming up and shaking her head to get water from her ears. She noticed a huge swell coming in. She dove in to catch it, body surfing the wave into the shore. She stood up once her chest and legs scraped the sand. She knew her suit would be full of sand. That's the way it always works when you ride waves into the shore. She slogged back out through the water until she was waist high. She reached in through her shorts' legs to pull at the crotch of her suit to dump as much of the sand that would rinse out. Deb swam up next to her. "Need any help with that?" Sam thumped the surface of the water, spraying her. "I'm pretty good at that. Just saying." Sam smiled, and she wanted Deb to do a lot more than pull at the crotch of her suit.

"I'm going back. Your outdoor shower is on for the season, isn't it?" Sam asked.

"Yes, but after you get most of the sand off, I can help you finish up." Deb's pitch was lower than usual. Sam was afraid she might come before she ever left the water.

"You'd better stop that. I have to make dinner tonight. You coming?" She regretted her words as soon as she said them and held her hand up in defense. She shook her head. "Nope. Don't say it. Whatever it is you were going to say...nope."

Deb shrugged and laughed. After shaking sand out of the towels, they dried off, donned their flip flops, and headed back. Deb unlocked her shower and showed Sam its eccentricities.

Sam stepped inside. The door latched when she pushed it closed, and she adjusted the water knobs, stiff from a season of inactivity and salt air. The fence-like walls afforded more privacy than she expected. Yes, feet would be visible, but the slats were adjusted and alternated on two separate wall layers that prevented seeing in or out. She almost regretted having shut Deb down. Deb had provided some soap, and Sam was able to wash nicely. Her hair would eventually need the salt removed, but it was fine for now. When she opened the door, Deb was leaning on a pillar, waiting. She handed Sam a clean, dry towel as she let her eyes gaze up and down Sam's body.

Sam knew exactly what Deb was doing, and she felt the electric rays hit her exactly where Deb would have wanted. "You really need to stop that," she whispered with broken breaths. She quickly dressed, Deb watching.

"We would have almost been finished in there if you had let me in with you," Deb teased, running her index finger down Sam's clothed body, between Sam's breasts to her pubic bone. "Should I invite myself to dinner?"

"If you promise not to distract me...be there at six," Sam answered, heaving a sigh of exasperation as she kissed Deb goodbye.

Chapter Twenty-One

A TYPICAL AFTERNOON AT Bea's place included Sasha reading to Sagal for her daily twenty minutes. Tom stayed at their place, taking his afternoon nap. Bea was looking at her mail. Even a one-pager took ten minutes for her to open the flap, work the contents out of the envelope, then read every word. After refolding and working the paper back into the envelope, she'd throw it on the stack of opened letters for Sam, who managed her finances. How Sam missed Jeff's culling of junk from the stack. No, not a big deal, truly. As a college buddy had told her, "It's the little things that bother us and put us on the rack. You can sit upon a mountain, but you can't sit on a tack." *Ha! Let it go, Avery.*

She began the process of prepping the veggies. She had lots to cut up for the five of them, making her Thai green curry with tofu. She had just washed the red pepper when her phone buzzed in her pocket. *I'm here. Are you going to let me in?* Sam felt the smile spread across her face as she left the apartment and took the few steps to the outside door.

"Hiya," Deb said softly as she handed Sam a bottle of pinot noir and they entered the apartment.

"Oh hello, Deb. I forgot you were coming to dinner. It's good to see you," Bea greeted her as Deb leaned to give her a hug.

Deb nodded at Sagal and Sasha, who took the excuse to close her book.

"Deb, this is Sasha." Sam gestured toward the child. "And her mom, Sagal. Tom's wife."

"Good to meet you, Deb. Sam has told us a lot about you." Sagal stood to shake her hand.

"I hope it was a good report."

"Aren't you the one who tried to give Aunt Sam a ticket?" Sasha stood with her hand on her hip, as sassy as she usually was.

"Guilty." Deb chuckled. "I think I've made it up to her though. And I did tear up the ticket, you know."

"Oh, gosh. Don't mind her." Sagal laughed.

"Can I stop reading now?" Sasha pressed her hands together in a mock prayer.

"No, ma'am. You have ten more minutes."

"Deb, can you help me chop some veggies?" Sam called from the kitchen area.

"Sure thing." Deb gestured a sorry to Sam and Sagal. "Please excuse me."

"And when you're finished reading, we have to finish up that math problem you were working on, remember?" Sagal said firmly.

"Aw, man. No fair." Sasha squinted and wrinkled her nose with a pouty frown.

"Thanks for the rescue," Deb whispered as she chopped.

Sam was grateful to be both close to Deb and to be busy with prep work. Bea had fallen back into another table nap. Sam heard Sasha's voice pronouncing each word, sometimes sounding it out.

"This is nice, Sam. This family time. I hope you realize it," Deb whispered to Sam.

"I know. I enjoy having this quiet time. Watching that one grow. It's sweet. I miss home, of course. And I'm always a little less troubled when I can keep an eye on Mom."

"Sure. I think I like the idea of being part of a family again."

"I'm glad to hear that."

"Okay, everyone," Sagal said. "This working gal has gotta go grab a nap before my shift tonight. Sam, Tom will be here for supper, and he'll take the girl home, of course."

After Sagal excused herself, Sasha came into the kitchen. "Deb, what do you do if it rains while you're out giving tickets to people?"

"Well, I wear a raincoat, and the little car I drive around has a covered cab. It's not too much fun if the rain blows in, but it's not such a bad thing."

"And do you ever have anyone else be rude to you the way Sam was?"

"Hey. Wait a minute. I wasn't rude," Sam interrupted. She bumped Sasha with her hip.

"She wasn't really rude as much as confrontational."

"Huh? Like mean? Or aggressive?"

"Hey!" Sam countered.

"You know what? I think we're getting in the way of our supper. Why don't you and I go sit on the sofa." Deb motioned Sasha out of the kitchen, following her.

"Great idea, but please stick up for me in that discussion," Sam interjected with a smile.

It was not long before Sasha was demonstrating her tumbling skills and rolling across Deb as she talked about school. Sasha was draped onto Deb's legs with her head hanging off and arms braced on the floor.

"You're not going to make Sam sad, are you? Dad said her last girlfriend made her real sad."

"Girl. You gotta stop with the twenty questions in there. Deb is a guest," Sam called out from the kitchen. Sasha pouted at the reprimand.

"I sure hope I never make her sad. You know, that happens sometimes when you really love someone—" Deb tried to explain.

"No, that person didn't really love Sam. I know that it's not very nice to hurt people."

"It isn't, Sasha. You're right about that. I think it would make me too sad if I made her sad." Deb's answer seemed to satisfy Sasha for now. "Now I need to go help finish cutting up vegetables so we can start cooking dinner." Sasha nodded and picked her book up and started reading.

"I'm glad you're not going to make me sad," Sam said softly, leaning her arm against Deb's. They kept busy with prep until Sam started cooking. Sasha seemed thrilled her playmate had come back into the room, and Sasha showed Deb a new game she was playing on her tablet. Sam mouthed, "sorry," and Deb just shrugged.

* * * *

Tom and Sasha left just before nine. Sam and Deb cleaned the kitchen, and Deb made Bea a bowl of ice cream.

"Bea, it's been so nice to spend some time with y'all. I appreciate your hospitality."

"You're family now. You're welcome any time. And Sam doesn't have to be here! I'm glad you came." Bea seemed sharp as a tack.

"I just might do that." She turned to say good night to Sam. "Hey you, don't look so dejected. Dang," Deb whispered. "Can you come to mine in a little bit? I mean, when you have Bea close to bed?" Deb asked.

"I want to. I'll plan on it, but if I need to stay...I'll text you either way." Deb nodded and kissed Sam on the lips. Sam blushed, but she did not pull away. "I'm glad you were here."

It was ten-thirty when Sam made her way to Deb's.

"I've freshened up the bedroom. Even changed the sheets!"

"Yes, I see that. And you've showered. Okay if I shower? I still have that salt in my hair."

"You don't need to ask things such as that, Sam. You know you're welcome to make yourself at home."

"Hey, I smell lavender. Smells nice. I love lavender." Sam began undressing and folded her clothes into a nice stack. Deb walked to the door.

"Hoped you wouldn't mind," she said, watching Sam.

"Gosh, no. When Mom was in the hospital last year, I sprinkled some oil around her room."

Deb smiled and cocked her head to the side. "Not the oil. Watching you."

Sam shook her head, pursing her lips, and stepped under the warm water. She called from behind the curtain, "No, I don't mind." It was weird not being young, knowing that one's skin sags, even if the muscle doesn't. To know that one has a few too many pounds, and that you just don't look the same as you might have even ten years ago. Odd to know that she could still be found attractive. These thoughts swirled around as she considered Deb wanting to look at her. That Deb found her attractive, even with her physical flaws.

"You still out there?" Sam called as she toweled dry. There was no answer. She grabbed Deb's robe from the door and wrapped it around her. Deb was leaning on the porch rail, looking out at the water. "Can I join you?" Deb signaled with a nod of the head and a smile. Sam walked close behind Deb and opened her robe as she leaned against her.

"That's nice," Deb said, smiling as she maintained her stance at the rail.

"It *is* nice. You know, when I was in the shower, I thought how weird it is to have someone find me attractive—"

"Oh God. You are attractive, Sam." Deb turned in place to face Sam's naked skin against her. She pulled the robe sides firmly to bring Sam even closer. "This doesn't hurt does it?"

"Nah, not really. Don't pull too hard, though. And the feeling is mutual, you know, but what I mean is this isn't how we would have looked…I mean our bodies don't look how they would have ten or twenty years ago. We can't bend our knees. We can't hold ourselves up the way we used to or contort into positions we used to be able to do." Sam dropped the robe from her shoulders.

Deb dove to pick it up, and Sam pushed Deb's head. "You can stay down there if you care to." Sam smiled, leaning against the rail. "The light's off. Nobody can see me here, can they?" Deb jumped up and covered Sam with the robe.

"Get inside. Sam, I told you, I live here," Deb said curtly.

"Sorry...Deb, I'm sorry. That was stupid." She walked toward Deb to hug her, and Deb stepped away.

"Let me cool off, okay? I need some time. Go to bed. You're tired. I'm pissed. Not a good combination. I love you, Sam, but I need to cool off. You just have to trust me. Really. Just go inside and let me have some time out here." Deb seemed sincere. Sam nodded and went back inside. *Fuck. There I go again.*

The last time Deb had been frustrated with her was the night she had taken the pain med with wine and had gone into Deb's hangout acting a fool. Here she was in Deb's territory, acting a fool again. Deb was not closeted, but she didn't care to have laundry aired either. Why had she been so inconsiderate? Sam knew this was not fitting end to Deb's short vacation—one Sam had wanted Deb to remember, but not this way. Sam felt horrible, but she had to trust Deb. She had to. She put on her sleep shorts and a tank and slid into Deb's bed. She tried to stay awake, but she drifted off before Deb came back inside.

* * * *

Outside, Deb sat in a rocker on the porch. "I know you will hear me, Angela, even if you're not out here, friend. You're probably in your rookery, sleeping, but still. I'm in love. I hate feeling angry. I know she was trying to make tonight special. I don't want people in my business, though. You know that about me. Miss you. You know I'm nervous too. No, I didn't tell her I have my usual appointment tomorrow. She didn't know that's why I would have been so keyed up. That's not fair to her, to have her think she did something that made me mad. Thank you, my friend."

Deb didn't feel convinced that her friend truly heard her in a parallel universe, but she didn't want to take a chance. And talking things through always seemed to help, even if she *wasn't* talking with her friend. She returned inside and prepared for bed.

She could tell by Sam's breathing that she was asleep. She loved Sam being in her bed. She slid in, hoping she wouldn't wake her. Sam turned and slid next to Deb, kissing her shoulder. "Mm. The lavender is nice. I love you, and I'm so sorry." Deb turned to face Sam.

"I'm the one who should be sorry, Samantha. I was keyed up. I get this way when I have any sort of appointment. It's one of my routine follow-ups. I get tense. I probably wouldn't have been so quick to react if I hadn't been processing that," Deb confessed.

They kissed. "Thank you for telling me that," Sam said softly, brushing Deb's cheek with her thumb. "Please talk to me about stuff like this. Okay? If I have to trust you—"

"I know. You're right. I'll tell you next time. It wasn't fair, Sam. Can we go to sleep now?"

Sam turned back to her normal sleep side, and Deb eased against her back, resting her arm on Sam's shoulder, stroking it gently with her fingers.

* * * *

The next morning, Sam wondered if they had spooned all night. She remembered waking once and facing Deb's back, but now they were in the same position as when Sam fell asleep. Sam stretched and pulled Deb's arm to her chest. Deb gently pulled her hand to Sam's face. Her thumb was warm and only a little rough against Sam's lips. She nibbled on Deb's thumb, then shivered as that thumb traveled down her chin and slid under her tank top. Deb's hand opened to caress Sam's left breast.

She thought of their discussion of how their bodies had changed. Deb drew her thumb along Sam's nipple, and it hardened in response. Sam sighed, and Deb cupped her breast in her palm as she lightly pinched and caressed. Sam's breathing grew ragged, though soft. Even in the moment, she noticed that her breast sagged toward the bed, and Deb ran her thumb again across the nipple. She knew Deb was receptive, as she breathed an unspoken 'oh' and turned so that half of her was now splayed on top of one side of Sam's body. Sam stretched and leaned firmly against her in this position.

Deb whispered into Sam's ear and neck how she loved how Sam felt. Her fingers gently caressed Sam as she gently rocked against her.

Sam's more audible sighs quickened with Deb's gentle movements. She gently rocked against Deb's hand as she climaxed, sighing soft, gentle moans. Sam slid her hand to Deb's and laced their fingers together. She pulled Deb's arm across her chest, in no hurry to leave the embrace.

Chapter Twenty-Two

AS DEB SAT IN the waiting room, she tried to look as if she were reading the entertainment magazine she was holding, but her focus was not on reading. Thoughts of the morning kept intruding. She remembered Sam's ample, soft breast cupped in her hand. How her nipple grew hard with her touch. Being aroused before her MRI was not what she had been expecting. It shouldn't have been surprising though, since breasts were on her mind, and she had certainly enjoyed Sam's that morning. Oh, how she had enjoyed them...and other things too.

She considered their trust discussion. She had not told Sam that she had noticed a small spot of discomfort just below her scar on the right. She couldn't tell if it was a small nodule or perhaps a small bruise from their most recent sex. Thinking of that rougher than usual wrangle did nothing to quell her arousal, but her concern for today's scan certainly brought her back to reality. Her doc would want to err on the side of caution. It was time for a scan anyway, so she wasn't lying to Sam. It was unnerving though, more so than her usual appointments. Also unnerving that she had kept her discovery from Sam. Was that right...or fair?

Deb decided her brain's way of taking her mind off worry was to keep bringing Sam into her thoughts. It wasn't a bad way to spend the time, she'd hand her brain that. Sam's whimpers, moans, and audible sighs had been so intoxicating, Deb was barely able to focus on bringing Sam to climax. She was surprised how easy it had been to pleasure herself to orgasm in the shower when she finally moved out of the bed, but then it seemed they both could find exactly what they needed in one another and in themselves. Her mind drifted back to lovemaking with Sam, and she again felt the burning ache of sexual craving.

She vividly replayed that rough encounter when Sam took her scarred chest into her mouth. She felt a jolt of desire that seared her and brought her to the edge of rapture.

Deb was so deep into her recollection that she jumped when the medical assistant touched her shoulder after having called her name twice. She was horrified, but the assistant allayed any discomfort with her calming presence. The compassion all the staff members showed made it much easier for Deb to comply with any follow-up. The assistant confirmed Deb's appointment in two days.

The office would never make her wait too long for results. She was always grateful for that. These were quick appointments, typically no longer than ten minutes, but her doctor had always told her that she wanted to share any results face-to-face—positive, negative, uncertain or inconclusive. If plans needed to be made, they could do so then, together—no waiting, but she also could address any remaining concerns.

Deb was to text Sam when her appointment was done. Since Deb was working the next day, she wanted to stay at her own place. The plan was for Sam to stay at Bea's tonight. It had been last night too, but they hadn't wanted to be apart. Deb's text would let Sam know if she was going to swing by Bea's or not. She opted on not going by Bea's.

* * * *

Sam sighed when she saw communication from Deb, but the message wasn't necessarily what she had hoped for. *Talk to you soon, I hope. Miss you already. Mwah*, Sam replied.

She pictured Deb in her khaki, cargo twills, tank, Oxford shirt and Sperry boat shoes, her long tanned legs and arms, short gray hair, and blue eyes—oh, those blue eyes. In this scene, Deb walked into the small, beach grocery store and bought a few items for supper and lunches. She leaned against the counter and discussed some beach issue with the clerk. She remembered how dark Deb's skin was compared to hers— that type of skin that had long been exposed to the sun. The skin looked almost tough. Age and the sun had reduced the elasticity, leading to minor sagging and minor wrinkles, but Deb's arms were muscular and strong, and Sam smiled at this image.

Sasha and Tom arrived, and Sam topped the pizza crusts she'd made in the afternoon. As she cut each pie into slices, her phone buzzed with a call. She recognized that it was a local exchange.

"Ms. Avery," the Kure Beach police officer greeted, "Just wanted to let you know that the man who assaulted you will be serving time for battery. You're not needed for additional testimony."

"He pled out, then?" she asked.

"Yeah. When the DA started talking hate crime, he pled to the battery...you know, lighter sentence and all."

"Thanks for letting me know. It's a relief. And thanks to you and your office. Truly appreciate it."

"Sure thing. Happy to help." The call ended.

"What's up?" Tom said.

"That was Kure Beach PD. That beer-can creep pled to battery, so he's going to serve some time."

"That's good news," Tom replied. "Wasn't sure anything would come of it." Sasha nodded, appearing to take in the discussion, never turning away from her tablet.

"I'm so glad to hear that. You'd better let Deb know. She'll want to hear that, I know." Bea looked up from her calendar-placemat, finger remaining on whatever date.

After Tom and Sasha had gone home and the kitchen was clean again, Sam excused herself to call Deb.

"Give Deb my love," Bea shouted. Sam considered again how lucky she had been to have had such a loving, accepting mom. Tears filled her eyes.

"Hiya," Deb said softly as she answered. "I was getting ready to read, and I wished you were here."

"Bea sends her love—"

"Is that why you called?" Deb teased.

"No, but I was glad to have an excuse to talk to you."

"You don't need an excuse to call, you know." Deb's voice was low and seductive, almost as if she didn't want someone in the house to hear her.

"I know on some level, but I think I have to prove to myself that I *don't* need one," Sam admitted.

"Hm. Then I say it's okay if you *do* need to. It's not unusual for people who love one another to want to communicate, is it?"

Sam thought of the question as rhetorical, but she wondered if she should answer anyway. "I suppose not. I still feel so funny, as I have said before...as if I'm a schoolgirl. I feel so excited when I think of you."

"If it makes you feel any better, I kept thinking of making love with you when I was waiting at my appointment this afternoon, and the assistant had to come tap on my shoulder to get my attention. She said she had called my name twice." Deb chuckled, but Sam could hear the strain.

"I hope I treated you well during that rumination," Sam said softly.

"Oh, you did. Oh my God, you did."

"Good. No, the excuse I used to call you tonight is that the Kure Beach police called this evening. That guy has been sentenced to some prison time for battery, and I guess he confessed or whatever, so I don't have to testify. The officer said as soon as the DA mentioned hate crime, he sang his guilty tune."

"I'm glad you let me know that. I wondered about that yesterday."

"I'm going to let you get back to your book and bed. Hope work is smooth tomorrow."

"Thanks. Me too...Samantha, thanks for calling. I love seeing your name on my phone."

"Yeah. I know that feeling...are we *really* in our sixties?" Sam chuckled. "I'll talk to you tomorrow. Hey Deb...I love you."

"Love you too. Night."

* * * *

It had been a busy couple of days. Sam had taken Bea for a day trip out of town to see one of her nieces, Irene. Annie, Bea's complex manager and friend, came by that night, as well as Tom, Sagal, and Sasha. Sam cooked seafood pot pies for them all. After the trip, cooking, and cleanup, Sam was exhausted. She was glad to have a break after everyone left.

She showered and retreated to the bedroom to read. Her phone buzzed with a text. She smiled when she saw it was Deb. *Hi. Can we talk?* Sam immediately dialed her.

"Hiya." Deb's typical, almost whispered greeting always made Sam's heart flutter. She was not sure why she loved the greeting so much—perhaps having heard it so many times from her huge celebrity crush—*Silent Witness* character Dr. Nikki Alexander.

"Hiya yourself. God, I swoon when I hear you say that," Sam admitted.

"I was hoping I would see you biking today," Deb said.

Sam explained her busy day. "If it's nice in the morning, I might make it on a ride. Can you come by after work and hang out?"

"I have a doctor's appointment this afternoon. We always meet face-to-face for the follow-up on my MRIs."

"An MRI, though? I guess I didn't realize that was a standard thing."

"Yeah. It's our routine. She's great to do the in-person thing. It makes me so much more comfortable than a call. No lingering questions."

"That makes sense. Dinner maybe?"

"Yeah. Dinner would work better. No reason I won't be home by four. You come by here?"

"I can use a cooking break. I'll come by after four."

"It's a date," Deb whispered. "Maybe I'll see you riding tomorrow, too."

"I hear your thoughts, so don't make some comment about Lycra." Sam chuckled.

"Mm. Don't remind me. I gotta get some sleep, you know."

"Ha. See you tomorrow."

"Yeah. I look forward to it."

So fuckin' sexy. Geez. Sam considered how amazing it was that her hormones seemed to have resumed their duties since first seeing Deb.

* * * *

The bike ride was great, and it was nice to be back on the saddle again. Sam made it down to the beach by eight, and it was already warm. She rode the eight-mile loop three times. On the second loop by the lot where she was parked, she spotted one of the beach's UTVs, then Deb, after she had gone past. She wheeled back around and pulled up to the UTV.

She always wondered what was behind the look Deb gave her—a look that made her feel she would melt into a puddle right there in the parking lot. The look was some combination of lust, love, and perhaps admiration.

"Hiya." Deb's smile formed from one side of her mouth to the other. Jaw clenched, she pulled her sunglasses to the top of her head and checked Sam out, head to toe, settling her eyes on Sam's lips.

"I just wanted to see you. I've got two laps to go, and it's getting hot, so I need to scoot," Sam said, returning the smile.

"I'm getting hot," Deb teased, tilting her head to the side.

Sam waved Deb away. "I'll see you later. We can talk about that then."

"Deal. Hope you don't mind if I watch you ride off."

"Incorrigible." Sam hopped on her bike and rode off.

* * * *

Once again, here Deb was, in the waiting room thinking of Sam—this time in Lycra—leaning against her car, Deb pressed to her as she caressed the Lycra hugging Sam's ass. Her radiologist, Frances Rowan, called her from the door rather than the assistant.

"Deb. Hi. Come on back." Frances motioned toward her office, rather than the typical exam room. A knot formed almost instantly in Deb's stomach. Rowan pulled up an image on the large monitor between them and turned the screen to make sure Deb saw it also.

"I suggest a needle biopsy." Frances pointed to a spot on the image in front of them. "I'm not convinced this is simply a hematoma." The black-and-white images of the tissue moved to show the different layers. Deb wasn't experienced in reading such images, but Rowan pointed out the round object throughout most of the layers. "I don't think it's fluid; it looks cyst-like. But we can't be sure without the biopsy."

"Okay..." Deb hesitated.

The doctor put her hand on top of Deb's. "Look. I can do it tomorrow if that works for you."

"Yes. I really don't want to wait days, or weeks." Deb blew out a breath. That was the extent of any relief.

"This might seem impossible, but I hope you won't worry. Statistics are in your favor, remember. You know I want to be cautious. Maybe overly so."

"I know. I always appreciate your candor, and kindness." Deb's eyes filled with tears. "I'll try not to worry."

Deb nodded, stopped at the desk for her biopsy appointment slip and some instructions, and went out to her car.

She closed the door. The ninety-degree temperature outside meant the inside of the car was probably one-twenty. She rolled the windows down and sat there for a minute. "Fuck," she said to herself, slamming her palms on the steering wheel.

* * * *

Footsteps coming up to the porch alerted Deb that Sam was there. Sam beamed when she saw Deb reclining in the lounger. "Hiya," Sam said softly, teasing her, while leaning in for a kiss.

"It's good to see you." Deb pulled Sam down for that kiss, trying to suppress any concern from her demeanor. "And really nice to see that dimple." She lightly touched it with her index finger. "Pull up a chair. I was thinking we'd just hang out until you're ready to eat. Let's go down to Bull's and after dinner take a walk on the beach. Okay?"

"Sounds nice. I could use the ocean right now." Sam breathed out heavily. "Let's start early, okay? I'm going back home tonight, much to my chagrin." She waited a minute or two as she pulled a rocker next to Deb, sighing again. "She's getting worse, Deb. I'm beginning to hate to leave even for dinner. Is it horrible for me to feel I don't want to be the one to assume this role?"

"It's how you feel, Samantha," Deb answered. "You love her. You're her daughter. You know she wants you to take care of her, or one of you guys. You can't blame her for that. I understand how it would be a tough position. Nobody relishes putting their parent in long-term care, but sometimes, that's the way it is. You said she had always told y'all to do that when she couldn't care for herself." Deb knew this wasn't a new topic, and she knew it would not be the last time they'd visit the idea. "It's tough."

"Fuck," Sam sighed out.

"You okay if I change the subject? And just say so if you don't want to talk about anything. I'm okay just looking out at the channel, and at you."

"I'm okay. Sorry, Deb. It helps, I hope, to vent. I know what I need to do. Shit or get off the pot. And it's okay to change the subject." Sam ran her hand down Deb's arm and laced their fingers. "How was work? Oh, yeah, shit! How was your appointment?"

"Are you hungry? Let's go have a drink." Deb's spontaneity did not seem to pique Sam's curiosity. She was relieved Sam didn't notice she was trying to avoid the subject.

"Drink sounds great. And you know me, I can always eat."

They gathered lightweight jackets, keys, money, and ID, and headed out. What a relief that Sam hadn't questioned further.

Jules was all smiles as they walked in, and Deb asked for an upstairs table, one with a view. They grabbed their menus and headed up. Jules followed them.

"Well, I'm glad to see you back. I'm pretty sure the last time I saw you, you were high as a kite." She chuckled as she held her pad to take the drink order.

"Oh God. That's so embarrassing." Sam sunk into the seat, a blush spreading from her neck. Deb laughed at her and gave Jules her order. Sam followed, shaking her head.

Jules leaned in and quietly said, "Don't feel too bad. This is a bar, you know. We've seen it before." Sam chuckled and nodded. Deb watched Sam's face, grinning, as Jules sauntered away to get their drinks.

"As pissed as I was at you, I think I fell in love with you that night. Not because you needed me, though. Because in that state, you said exactly what you were feeling. Well, what I thought you were feeling, maybe what I wanted to hear, what I had been scared to hear." Deb's gaze averted toward the ceiling. "I wonder...I was pissed, but I would never have let you hurt yourself or anyone else."

"We've become close so quickly. I guess that's the norm, right? Rental truck on the second date, and all that?"

"Maybe not quite, but I know what you mean. Look at older straight couples. Haven't you seen someone's dad pass away and all the church widows shower the poor guy with affection, meals, and sweets?"

"I have...so, are we elderly, then?" Sam joked.

"Oh, stop. We've talked about this. We have experience. We know what we want, what we need, and how to make that happen, right? If we feel this way, why shouldn't we act on our desires?"

Chapter Twenty-Three

THE BREEZE WAS COOL, even with the muggy air. They each held their shoes as they strolled along the water's edge, wet sand oozing between their toes. Sam closed her eyes and inhaled the salt air, still buzzing from the two whiskeys. Deb pressed her lips against Sam's. Sam seemed surprised, but she gave in. She slowly ran her hand down Deb's arm. Deb's tongue found hers, and Sam's sigh was audible. She leaned backward into Deb's arms.

"Deb," Sam whispered. "Those two young women, sitting on the blanket looking at us."

"I know. I saw them. That's why I kissed you then. Give them something thrilling, encouraging about the future, or even the present."

"They're adorable."

"Uh huh. They are." Deb nodded toward the blanket, and they smiled in return. One of them reached for the other's hand. "You remember how horrified we would have been to do something like that at their ages? How scared we would have been that we would be arrested, or worse?"

Sam nodded. "It was a relief in college to know those few people you could hang with. Typically music majors, artists, or athletes for me. You?"

"Same, but usually for me, just athletes," Deb replied. "God, I'm glad I can marry someone I love now. Makes it so much easier for folks to have to accept...well, *tolerate* our holding hands. Maybe not so much making out on the beach, though." Deb laughed.

"I seem to remember your anger with PDA not that many days ago." Sam turned to look at Deb's face.

"Sorry. Yeah, I did get a little hot, didn't I?" She grimaced.

They continued their stroll, holding hands. Deb turned around and looked back at the two women, smiling. She wiped some tears from her eyes with her other hand.

"Samantha, I need to tell you something," Deb said in a serious tone. She dreaded the revelation and dreaded even more how Sam might react. Would this be the moment Sam washed her hands of the relationship all together? Honestly, who would want to face their new lover having a breast cancer diagnosis?

Sam looked at her. "Sure."

"At the doctor's today..." Several beats passed. "I have to go back tomorrow for a biopsy. There's a small cyst just below one of my scars." Deb stopped talking as Sam pulled her to a stop, no longer smiling.

"What do you mean? You said it was a routine thing." Sam seemed miffed and let go of Deb's hand.

Her stomach churned as she searched for a way to downplay the cyst. She continued walking, slowly, not wanting a scene in front of the younger women. "It *was* a routine visit. It happened to be conveniently timed to my having a small, sore spot. I thought it had been from my lover's voracious lovemaking of my chest." She looked up smiling, but Sam was not. "I didn't think too much of it. Maybe part of me didn't want to, but the doctor wants to check it out. She said to think of it as being overly cautious. So, let's do that." Deb tried to sound as positive as she could.

"I wish you'd told me, Deb. I—"

Deb stopped walking, took Sam's hand, and faced her. "Samantha. I understand how you feel, but I don't want to have a long discussion right now." A beat passed. "If you ask me questions though, I'll answer them. I'm still processing this myself, you know." She took Sam's other hand and looked straight into her eyes. "I'm scared shitless. I simply want you to be there for me right now. I need someone. I'd prefer that was you."

Sam looked away, then back, tears welling. "I'm so sorry, Deb. Of course, I'll be there for you. I'm such an asshole. You were...*are*... probably terrified. I mean, I am also now, but you're right. Let's stay positive." She pulled Deb's arms around her. "I'm so sorry."

"Thank you," Deb whispered. She blew out a breath, lowered herself to her knees, and sobbed into her hands. Sam knelt next to her, putting her arms around Deb's shoulders. "It's hard to think about it," Deb admitted, "much less say something about it. I have a favor to ask, though."

"Anything."

"Would you please let Peg know? She would want to know...even if it's nothing. I don't mind if you tell your family if you want to or need to, for *your* piece of mind, but Peg was a rock for me then." Sam nodded, and Deb wiped her eyes and stood, pulling Sam up. "Thank you."

"Of course, I'll let her know. I'll make sure she knows *you* wanted her to know. I hate it, but I need to get back within the hour. I wish I could stay with you." Sam looked out at the waves. "I wonder how many people are looking out at this ocean today, sharing some sort of joy or heartache or rebirth." Another few beats passed. "You're such a kind person," Sam continued. "This was the perfect place to talk to me…but you knew that didn't you?"

"I did," Deb answered softly as she looked out over the waves, taking in the perfect balance of power and serenity.

"You know you're kinda…*sweet*…don't you?" Sam asked softly. "Even if most people think you're a bitch for giving them tickets." Deb lunged, and Sam took off running back up toward the pier. Deb chased her and had almost caught up, when Sam stopped short. Deb crashed into her, knocking her down. They laughed, completely out of breath.

"You planned that!" Deb managed to say through her laughter, both rolling around, trying to get up. The intense laughter was a release from the tension Deb had felt. They were covered in sand when they finally stood. "Let's go. You can rinse off before you leave." They brushed what they could, still breaking into chuckles. The cute couple was still there, watching with sincere enjoyment.

Deb pulled on Sam's arm, "Come with me for a second." They walked to the blanket, and the couple at first looked surprised, tentatively optimistic. "I'm Deb. This is Sam. We're in our sixties, and we've only known one another a few months. I love this woman, and…" Deb paused to raise a hand as if Sam wouldn't be able to hear the fully audible secret she was relaying. "I hope she is going to marry me when I ask her." She raised her finger to her lips as if to entreat their cooperation.

"Y'all look happy. If you're right for one another…well, you might not know that yet. You're young." Deb dropped down to one knee. "But if you want to take a chance to see if you are, communicate. Don't keep secrets. Set aside some time each week where you discuss what happened, air any sorts of irritations. Make it as important as whatever else you protect time for. It's a time for you to grow what you have. It won't happen if you don't make time to communicate. And have fun. Laugh. And don't blow my secret, okay?" She reached for Sam's help to stand, groaning as her knee rebelled against her former position.

The couple nodded with wide eyes. "Thank you for stopping. You two look happy too…even when you looked serious," one of them responded. The other put her hand up as Deb had done. "And your secret is safe with us." The couple kissed and hugged one another. Deb snaked her arm around Sam's waist, and they walked toward the house.

Sam leaned into Deb's arm with her shoulder. "You really are sweet," she said. "I have a feeling that someone might just say yes if you asked her." Deb wiped her eyes as she walked, overcome by the gravity of the moment.

* * * *

Deb unlocked the outdoor shower door before she ran up the stairs to grab towels. Sam pulled her clothes off, shaking each piece as hard as she could to get most of the sand off. She hung them atop the door. As is often the case at the beach, one often wonders what remains by the ocean once the piles of sand are washed off during the shower. Sand was everywhere—in her ears, in her nostrils, in her armpits, her groin, her toes, behind her knees. The warm water felt nice, and she considered she was having an exfoliation treatment as she rubbed all the sand and salt off with the water. She reached for the knob to turn the water off when Deb rapped on the door. She slipped in before Sam could answer and pressed their bodies together.

Sam shook her head as she reached up to pull the sand through Deb's hair. The water rolled down, carrying an equal amount of sand. "I'm going to take your clothes off, or you'll never get the sand off you," Sam whispered. Deb just stood, eyes closed, letting the water stream down on them. Sam unbuttoned Deb's shirt and pushed it off her shoulders. She pulled at the tank, and Deb raised her arms, releasing it over her head. More sand ran down Deb's head, and Sam, once again, pushed the sand through her fingers. Sam raised each of Deb's arms, then turned her around and gently stroked and kissed her back. Once she felt the sand was gone, she turned Deb around again and ran her palms gently down her chest. Sam squatted and ran both hands down either side of Deb's legs, brushing more sand down toward her feet. Deb stepped out of the muddy pile of boy shorts.

"I could easily move this moment to something else." Sam looked up at Deb's face, water splashing into her eyes. She shook her head to clear the water from her face.

"And I would probably let you, but...can we simply be close right now?" Deb helped Sam stand from the squatting position.

"Friggin' knees," she huffed. She slid along Deb's body. Deb pulled her into a firm embrace, running her fingertips along Sam's inner thighs, slippery and warm. "What happened to just being close?"

"Mm. Yeah. About that. I think you're not making it to Bea's on time." The rough passion of the kiss conjured a guttural moan from Sam and signaled Deb to continue.

After lovemaking, Deb turned the water off and pulled the thick, oversized towel around Sam. Deb towel-dried Sam's hair, kissing her face and neck. She worked her way from head to toe until Sam was dry enough to step into her clothes. Sam could still feel sand against her skin, but she was dry enough that scratchiness wouldn't bother.

Deb then dried herself and pulled the towel around her like a dress. She squeezed the excess water from her clothes, and once she was out of the stall, she threw the ball up the steps to the porch landing. "Hope your night is okay." She kissed Sam's nose, then her mouth. "Be careful going home, okay?" Sam nodded.

"I wish I could stay," Sam said sadly.

"Me too. Thank you for staying a little past your curfew." Deb pulled at Sam's shorts.

Sam grabbed her wrist. "Oh, God. Don't even. Your body is so...I mean...so incredible. I am still on fire to make you come again, like you wouldn't believe."

Deb laughed. "Oh, I believe. Get out of here before I start begging." She kissed Sam again.

"How does she do that?" Sam yelled to the universe as she pulled onto the main beach road. She leaned against her seatback, arms outstretched and locked, hands on the wheel. She blew out a breath. "How?"

Chapter Twenty-Four

WHEN SAM ARRIVED AT Bea's, Tom and Sasha were still there, and it was ten o'clock. Sasha was asleep on the sofa. Bea was slumped at the table, as expected.

"What gives? I thought y'all would be long gone."

Tom waved for her to come out of the room. "We were. Mom called me three times by mistake. I didn't want to bother you. I knew you'd be back, but I just couldn't figure out what was going on. When we came back, the toilet had overflowed, and it confused her. It was a mess, Sam."

"Aw no, Tom. I wish you had called." She grimaced, but inwardly she was thanking her lucky stars.

"I cleaned the bathroom, pulled out one of the outfits, and settled her at the table."

"She had eaten?"

"No. At least I couldn't find evidence of it. I gave her the meal from yesterday that she hadn't eaten."

"I'm so sorry. You're a good boy." She patted his shoulder.

"Just don't know what we're going to do. Seems that she needs more and more." He ran the fingers of both hands through his hair.

"She does, I know. We should probably discuss long-term." She walked Tom back into the living room.

"I don't know what y'all are talking about back there, but I am just fine." Bea shook her finger at them.

"We gotta go. School night, you know. I'll wake Sasha." Hunched shoulders marked his distress.

"Thanks again, Tom." Sam patted his back as he hugged Bea.

How quickly a wonderful evening could be overshadowed, she thought. She called Deb. When she picked up, it was clear she had been asleep. "Hiya. You home okay?" Deb asked.

"Yeah. Just wanted to let you know. I'm sorry I woke you," Sam replied.

"I fell asleep in my chair. When I woke up, I made my lunch for tomorrow and pulled out my clothes. I'm still in my towel. For some reason I was completely relaxed." Sam could almost hear the smile through Deb's tone.

"I'm glad...can I come with you to your appointment?" Sam posed the question tentatively, worrying she was overstepping.

"That would be really nice, Samantha, yeah. Thank you." Deb's voice caught as she answered. "Night." Her voice was soft, and Sam felt the electricity of the tone.

"Night," she replied softly. She sighed when she hung up.

"Did you tell Deb hello for me?"

"I woke her. I just told her I was here."

"What'd y'all have for dinner? Did you eat at the beach somewhere?"

"We did. We ate at Bull's again, near the pier, then we walked on the beach. After that, we went back to Deb's and talked." *Talked. Hmph.* She felt warm again and caught herself closing her eyes.

"I need to go to bed, I think." Bea pointed at the refrigerator. "Would you bring me some water?"

Sam helped her mom with her evening pills and prepared Bea's bed with incontinence pads and clean sleep clothes. Bea was brushing her teeth, and Sam started the Barry Manilow CD. She locked the apartment door, turned on the night-lights, and turned off the overheads. Bea would be another twenty minutes in the bathroom, so Sam changed into her sleep clothes. She would be asleep before Bea came out.

Sam woke up at one o'clock for a restroom visit. Bea was watching MSNBC and eating from a carton of ice cream. "Mom, you were headed to bed when I went to sleep. You had already brushed your teeth."

"I wanted ice cream, and Rachel was on."

"You should go back to bed, but you really should at least rinse the ice cream out of your mouth."

"I will, Momma."

"Ha-ha. Very funny."

Sam put away the ice cream and turned the television off. She waited while Bea slowly made her way to the bathroom. Sam checked Bea's bed pad and changed it from the wet one. She pulled out another pair of pants and handed them through the door to her mom.

"Change into these, okay? The ones you have on are wet."

"They are? I didn't realize. Thank you." At least Bea had been in bed for some part of the night. Sam pushed play again on the CD player as Bea made her way to her bed. She hugged Sam good night and sat down on her bed, fixing the pillow.

The next morning, Sam checked for yesterday's mail at the box. She was sorting through the usual junk when Peg walked up. "Hey girl. Good to see you back again."

"I'm so glad to see you. I was going to find you a little later. Wasn't sure if you slept as late as Mom...you know, noon."

Peg laughed and shook her head.

"Not the greatest way to say hello, but Deb asked me to tell you that she went to her follow-up appointment. She's going to have a needle biopsy today. She wanted to make sure you knew. Evidently, she had a sore spot just below the scar on the right. Her radiologist thinks it's a benign cyst, but she wants to be cautious." Sam tried to be upbeat but concerned.

"Does she seem okay about it?" Peg's worried expression was obvious.

"She's apprehensive, sure, but she wants to stay positive. I'm going with her after she gets off work."

"Sam, I'm so glad to hear that. I know she's told you how tough that time was. She was a trooper, but it was scary as hell." Peg shook her head and wiped a tear from her eye. "You two have been spending a lot of time together. If I were a betting woman, I'd say you're an item."

"You'd be right." Sam's widening smile emphasized her agreement. "I love her, Peg. I can't believe we have found one another."

Peg gave her a high five. "Look at that grin. I tell you, Deb is one of the nicest people I have ever met. You are one lucky lady."

"I will agree with you on both counts. We probably won't know results for a few days, so when we find out, I'll make sure to let you know." Sam recorded Peg's cell number before taking the elevator back to Bea's floor.

Deb's text that morning had said to meet at her place at two, after work. Sam would drive her to the two forty-five appointment. She had plenty of time to get Bea up, bathed, dressed, fed, and ready for the rest of her day.

When Sam arrived at Deb's, she could sense her anxiety. They hugged and kissed. "Now I can look at you, rather than just think of you while I'm waiting," Deb teased, trying to lighten her mood.

"Yeah. You think about yesterday. I sure have...shit, that was hot." Sam's voice softened. Deb squeezed her hand.

"It was," she said, almost in a whisper. "Let's go do this."

* * * *

"I wasn't expecting to be so sore." Deb touched the bulky bandage.

"Well, that's what your pre-op papers said. You didn't remember that?"

"Not really. I think I was too anxious to take it all in." She looked at the passing scenery from the car window. "Hope you know I'll be out of the game for a few days."

Sam played at pouting, but then smiled. "As I recall, pretty vividly, you don't need to use your arms or hands to be in the game." Sam nodded her head as she spoke.

Deb looked at Sam intently. "I have half a mind to try it right now."

Sam shook her head. "No ma'am. Let's get home safely. We'll see if you're such a big talker later."

After they arrived at Deb's, she helped settle her in, making sure everything was at her side. "You'll be sleeping the rest of the day. I'll be at Mom's. Call me if you need something, okay? And let me know if, or as soon as you hear something, okay?"

"Sure. Thanks, Sam." They kissed, and Sam reluctantly drove back to her mom's.

* * * *

Sam had done internet research on cancer recurrence statistics after mastectomy and hysterectomy with salpingo-oophorectomy. She and Deb had discussed that previously, when Sam had asked her why she didn't have a hysterectomy scar. Deb had had a vaginal hysterectomy, so she didn't have the long scar like Sam did, down the middle of her abdomen. And the removal of her tubes and ovaries wouldn't have shown additional scars. Sam thought about how more scarring would have been an even bigger deal for Deb. Hadn't her self-esteem suffered enough from surgery scars? While her own was noticeable, it had been more than thirty years before, so practically forgotten. Even when they discussed Deb's scar, she hadn't considered her own. At their ages, they likely had seen at least one date with a telltale abdominal scar, even if it had been from a C-section.

She wondered if she would have felt differently if she had known Deb before her surgeries. Would having been intimate with Deb's breasts made her feel *she* had lost something too? She couldn't imagine how someone could shun the one she loved after such a cruel physical insult. She met Deb long after the physical scars had healed. There was really nothing to miss, per se. Deb's body was beautiful in its uniqueness.

Sam let herself cry. She wasn't sure if the tears were for Deb and Deb's loss, for Deb's fear, or for her own fear. She knew her emotional strength was tenuous, anyway, since she was caretaking Bea. Sam dialed, smiling when she heard Liz's voice.

"Hey. This is a surprise. Everything okay?"

"Yeah, but I think I'm having a bit of a hard time with Mom's decline. I've seen it before, in my long-term hospital patients, but it's harder with your own mom."

"I imagine it would be. You took care of a lot of elderly patients?"

"They've always been my favorites. It's funny. All those seventy-five-year-old patients seemed to forget whatever was going on when I came in. It wasn't me, though, it was my hair. Those short gray curls. Seemed to shift the focus. They asked me where my hair was cut or if it was a perm.

"In the Northeast, it was my accent, though. Staff nurses would ask if I would follow up on patient complaints. When I walked through their doors, it was as if the complaints never existed. They would comment on my accent and ask me to say something else. Of course, that worked with many ages, not just the elderly.

"Really though, I learned a lot from Bea. She's positive, caring, kind, and empathetic. That's one of the things that gets me now. She's become more gloomy, almost apathetic, except when she's at a doctor's office. Then she's all upbeat and 'I'm great.' I remind her she's requiring more pain medication or has a particular wound. I even had to remind her of the surgery she had a few months ago after she broke her arm. Oh, shit. I'm just feeling sorry for myself."

"I'm glad you called, then. You know we love you. You call anytime."

"Thanks. I feel better."

"And that's what we can hope for. Bye, friend. We'll talk soon."

Sam returned to wondering about Deb's biopsy results. She should hear today, though likely Deb wouldn't even check her phone until after work. She was irritated Deb had gone to work. Sam knew the instructions said she could do that if she was up to it, but she didn't like Deb's instructions. Sam certainly understood that Deb might put off checking her messages, or may not be able to pick it up right away. Deb might dread knowing a message was waiting while she was working.

Deb had promised to call or come by when she knew something, and Sam needed to trust that would happen.

She showered and tried to wash away her sorrow. When she felt sad or overwhelmed, she would say that it must be time for her period. Since she had no uterus and had long since waved goodbye to menopause symptoms, she wondered if it was still possible that what must be shriveled up old ovaries were occasionally making some last-gasp effort, but stress could also trigger these same symptoms, so she typically settled on that.

There was a long list on the refrigerator, so she prepared for a grocery outing. Bea was set up to eat and had meds in a cup in front of her. List, car and door keys in hand, she headed out. Sam was in the middle of the store, when her phone alerted her to a text. It was Deb. She took a deep breath. *Your car isn't here at Bea's. Where u?* She responded, *Food World up at corner. Almost done, then back to Bea's. K I'll wait here.* Sam opted for the real thing, rather than taking the time to send a lips emoji. She smiled at the thought.

She was back at Bea's in fifteen minutes. It was so hot, she felt bad that Deb had to wait in the car, but when she got there, Deb was up on the stoop talking with Peg. Deb stood up, said something to Peg, and bounced down the steps. She met Sam at the back of the car and grabbed a couple of bags. "Hiya," she said, smiling as she kissed Sam.

"You gonna get Bea thrown outta hea withat," Sam teased. "Woah. Okay to pick up those groceries?"

"Yep."

Sam grabbed the other bags and they headed up the stairs. "Afternoon," she greeted as they walked by Peg.

"Y'all are right, damn cute." Peg unlocked and held open the door.

"You ain't so bad yourself." Deb returned the smile. "Thanks. See you later."

Chapter Twenty-Five

"LET'S GO TO THE back and talk. It must not be simple if you haven't already told me the results." Sam looked concerned, but Deb just kept smiling at her.

"Same ol' position, eh? Slumped over the table. How can that be comfortable?" Deb asked, noting Bea napping.

"I don't have a clue, but that's Mom." Sam walked to the table to gather the dishes from her mom's previous meal. "At least she took her pills. That's good." Deb followed Sam to the back room.

"Okay. What?" Sam hoped she sounded more concerned than irritated.

"They had to send the sample for molecular testing. The cells were considered atypical." Deb sighed. "So, more waiting."

"Why were you all smiles then? You're not worried? How long will it take to get those results?" Sam was trying to read Deb's face for some covert sign of concern.

"I was smiling because I love you, and I am *with* you. You make me feel good." Deb kept smiling, seemingly looking more at Sam's lips than anything. She kissed Sam as a smile formed. "That's more like it," she whispered as their lips touched.

"What about the worry part?" Sam whispered back, slipping her arms around Deb's neck and relaxing into her embrace.

"It comes and goes. Mostly goes when we kiss." Deb's kiss was much firmer. Sam moaned softly when Deb's tongue found hers. "Feel free to keep my mind busy any time you choose," Deb teased. "You know, I missed you."

"Me too...you're welcome to stay here, but I wouldn't wish this mattress on my worst enemy." Sam chuckled and shook her head in dismay.

"Quite a seductive invitation there, Samantha."

"Do I hear voices back there?" Bea called from the living room. They pulled out of the embrace and walked down the hallway.

"Hi Bea," Deb said.

"Oh, Deb. It's so nice to see you." Bea stood to greet them, and Deb gave her a big hug. "I just love a hug," Bea said. "That's one of the worst things about being old and alone. You miss having someone touch you. It's depressing if you focus on it too much."

"I've never considered that, but I certainly can see how that would be the case." Deb smiled. "I'll try to make sure I come by from time to time, just for that reason."

"Please excuse me. I have to go potty." Bea began her arduous trek the short distance down the hall from the table. Sam closed the door for her. She turned around and saw Deb sitting in the rocker, long, tanned legs outstretched and crossed at the ankle.

"I could look at you all day. Look at those long legs." She sighed. Deb shook her head, feigning embarrassment. "You don't have to stay, you know," Sam offered.

"Thought I'd have dinner with y'all...or you...whoever shows up." Deb threw her hands up in a shrug. "I can go pick something up for everybody."

"What did I do to deserve you?" Sam looked down at her. "Isn't there some song about heaven missing an angel, something like that?"

Deb laughed. "Let's not go *too* far." She sat upright, uncrossing her legs.

Sam kneeled between them. "Thank you for being here." She had closed her eyes as Deb kissed her, then her phone buzzed. "Text from Sagal. They're at the door." Sam stood, stole a kiss, and let Sagal and Sasha in.

Before they could even take the four steps through Bea's door, both had hugged Sam, and Sasha was draped around her waist as they entered. Deb laughed. "It's nice to be loved, Samantha. Just keep that in mind." Sagal hugged Deb and sat on a stool at the counter.

"Samantha? You call her that?" Sasha was incredulous. "Lesbians have short names. Sam. Deb. Liz. Right?" Sagal was laughing and waving her hands in front of her as if to say she wasn't going to claim her daughter or take responsibility for what she was saying. They all laughed, with Sasha looking at them as if she was the one who held the facts of the case.

"I look at it this way, Sasha," Deb started her explanation. "Samantha is a beautiful woman. I call her Sam sometimes, but I love to call her by a name that more accurately reflects her beauty."

"Oh boy, it's getting deep in here," Sam replied. Sasha immediately ran to curl up beside Sam on the sofa.

"She *is* a beautiful woman. I will try to remember to call you that too...Samantha." Sasha looked at Deb and then looked back at Sam, eventually settling in with Sam's arm as her pillow.

"How's Bea doin' today?" Sagal asked.

"Pretty good today, at least mentally. I told Tom we need to consider her increasing needs, though."

"You all could probably use the peace of mind if she were in long-term care. I just hate to think of that, you know? Especially since I work in it."

"I'd like to eke out as much time as we can, her being at least somewhat independent. She always told us—years ago, I mean—she didn't want us to worry for her safety or sanity, that she'd be willing to go somewhere. But now that the time is here, she's not so ready."

"Can't blame her," Sagal replied.

"It's wonderful for her, really. Y'all take such good care of her. Nothing terrible has happened yet. Even with her falls, she doesn't seem to be stuck on the floor, does she?" Deb looked at Sam and Sagal for an answer.

"Other than that arm break last year, she usually can get herself up, eventually., but this visit…like I told you, she's already fallen twice. I had to assist her and counsel her on how to get up. Annie had to help once."

Sam changed the subject. "Hey, we need to get a supper order. Ordering from Tom's favorite steak house." Sam took everyone's request. Sagal knew what Tom would want, and Sam knew what Bea would want. "And we have a lovely delivery driver here today," Sam added. Deb took Bea's door keys and headed out to pick up the order. Sam mouthed *thank you* as Deb left.

"That Deb seems to be a nice one, Sam. She's good to y'all, and to Sasha," Sagal noted.

"She is. It's getting pretty serious."

"That's not too difficult to determine, you know," Sagal said with a laugh.

"Sam loves Deb. Neh, neh, neh, neh, neh," Sasha chanted.

"You're right. She does," Sam said softly. When Sasha realized Sam wasn't going to engage in the back and forth, she picked up her tablet and started playing her game.

"So y'all are going to do the couple thing, then?" Sagal asked.

"Sure looks that way."

"What about the two households? Y'all doing a back and forth, or has that been determined?"

"We're not sure yet for the long-term, but short-term, back and forth. At least that's how it looks now. We've considered cohousing with some other good friends long-term. You know, so we can take care of one another. We sure aren't getting any younger." She chuckled.

"That's an interesting concept, but I'm too private. I don't want people in my business. And eating in a big room with everybody. Nah. That's too much like long-term care to me." Conversation waned as Sam busied herself preparing the table and beverages.

When Deb returned, Sam plated to-go orders and served everyone. Tom arrived, and Bea had finally emerged from the bathroom. Sasha, chatting away with Tom, decided to address the room, obviously not oblivious to Sagal and Sam's discussion. "Dad! Sam and Deb are going to get married."

Deb turned in her chair quickly and looked at Sam. They both laughed. Sagal looked horrified. "Sasha. That was not exactly the way the conversation went. You were playing your game, so you really didn't hear everything right."

"I certainly hope that will happen, but she has to say yes first." Deb was still laughing.

"I would think there has to be a question before there could be an answer." Sam's grin belied her matter-of-fact reply.

"And I think someone would have to have picked out a ring or something before a question could be asked," Deb replied.

"All right. Sookie, sookie, now," Sagal said, laughing.

"Mom." Sasha drew out the short word in exasperation. "Don't you want Deb to ask Sam tonight?" Everyone laughed again.

"Usually, Sasha, you know like on TV, when somebody asks, they usually do it quietly somewhere, or maybe at a baseball game," Sam explained.

"Yeah! And the one asking gets down on a knee, right?" Sasha asked.

"But when it's hard to get down on your knees anymore, you might have to find another way to make it seem romantic, I guess." Sam added. Everyone chuckled except Sasha. She looked pensive, then shrugged and continued eating. Tom smiled and shook his head.

After Sagal, Tom, and Sasha left, Deb helped Sam clean the kitchen. Bea was coloring at the table. "I gotta go, babe," Deb said. "School night and all."

"What kind of ring do you want?" Sam asked quietly as she looked in Deb's eyes.

"Plain band's okay with me. I just want you to marry me." Sam pulled Deb by the arm to the back room.

"Are you asking?" Sam's look was one of surprise.

Deb tilted her head and smiled. She put her arms around Sam's waist. "I can't. I don't have a ring."

Sam pulled her close and whispered, "Wally World is open all night." Sam sighed as they kissed.

"I really gotta go, but this is a promising topic for sometime soon."

"Yeah, it is. Maybe sometime when I can really show you how I feel when I'm with you." Sam pressed herself firmly into Deb's body. "I wish I could be with you tonight."

"Me too," Deb whispered. "Night." She kissed Sam again before she returned to the living room and said good-bye to Bea, who stood to get her hug.

"Now you be sweet," she said as Deb left.

* * * *

The cold front that came through behind the potent thunderstorm during the night brought a beautiful cycling morning. Sam was grateful for a day starting in the sixties, a good ten degrees cooler than usual, and much less humid. She was at the beach parking lot by eight and well on her way by eight-fifteen. While she was tempted to detour by Deb's, she knew Deb would be in work mode and would appreciate the morning to get ready without distraction. Plus, Sam needed a good ride. This would be the first ride in several days.

The winds were low, and she focused on keeping up her speed. She was a good two miles an hour quicker than her average. It felt great. She had made it past her car's lot, down to the circle, and back up toward the lagoon area, when she saw a great blue heron fly close by. She pulled off the road and walked her bike the short path to the water's edge. The heron preened, and when finished, it stood looking into the water's shallow edge, waiting for the next minnow or small fish to brave its way near enough for its darting beak to snag it. Sam was enthralled by the heron's slow, deliberate dance.

She heard the puttering of a UTV slowing down behind her. It was Deb, and Sam was afraid, if she spoke, she would scare the heron. Sam put her finger to her lips in a shushing movement, then motioned for Deb to come look, pointing behind the reeds. Deb tiptoed to her. Sam was glad Deb appreciated the heron, but was a little surprised by her beaming smile and tear-filled eyes. Deb leaned and whispered, "Meet my buddy, Angela. I've been wanting this since our first date. I firmly believe that bird is my best friend come back as her spirit animal."

Sam wiped tears from Deb's eyes and leaned back against her. "How do you know it's the same one?"

"Look at the wing on its right side. See that little place where the feathers look torn or scraped? This one comes to the bulkhead in front of my house, often. And it's almost always when I'm wrestling with some dilemma. Just like it always was when she was Angela."

"I don't need you to get in trouble for slacking off. I could stand here the rest of the day, but I want this ride. Can I come to your place this evening? Tom said he'd come for dinner, and that he and Sasha would spend the night."

"That would be nice. I was going to come to you again, but—"

"I want to sleep with you, if that's okay."

"Hmm. I'll need to consider that...*not*. Of course. I'll call you later, when I'm off work and home."

"Deb. Thank you for sharing that about the heron. I love it when I learn some other sweet part of who you are." A loud, harsh honk arose as the heron lifted from the water's edge. Long, stunning wings carried Angela slowly and gracefully down the channel. "Wow. So cool." Sam squeezed Deb's hand, then rolled her bike back to the road.

"I'll see you later," Deb called as Sam rode off.

Chapter Twenty-Six

THE CALL FROM THE doctor's office woke Deb from a nap. She had been so tired after work she sat out on the porch and closed her eyes. She wasn't expecting to fall asleep, and she certainly wasn't expecting to have slept for an hour. The warm sun on this cool, dry day had made for the perfect porch napping weather.

"Hi Deb. It's Sandy," said the voice on the other end. "Dr. Moore wanted me to see if you could swing by today, maybe at four? She has a cancellation. Otherwise, is there a time tomorrow?"

"I can come by today. If she wants to see me before our scheduled follow-up, I'm figuring that isn't good news. I'll be there." Deb said.

"We'll see you at four then." Sandy ended the call. Deb noted to herself that Sandy didn't address her comment. Sometimes omission was worse than having the news. "Shit." She punched Sam's number.

"Hey. When are you heading over?" Deb asked matter-of-factly when Sam answered.

"Well, hiya to you too. I was gathering my things now. Leaving a note for Tom. I was surprised you hadn't called, but I'm glad to hear from you now." Sam's upbeat voice calmed her only slightly.

"Sorry, Samantha. I fell asleep on my porch after work. My doctor's office called. They want me to come in at four. My guess is that means something's off. Can you come now and go with me?"

"Jesus. Of course. I'll be there within a half hour, okay?"

"Thanks." Deb punched the call's red button quickly. Whatever upbeat tone Deb had before sounded more like beat up now.

* * * *

Sam tried to focus on making sure her note made sense and that Bea had what she needed until Tom arrived. She didn't want Bea to detect her anxiety, when she reminded her she was going to Deb's for the evening.

"Mom." Sam lightly touched Bea's shoulder to wake her. "I'm off to Deb's. Tom will be here by six. Remember he and Sasha are spending the night with you."

Bea stood to get her hug. "I love you so much. Tell Deb I love her too, okay?"

"I will."

"Now you be sweet."

Sam chuckled that she so often forgot Bea's salutation. Traffic was worse than Sam had expected, and it annoyed her that she couldn't get to Deb's any sooner. It wasn't that she didn't have enough time, and she tried to calm herself. She felt it was important to be calm for Deb. And they really didn't have any news yet, but wasn't that always the way it goes when you're waiting for news? Especially news regarding a diagnosis or prognosis. It never comes fast enough, and then, when it is imminent, it's still nerve-racking.

Deb was pacing. She stopped long enough to take the bags from Sam's arms and put one in the kitchen and one in the bedroom. Sam took a bottle of white wine from the kitchen bag and put it in the refrigerator, then walked to where Deb was looking out the window. She put her arms around Deb's waist and her head on Deb's chest. "I know that saying try not to worry is crazy. Deb, I love you, and I'm here." Sam couldn't see a reaction on Deb's face, but Deb did put her arms around her.

"Can you drive?" Deb asked. "I can't think straight."

"I'll bet you never did," Sam offered with a smile. Deb managed a weak smile and pulled Sam tighter.

"I'm scared shitless, but I'll tell you right now..."

"Come sit down with me. Breathe. Just breathe." Sam led Deb to the sofa. "Now, what were you saying?"

"Samantha. I just want you to know. I'm not going through all that shit. I'm not going to be sick the way Mom was. I'm just not going to do it. You have a right to know that. If you want to leave, I understand." Deb seemed beside herself, and tears were welling up in her eyes.

"Shh. Let's wait to hear what the doc has to say, okay?" Sam's voice was calm, and she squeezed Deb in a hug and held her there. "I'm with you no matter what. Not going anywhere."

"Fuck! Fuck! *Fuck!*" Deb shouted. Sam wiped the tears off Deb's cheeks. Deb jumped up and went out to the porch. The door slammed behind her. She looked out at the water, staring. Sam followed her out and stood close behind her, running her hands up and down Deb's arms.

"Hiya," Deb said softly, chuckling. "I love you."

"I know."

"There can't be anymore PDA out here for a while," she said, continuing to look straight ahead. "The houses around are almost always rented now, so there's no privacy."

"Okay. I'll limit making a fool of myself then."

Deb chuckled again and turned to hold Sam. "Fuck 'em," she said as she kissed Sam. After Deb's PDA pronouncement, Sam wasn't expecting the hunger in Deb's kiss. It took Sam aback, and a sound escaped from her throat. Her body instantly yearned for Deb's.

"We need to leave in twenty minutes," Sam was able to say between breaths. Deb pulled Sam's arm to lead her back inside. She pushed Sam against the hallway wall and pushed her hip bone between Sam's legs. "Oh my God," Sam whispered as Deb pulled her shirttail out and ran her hand to Sam's breast. Deb bit Sam's lower lip gently, and her tongue flicked against Sam's upper lip. When her mouth took Sam's, Sam uttered a deep, feral "oh."

Deb pulled back, as if worried she'd hurt Sam. "I'm sorry," she said softly.

"Don't be," Sam whispered. "I think we need to...I need to get ready to drive."

"I felt so...so tense...I needed some sort of release, I think. I hope I didn't hurt you." Deb's concern seemed sincere, her head shaking as if waking up.

"Look," Sam said, still trying to catch her breath. "If you need to do that...anytime...I'll buck up under the strain." She smiled at Deb, pursing her lips as she exhaled. "Just let me say...mind blown." Then in a whisper, "Wow." Deb pushed up against her again, but the kiss was gentle.

"I hope I'll be able to drive. And if I get us there, I hope I can listen to what is being said." A beat passed, their bodies still close. "Save some of that for later." Deb kissed her again, gently, and her tongue lightly brushed Sam's. Sam moaned again.

She pulled away and washed her face in the bathroom. Her eyes looked glazed. She chuckled and slid her hand between her legs to straighten her pants. Luckily, they were still dry on the outside. She smoothed her shirt and tucked it back inside her waistband, then walked to the full-length mirror and turned around to check herself.

"Wow...did I already say that?" she asked rhetorically. "I think I can get us there."

Deb grabbed her wallet and followed Sam to her car. She swallowed audibly, opened the door, and slid in. It was a quiet trip between them. Deb sat looking out the passenger window, but she held Sam's hand almost the entire way. When Sam needed it for driving, she rested her hand on Sam's thigh. The weight of Deb's hand on her leg kept the fire active between Sam's legs. She halfway expected Deb to slide up her shorts. Luckily, or not, Deb was preoccupied. When they pulled into the office lot, Deb heaved a big sigh through pursed lips. Sam put her hand on Deb's back as they walked in. Deb checked in and joined Sam in the waiting room. Deb nervously wiped her palms on her upper legs. Sam reached to hold her hand, but Deb shook her head almost imperceptibly. Sam picked up a magazine and flipped through the pictures.

At four o'clock on the dot, a woman Sam assumed to be the doctor's assistant poked her head out of the door and motioned with her head for Deb to come on back. Deb took Sam's hand and led her back, following the woman. "Come on into her office," she motioned with her hand to sit in the chairs across the desk from the large chair that was presumably Dr. Moore's. "She'll be right with you."

Deb heaved another large sigh and wiped her hands on her pants again. She rested her palms there. Sam reminded her to breathe regular, even breaths. Deb nodded.

Dr. Moore walked in and stood next to Deb and stretched out her hand. "Deb," she said simply. "This is?" she said, looking at Sam.

"Dr. Tina Moore, this is my fiancée, Samantha Avery. I want her to hear whatever you have to say. Not just because I care for her, but because I'm so damn nervous, I need another set of ears."

Dr. Moore nodded and reached out to shake Sam's hand with both of hers. "It's nice to meet you, Samantha. Deb has a special place in my heart. Now, so do you. Thank you for coming with her today." Rather than sitting across the desk, she rolled her chair around to their side. Sam turned her chair so that they would be facing one another.

"Sandy told me you suspected the news wasn't good," she started. "It's complex, actually. The test indicates the cells are not what we would classify as truly cancerous at this point. They are atypical, meaning suspicious and not what we expected. There is still research being done on this type of cell presentation, but Deb, I think...my recommendation is..."

"You want me to have the full monty?" Deb asked. "Surgery, radiation, chemo?"

"You know me well enough to know I'll respect your wishes, but that cyst needs to come out, Deb. That's the safest thing for you. Bottom line." She looked at both of them and put her hand on Deb's.

"Dr. Moore, if I'm hearing you, you advise her to have surgery to remove the cyst, but I haven't heard your specific recommendations regarding chemo or radiation." Sam put her hand on Deb's elbow and met Dr. Moore's eyes for her opinion.

"I recommend starting an oral chemotherapy agent after the surgery. Deb, you know I wanted you to take it before, and you know something of the side effects. They're not necessarily as severe as the ones we discussed in your mom's case. You were late to the mastectomy, and that was understandable. They hadn't done any genetic testing on you prior to your first visit with us."

"I need to think about it, Doc," Deb interjected. "Sam and I will discuss it and weigh some options, okay? In your opinion, and I understand the inability to back it up, but your gut, Doc. What are the chances that one, the cyst becomes malignant, and two, if I have the surgery but don't choose the chemo, that another cyst will develop, or that I'll have mets somewhere?"

"You know I can't answer that with any sort of confidence, Deb," she answered.

"If Deb were your sister, what would you advise, Dr. Moore?" Sam's request was a reasonable one. Dr. Moore nodded, looked down and closed her eyes.

As she spoke, she opened them and looked at Deb. "I'd say get that cyst out of there, and do it quickly. I know your resistance to further treatment, but if that cyst stays, I think the likelihood of metastasis is too great, whatever the percentage." She swallowed. "Just call me. If you elect to have the surgery, I'd feel better if we get it scheduled quickly. I'll call Cammy Gates again and have her get you in soon. It'll be outpatient is my guess, but she'd have to give you details. Deb, I know it's not what any of us want to hear."

Deb and Sam stood, speechless. Dr. Moore pulled one of the cards from her desk, pulled out her pen and wrote something on the back. She handed the card to Deb. "That's my personal cell, Deb. Call me when you decide, okay? You know what it's like here, so don't feel you can't leave a message. I will call you back when I'm able, but go ahead and tell me what you're thinking. If you want the surgery, I want to call Cammy and get this started. And Deb, call me if you have any questions. Okay?"

Sam nodded. "She will."

Deb appeared to be thinking. She reached out to shake Dr. Moore's hand. "Thanks, I'll let you know."

The drive home was almost as quiet as the drive to the office. This time, Deb's arms were crossed on her chest. Sam considered her body language. She recognized Deb's self-protection against some force beyond her control. An onslaught from her own body.

Chapter Twenty-Seven

WHEN THEY ARRIVED AT the beach house, Deb walked immediately to the porch and sat in the lounge chair. She handed Sam the keys and motioned for her to turn on the porch fan. It may have been cooler and dryer, but there were still no-see-ums and mosquitos.

Sam sat in the chair next to Deb when she returned to the porch. Deb's arm rested across her eyes. Sam reached and stroked Deb's other arm with her fingertips. "You want a drink before I make supper?"

Deb nodded. "In the cabinet. Get the Angel's Envy. Rocks. A double. I think I need the best."

"Agree. Consider it done."

They clinked their glasses together, but neither uttered a toast. Sam took a sip, and she was reminded why Deb would have kept this bottle for special occasions. She slipped back inside to warm the Asian-inspired leftovers from a recent supper at Bea's. Deb seemed to be putting one foot in front of the other without difficulty, and she came inside when Sam told her dinner was ready.

Hoping to have some sort of normal conversation, Sam relayed Bea's message of love to Deb.

"Your mom's a sweet lady," Deb said. "I see where you got that."

"What are you thinking Deb? Are you okay talking about it?" Now was as good a time as any to test the waters of heavy discussion.

"I don't want to, but I'll have the surgery...fuck it, though. Fuck it. Haven't I been cut enough?" She put her fork down on the plate firmly, as if she were trying not to throw it. "Just what I need is another damn scar. But I told you, Sam, I'm not doing that other shit. I'd rather take my chances."

"I get that," Sam said calmly. "I told you, and I mean it. I'm with you whatever you decide, but I'm glad you're agreeing to the surgery." She reached and rested her hand atop Deb's. "Maybe you'll fight these little pop-up cysts for years. Maybe an oral agent will prevent them, or lessen the number of them, or maybe it won't. But that cyst sounds as if it's no joke. That scared me."

"Yeah. One thing with her, she'll call it as she sees it," Deb said. "I'll call her in the morning." After a minute or two, Deb looked at Sam. "Thank you again for coming with me...for being here."

"Where else would I be? I can't imagine any place I would rather be than with you." A beat passed. "Look. You may not want to, but it's early still. Why don't you give Dr. Moore a call? I worked around doctors enough to know. She's concerned. And your surgeon...Gates, was it? She'll still be at the hospital, I bet."

"Yeah, you're probably right." Deb pulled her phone from her pocket and stepped to the porch. "Done," she said. "Had to leave a message, but done."

"Thanks, babe. I appreciate that."

"It's really some sort of relief." Deb looked out the window again. Sam nodded.

"Samantha," Deb said with such an earnest tone that Sam was somewhat unnerved. "I want to really start working on my bucket list. To do that, I'm going in to talk to Jim. See if I can cut short my retirement notice. I'm going to be out a couple of weeks anyway, after the surgery. So why not?"

"Wow," Sam interrupted. "That makes sense, really."

"I had one item on the list already, and in the past few weeks I've added a few things. After dinner, can we go for a walk, and I'll tell you some of them?"

Sam nodded at the promise of a welcomed distraction. They finished dinner and cleaned the kitchen together. Deb grabbed a small messenger bag that appeared to be stuffed with some sort of outerwear.

They walked down past Bull's, out under the pier, and turned toward the section of the beach where it was surprisingly less populated. It had become darker. Sam's eyes adjusted pretty quickly, and there were enough exterior lights to provide what the moon was not contributing to the night. The waves lapped against the shore. Out past the sandbar, they rolled in a little louder, and the reflection from the pier's floodlights flickered across the water.

Deb stopped and grabbed what turned out to be a beach blanket and spread it on the sand. She pulled at Sam's hand to join her. Deb sat next to Sam, shoulders touching, and her arms held her knees to her chest. After a few minutes, she turned toward Sam. "I love you Samantha. I want you to marry me. It's been incredible having your support, the kind of support one gets from her partner. Someone I know wants to be there...wants me. I want to be married when I have this surgery. Will you marry me, Samantha?"

Sam threw her arms around Deb's neck and kissed her. "Yes, I will marry you. Have you—"

"I want to be married in my yard, Sam. You can pick a honeymoon spot, but I really want to marry you there in my yard. I know Angela won't likely show up, but you know how I use that view for peace."

"Okay, sure. I love that space. And then I say we honeymoon in Maine. We can go after the surgery if it works better that way...yeah, I'd love that. It's been so long since I've been there. As I told you, I still have friends there. I know some great spots."

"Should we call Liz and Monty...and Peg? Liz can perform the service if that's okay."

"And Monty and Peg can be witnesses. Maybe Sasha would agree to be an attendant."

Deb reached to wipe tears from Sam's cheeks. "Do you trust me, Samantha?"

"Of course. With my life. Why?"

"Follow me then." She began packing everything back into the bag, Sam helping and shaking off the sand. Deb removed her shoes and tucked them in on the blanket. Sam did the same. She led Sam to the water's edge and pulled her close. "Bucket list item number one," Deb said softly as she kissed Sam. The kiss was gentle at first. "I'm going to make love with you right here, right now," Deb whispered.

Deb led Sam into the water, up to their waists. The wind was low, and waves were breaking gently on the shore. After adjusting to the water temperature, Deb pulled Sam's shirttail out, then unbuttoned and unzipped Sam's shorts. Sam gasped as Deb's fingers slipped under her panties and against her wet flesh. Sam fell backward into Deb's arms, and when she came, she held Deb's hand against her.

"So much for no PDA," Sam whispered, breath still ragged. "We'll be lucky if videos aren't posted. I know I sure wasn't paying attention to passersby."

They made their way back to Deb's, blanket wrapped around them both. Sam hoped Deb shared the feeling of so much tension washing away with the warm water of the outdoor shower. She was grateful Deb had left some shampoo there so she wouldn't have to shower again upstairs. She could simply brush her teeth and slip into bed.

By the time Deb showered and made it upstairs, Sam was already feeling the pull of sleep. Deb didn't seem frisky when she slid beside Sam. Sam turned and rested her head on her arm facing Deb. She lightly stroked Deb's chest with her other hand. "Is this where it hurts?" she asked.

Deb pulled her hand and pressed Sam's index finger to the cyst's location. "There." Deb let go and stroked Sam's shoulder.

"Does it hurt when I touch it?" Sam pressed lightly with her fingertip. She brought her middle finger up to see if she could feel the curvature of a cyst.

"Sore, mostly, but if you press hard, it will hurt. And if you keep stroking my chest much longer, I'm going to ask you to press somewhere else." Deb smiled.

"I will," Sam offered. She rolled off her arm and pushed herself up. "I think I like your bucket list...so far, anyway." After a luxurious kiss, Sam used her fingertips to stroke Deb's scars, then slid her fingers down Deb's body, stopping at the pubic bone. Deb breathed in deeply and exhaled in short, broken sighs. "Shall I?" Sam whispered. Deb pulled her up, and her kiss gave Sam her answer.

Chapter Twenty-Eight

THE 'OLD PHONE' RINGTONE was startling most any time, but especially at one o'clock in the morning. Sam jumped up and ran to grab it from her purse in the kitchen. She had only just fallen asleep. Deb didn't seem to wake, and for that Sam was grateful. It was Tom, so she immediately answered.

"Tom?" she asked.

"Sam, I'm sorry..." Then silence.

"Tom?" He didn't respond. "Tom?" She heard what she assumed was the stifling of a sob. "I'm guessing it's Mom...did she pass?" Sam's voice was soft and conveyed compassion.

He cleared his throat. "Um. Yeah. She was sitting at the table, you know. Slumped over, asleep as usual...When I woke her to go to bed, she didn't move. At first, I thought she was asleep..." He cleared his throat again, obviously trying to hide his emotion. "Do I call someone? It doesn't seem to be a 911 call."

"I'll be there within thirty minutes. I'll call EMS when I get there, okay? She's not going to be any less alive...I know that sounds crasser than I want it to. See you in a bit. Love you."

"Okay. Sasha's still asleep in the back." Tom ended the call.

Sam heaved a big sigh. She debated waking Deb, but she knew it would be expected. She sat on the side of the bed where she could see Deb's face and stroked her cheek with the back of her hand. "Deb," she whispered.

"What?" Deb woke with a start.

"Sorry. I really didn't want to wake you. Tom called a minute ago," she started.

"I didn't hear the phone ring. What? What is it?" Deb was clearly trying to process the situation.

"I've gotta go. Mom passed away. He hasn't called EMS or anything yet. I gotta go."

"Let me come with you..." Deb insisted.

"No. You go back to sleep. I know you have to go to work. We'll have calls to make in the morning, first thing, and I want to call my other brother, Jeff, before the morning. It's daylight for him right now. I don't know if he'll fly home or not. I'll nap on the couch there. I want to clean her up, you know."

"I'm so sorry, babe." She pulled Sam down for a kiss. "I love you."

"Me too. Sorry. And I love you. But it's what we had been expecting. I hate I've kept you from sleeping. You were sleeping so sweetly." She leaned and kissed Deb good-bye.

When she arrived at Bea's, her mom was still in the slumped position. Her body was warm, and not yet stiff, so Sam estimated less than three hours. Tears rolled down her cheeks as Tom walked up and put his hand on her back.

"You're so together...calm. My stomach's a wreck."

"It's what we do. Nurses, I guess. Maybe women in general. We just have to push forward." She wiped tears from her face with both hands. "She was a good mom, Tom." She wiped her face again. "I'm sorry I wasn't here. Is Sasha still asleep?"

"Yeah. She conked out early, nine-thirtyish. I texted Sagal. She's at work, but I wanted her to know. Nobody else knows though." He sunk into the sofa cushion and sobbed into his hands.

Sam was fighting her own battle with that, but she sat next to him and ran her hand across his back as she might have when he was a young boy. She stood and reached for tissues for both of them and handed Tom a few.

"I'll go ahead and call EMS." Tom stood to hug Sam, then sat right back down. She knew it would be hard on him. He was the one who lived in town and saw Bea the most. Tom was the youngest. Even in his fifties, Bea still called him her baby. A six-foot, 300-pound baby, his once curly, dark-brown hair, now gray. She hoped she'd be able to keep it together long enough to make that call.

The dispatcher said she would notify EMS and the police. Both would likely respond and look at the DNR paperwork. All of the residents kept their emergency papers displayed in a packet on their refrigerators. The EMS teams knew they'd find doctors' numbers, medications, living wills, and do not resuscitate orders.

Bea had planned her death years before. In her important paperwork file, there was information regarding her desire for cremation, the program information for her closed-casket funeral service, and a direction to bury her next to Sam's dad. There was also information regarding the funeral home. Her mom had even painted the burial box for her own ashes and kept it on the bottom shelf of the living-room bookcase.

EMS took Bea's body for pronouncement and funeral service pickup at the hospital. Tom returned to the bedroom to sleep for a few hours. Both he and Sasha were deep and long sleepers. Sam was grateful she could grab a few hours' sleep, but she called Jeff first.

The international call had a bad echo and delay, but she gathered Jeff would text or email her with his return itinerary. She was exhausted and drifted off to sleep on Bea's sofa, fully dressed.

Her alarm was not a welcomed interruption at eight o'clock, but she knew she needed to get some things together. She called the complex manager first. Sam knew Annie was typically up before six.

"Don't you worry. I'll take care of calling everybody here, and we'll take care of your family during this time."

"Thanks. I wasn't sure who all to notify. I was just going to look at her tenant list on the refrigerator."

"Really, don't worry about anything here. As I said, we'll take care of all your meals until the day of the service."

"Thanks again, Annie." She felt a burden off her shoulders after those calls, but there was still a lot to consider. All the stuff. More than ten years of stuff. Ugh.

At nine, Sasha shuffled into the living room, rubbing her eyes. She sat on the couch, curled up at Sam's side, and noticed the tears on Sam's cheeks. "Are you okay?" Sasha asked, rubbing Sam's hand.

"Grandma died last night, so I'm sad," she replied simply.

"She died? What? Where is she?" Sasha was still half asleep, but her expression indicated she well understood what Sam had said.

"Your dad went to wake her up when he was coming to bed, and she had died in her sleep, right there at the table." Sam described the EMS visit, and that Tom had finally gone to bed after they left. Sam's phone buzzed. Sagal was at the door. Sam was grateful for the perfect timing. Sagal could comfort Sasha. Sagal had come directly from work and was still in her scrubs.

Sagal's eyes were wet, and Sasha ran into her arms. Sagal gave her a big hug, then hugged Sam. Sasha joined in, and the three of them stood there crying.

"Oh, Sam. I know we knew it was coming." Sagal wiped some tears from Sasha's cheeks. "It doesn't make it easier, does it?"

"No, I'm not sure it does." Sam pulled out of the hug and brewed coffee.

"I'm going to rest for a bit and watch television until Tom's awake." Sagal continued to hold Sasha in a hug as she drank her coffee. "Grandma's in a better place now. No more suffering, right?" Sasha nodded but held Sagal tightly.

Sam had barely ended the call with the funeral home when the knocks on the door started. Bea was well loved, and Sam knew that, but she definitely had not prepared for the number of food dishes that appeared. She had a seemingly endless list of phone calls to make, and she and Sagal could barely handle the food plates arriving. She couldn't even stop to think how all these people had food prepared in less than an hour of being notified of Bea's passing. Most things were finger foods, which was helpful, but they still required making a list so that thank-you notes could be sent later.

She was almost ready to put a *Do Not Disturb* sign on the door, but she answered the next knock. "Hey girl, I found this at the front door. Thought you could use it," joked Peg with a hug, delivering Deb to the door. "I'm so sorry about Bea."

Sam began crying again, and Peg broke the hug so that Deb could pick up. Deb held Sam for a few minutes while she cried, simply stroking her head and back. Peg and Sagal had a chat that Sam couldn't process, and Peg began organizing the food. She grabbed a notepad from Bea's stack on the bookshelf and a roll of masking tape from the drawer. She checked the bottoms of plates to make sure they were marked. If they were not, she put a piece of tape with the owner's name and room number if it was one of the complex's tenants.

"Sam. You go on into Bea's room and start making your calls. We'll hold down the fort here," Peg pointed to Deb and Sagal, who nodded in agreement, motioning her into the other room. "Use this." Peg handed Sam another pad and pen. "Write who you've called and their number, the time, and indicate on this side if you've had to leave a message, if you spoke to someone, or if there was no answer and no machine. That way, any of us can go back and follow up."

"I guess, as long as Mom has lived here, y'all probably know her better than I know her in some ways."

"Maybe close to that," Peg replied. "But we've also all dealt with this scenario much more than you have, I bet. We've got it down to a science...unfortunately. In our experience, the sooner you get the stuff settled, the sooner you can really process your loss, and get back to your life. You don't have this hanging over your head. And if we're in your way or you don't want us to continue, let us know. We all get it."

"I've never considered that. All the stuff....dreaded thinking of it. Pretty much, we have everything we want. Jeff may want a few photos, but..."

"We're putting the art and photos in the back room for you all to discuss. And if you know of anything big, just tell one of us. But you know, she's told most of us what she wants, and she has her list in her papers. Believe me, we've all seen it!." They all laughed.

Tom eventually came in and began feasting on the newly arrived and ever-growing smorgasbord. Sasha jumped up from her television show and joined Tom's eating.

When Sam and Tom returned from the funeral home, Bea's apartment had been transformed. Shelves had been moved out, and folding chairs set out with the other furniture to form a large circle for visitors. Several people were there, and Sam could hear voices from Bea's room. Deb and Peg walked out with large garbage bags, obviously filled with clothing.

"All the clothes from the table, we put into these bags," Deb said as they dragged the bags across the floor. "And we've boxed up all the churches, angels, and other items."

"We let everyone who's come by thus far—they're all from here— look through and take anything they wanted."

"And the shelves have already been taken to the donation center. We're putting these bags in the back of the truck now. We'll take them and be right back. Okay?"

"Oh Deb. Of course. This is such a relief." After a brief kiss on Deb's cheek, she turned to Peg. "Still there for her. You're still there."

"You know it, girl." Peg hugged Sam. "She's been my bud a long time. And she clearly is crazy for you. So that makes me care for you, too."

"I'm one lucky lady, for sure." Sam covered her face and cried again. Deb and Peg held her in a sandwich hug for a moment.

When they left with the bags, it gave more room. Once visitors cleared out for the night, Tom and Sam would be able to sort through the more personal items. Sam noticed Tom had a big smile on his face.

"What?" Sam asked.

"See, we had just been discussing how we were going to tackle this mess."

Sam burst into tears again. "There I was worried how I would even begin sorting, and you guys have just—boom—taken care of it."

"Oh, don't worry. Y'all have plenty to do," Deb said with a chuckle.

"Yeah, probably a minimum of ten photo albums...make that at least twenty. And boxes of photos that were under the beds," Peg added. "But the books and videos are already in boxes in the back of Deb's truck."

"We're headed out for our second run, and then we'll call it a day and come back and help host visitors." Deb feigned a salute.

"Thank you," Sam said softly, pulling Deb into another hug.

"Thank this one." Deb nodded toward Peg. "She's the get'er done woman." Sam hugged Peg.

"You have no idea, Peg. Thank you so much." Sam hoped Peg would recognize her sincere gratitude for helping with this overwhelming part of Bea's death.

"We've reserved the community room and building entrance for a gathering after Bea's funeral. I heard Tom tell someone it would be in four days."

"Yeah, Peg. The announcement will be in the paper tomorrow, and the big obituary the day of the service, but we had to wait until Jeff could get back."

Sam was finally able to get a shower. Tom ate again, then left. Sagal and Sasha had already gone home. When Sam came out of the shower, only Toots and Ida were in the apartment, and they were manning Bea's phone and the door.

"Hey girl. We'll stay as long as you need us. Just let us know, and we're out of here. Don't want to be in the way. We've all been where you're at one time or another," Toots said.

"We've changed the sheets and are washing all the linens. We're hoping you have time for a nap. The other Barb will be back after the wash. She's ready for her shift here." Ida smiled at her.

"I still can't believe the organization at work here. Y'all are amazing." Sam didn't care who had taken charge. She wasn't sure she even knew, but she knew it was a bigger relief than she could have imagined. She acquiesced to taking a nap, and sliding into the clean, crisp sheets was delightful.

A light knock on the door woke Sam. She had no idea how long she had been asleep. Deb opened the door. "You okay to wake up? A cousin is here to see you. Bea's sister's daughter? That's what she said, anyway."

"Shit. What time is it?" Sam looked at the clock, not believing she had slept for three hours.

"It's five-thirty." Deb handed her a wet facecloth.

Sam jumped up and wiped her face. "My God. What would I have done without y'all? I have never been so cared for." She kissed Deb. "I'll brush my teeth and be right out. Let Irene know."

She didn't focus as she ran into the bathroom, but she noticed several chairs were occupied. After a quick toothbrushing and hair adjusting, she was presentable enough to begin greeting duties. Her eyes still looked puffy, but no one would expect anything less.

Irene, also a retired nurse, asked a few technical questions. Then Frances, Bea's longtime best friend from youth, greeted her and reintroduced her to a few of Bea's high school classmates that Sam hadn't seen since her dad died.

"Excuse me, Irene. Sam, you need to eat." Deb handed Sam a plate of food and a glass of wine.

"Yes, Samantha. Don't let yourself get worn down," Irene advised. "I remember how it was when Mom died. Everything is on you right now. Same as me. The oldest and the only female."

"I feel so exhausted...and sad, of course."

"All the more reason to take a break. Come on and sit down. Nobody is expecting you to entertain them," Deb added.

Mostly, people were telling stories of Bea and her antics. Sam was glad others could function during this type of situation. She saw herself simply floating along, talking to others, but she wasn't sure she would be able to remember any of it.

"Deb, is someone keeping track of who is here, and who has been here?"

"Honey, don't give it a second thought. The funeral home people came by and put a stand with a book outside of the apartment door. People know to sign."

"Sam, you don't have to remember a thing." Peg walked up, obviously having heard the conversation. "Everything is in the book or on a list."

"Amazing. I can't thank y'all enough." Peg patted Sam's shoulder and lightly rubbed her back. "We loved her, Sam. Folks here are grateful she didn't suffer. And no one has a bad thing to say. We're all glad to pitch in."

"That's so nice to hear."

Tom, Sagal, and Sasha came back in, and greetings and condolences around the room started anew. Tom and Sasha immediately made plates of food. When Sam looked and smiled at Deb, she realized she had not introduced her to anyone. Her strained look prompted Deb to walk back to Sam's chair.

"What's going on?" Deb whispered.

"I haven't introduced you to anyone, Deb. I'm so sorry."

"Don't worry." She waved her hand in disregard. "This is all for Bea, okay?"

Sam shook her head. "What did I do to deserve you?"

Deb shrugged and refilled Sam's wine glass. "I ask myself the same thing regarding you, you know."

By nine that night, it was just the usual immediate group and Peg remaining. Deb's phone buzzed, and she walked out of the apartment to take it. When she returned, Liz and Monty followed her in. Sam stood up and began sobbing again, and the two of them group-hugged her. Deb poured wine for them, and they joined the seating circle. Monty introduced herself and Liz to each of Sam's family members.

"Seems like I know you already, based on what I've heard," Monty added. Everyone chuckled.

"Hope Sam wasn't too hard on us," Tom said, smiling.

"How long will y'all be here?" Sam asked.

"Until after your service." Liz leaned over and whispered, "Do the rest know...your service...not your mom's?"

Sam put a finger to her lips.

"Where are y'all staying?" Sam asked.

"Hey, wait a minute," Sasha said. "What service? You weren't talking about Grandma's funeral?"

"Hey, can't answer but one at a time," Monty quickly added, coming to Sam's rescue. "We have a room close to you, right near the pier. Deb said your brother is coming and that's why you've held back the funeral."

"Yes. Jeff will be here in a few days." Sam responded.

"What service, Sam? Don't ignore me." Sasha insisted, hands on her hips.

"Since it's just us right now," Sam said, "I want to let y'all know...Deb and I are getting married Saturday. Liz is performing the ceremony, and you're invited. We're getting married at Deb's place at the beach. It'll just be us here in this room right now and Jeff. Sasha, if you agree, we want you to be our attendant. Monty and Peg will be witnesses."

Everyone began chatting and congratulating. After that died down, Deb garnered the group's attention by clearing her throat loudly.

"I have an announcement also. I don't want any of this to overshadow our celebration of Bea's life," Deb added. "One of the reasons we've decided to marry now is that I'm having surgery next week to remove a suspicious cyst."

"Oh, shit, Deb. I'm so sorry," Sagal said with a grimace.

"My own mom died of breast cancer. I had surgery to try to prevent it. I've been clear, luckily, for a few years. And it may be nothing, but we can't take a chance."

"We didn't know," Tom said.

"Yeah. I don't usually share it. Peg was there two years ago when I found out I was positive for the gene that causes the cancer. I couldn't have made it through then if she hadn't been encouraging." Deb held Sam's hand tightly as she discussed the why's and how's and when's. Everyone nodded, and Monty led a toast to Bea and another one to Sam and Deb.

By eleven, only Sam and Deb remained. The quiet of Bea's absence seemed deafening. Deb led Sam to the bedroom and held her until the sobs subsided and she fell asleep.

Chapter Twenty-Nine

JEFF EVENTUALLY MADE IT to Wilmington, twelve hours before Bea's service. His plane had been delayed in Cebu, which caused him to miss the day earlier flight to Atlanta. The forty-eight travel hours had been grueling, but he was his usual jovial self when Sam and Deb picked him up. Jeff was an easygoing guy, and he and Sam had always been close.

Jeff entertained them while they waited at baggage claim with stories of several flight attendants showering him with attention because he'd sobbed almost continuously.

"I think they were so moved by my sorrow, they kept that booze flowing. You know I didn't mind that one bit." Jeff looked at the baggage belt and pointed. "There they are now." He and Deb moved to grab a bag each, and they headed to the car.

"Well, Jeff, Sam has told me quite a few stories." Deb turned to face him in the back seat.

"Oh no! Don't tell me that." His hearty laugh proved infectious.

"Jeff, it's so good to hear that laugh. I've needed it these past few months."

"Shoulda called me, Sis. I can video call with the best of them, as long as we have power. That is kinda iffy sometimes."

"You guys must've been pretty close as kids, too, then?" Deb observed.

"Oh yeah. We shared the same playpen, the same toys, and stuff like that," Sam added.

"Yep. And she always blamed her antics on me, so I'd be the one getting punished. And she was mean." He laughed again.

"Shoot. You were the one who always got me in trouble," Sam protested.

"I came out years before Sam. Those times were tough. Dad made Sam take me everywhere to keep an eye on me. Day I turned eighteen, she was away at college. I drove my car down that long driveway for the final time and moved out."

"Gosh. I remember that day. I could only picture it, of course, not being there, but I remember I called to wish you happy birthday, and you told me as soon as you hung up, you were headed to your own place."

"I think a lot of what made us close were those times...the number of discussions related to my coming out and being frustrated that I was living in a virtual jail."

"That sure doesn't always happen in teen years between siblings...the becoming closer, I mean."

"No, Deb, it doesn't. I just couldn't breathe anymore."

"Speaking of keeping you boozed up." Deb pulled out a strong whiskey cocktail from the cooler she had packed in the car before they left the house.

"Man, oh man, Sam. She *is* just as wonderful as you said. Thank you for this. I don't care if it is zero dark-thirty in the morning." A few minutes of quiet followed, only the sound of tinkling ice breaking the silence. "Sam, you know I've never cared for family-type gatherings, but I'm happy to be in town for your ceremony. And Mom's too, really. I'm sorry that I can't keep from crying, though."

"Sure doesn't surprise me," Deb said. "It truly runs in your family."

"We try to hold it together," Sam said. "And then a sappy cola or coffee commercial comes on the television and the waterworks begin."

Jeff's hearty laugh indicated he agreed.

"Here we are," Sam said as they drove into the lot.

"What's the plan, Sam? Should I book a room?"

"No. That's taken care of. We've booked two, two-bedroom suites for the family for the remainder of the week, through the wedding. Our friends Liz and Monty, you, and Deb and I have our own rooms. The suites have kitchenettes and shared living space. There's one empty bedroom in case Tom and Sasha want to stay with us. Sagal has to work...or will take her refuge in their quiet apartment." She chuckled.

"After Liz and Monty return home, you'll stay at my place at Wrightsville," Deb added.

"I'm not sure how much longer I'll be in town, but likely until after your surgery. You sure that's okay?"

"Absolutely. It'll be nice for the three of us to hang out."

"I look forward to it. And I always like Wrightsville when I can stay put. I'm not thrilled at how busy it is these days."

"I remember those earlier days too. I knew everyone who lived there year-round. And the traffic. Crazy now."

"But I hear you enjoy giving tourists those parking tickets." Jeff laughed and tapped Deb's back.

"No, you didn't," Deb said with a smile.

"You ready to do this thing?" Sam asked Jeff.

He blew out a breath. "Not really, but let's do it." They walked up the stairs. Sam was grateful the old gang wouldn't be sitting at the top of the stairs at this time of the morning. She knew seeing some of Bea's friends would elicit even more tears, and Jeff was already exhausted.

"Holy crap." Jeff looked around the empty room. He walked through the bedrooms, touching the remaining things. Once again, tears streamed down his face. Sam pulled him into a hug, and the two wept softly. After a minute, he pulled away and wiped his eyes and nose.

"What happened to everything, Sam? How did y'all get this done so quickly?"

"Definitely a group project. Annie took any durable medical equipment to the room here at the complex where people can borrow them. ReStore is picking up the remaining furniture tomorrow. Deb, Peg, the two Barbs, and Ida organized a few times when residents filed through and took whatever they wanted."

"Your mom had some mighty good friends, that's for sure," Deb chimed in. "Truly, with all the hands in the removal process, the only thing left after tomorrow is the cursory cleaning. Annie let us know, in no uncertain terms, to avoid any heavy-duty cleaning."

"Wow. That's hard to believe."

"I guess Mom's been here so long, they have to do some major remodeling."

"Peg and Annie said that even some of the appliances should be replaced by newer models."

"That's incredible." Jeff's eyes welled with tears again. "There is so little left to do. I mean, I'm grateful, I really am, but at the same time..." He choked back a sob. "It's so striking. Makes it so clear that...she's not with us anymore."

"C'mon, let's get ready. We have a service to attend, way too soon. Grab a short nap." Sam wiped Jeff's face with a tissue and hugged him again.

* * * *

After Bea's services, everyone met up at the apartment community room. The residents and Bea's church pals had yet another enormous smorgasbord for family and friends.

Sam sidled up to Tom and Jeff, who were chatting. "Even with all this love, I'm so glad to be going elsewhere for the evening. I know you're beginning to think of that nice bed."

"Luckily, I had one of those second winds after the nap. Maybe fourth or fifth. It has been an emotionally and physically exhausting day...days, really."

"Don't know how you could do it. I'd be asleep on the floor up at Mom's if I had just done that trip," Tom added.

"It's winding down. I guess we best begin saying good-bye and cleaning up." Sam looked around the room at the diminishing crowd. Monty and Liz joined their group.

"Y'all go on and do your goodbyes. You won't need to clean up. The gals are doing that for you," Monty said with one hand on Jeff's shoulder and one on Tom's.

"That is the best gift of the entire ordeal, I think." Sam looked at Deb. "That and you."

"Okay, now. Don't get too sappy. I'll start the waterworks again." Jeff laughed at his own joke, and the others joined in.

While they could only imagine how exhausted Jeff might be, Deb and Sam were first to excuse themselves from their joint living room in the suite. They did manage to say good night to their buddies in the adjoining suite. Once alone, they showered and went straight to bed.

"You know, I don't think I have even one more drop of water left in my body."

"You've cried a good bit, Sam, but I think it's good to share your grief...to be able to share your grief...especially with your friends and family. Not everyone can process so immediately."

Sam wasn't sure if she answered or just thought she had answered Deb's observation. Sleep was advancing strongly as she relaxed into Deb's arms.

* * * *

There had been little time to plan for tomorrow's service. Deb and Sam had secured a marriage license, and Sagal and Sasha had helped them invite their friends and cousins to the party after the service. The inner circle had agreed to meet at Deb's place at two.

"Thank goodness we found matching linen slacks and jackets." Sam pulled on her sleeveless tee and straightened it, letting the hem fall just below her waistband.

"Yeah. It's going to be a hot, humid one. Luckily overcast, though." Deb helped Sam into the jacket, then pulled Sam against her and hugged her from behind.

"Thanks." Sam turned in her arms, pulled out, and checked out Deb, top to bottom. "You look great."

"You too. Are you sad we're not doing the dress thing and all that formal stuff?"

"Deb. C'mon. Me? Hell no. I'm glad we're doing this casual-like. It's just too hot for any of that. Island wear always trumps dressy down here, doesn't it?"

"Usually, but you'd be surprised how often you see the whole flowing white dress, tuxes, and bare feet."

"That's an okay thing for some people. We're not that traditional." A few beats passed. "Deb." Sam looked into Deb's eyes. "I know I'm probably going to cry. I mean, I wish Mom were here, you know."

"Of course you do, but all your other real and chosen family members are going to share this with us. And nobody's going to have one iota of anything but love if you shed some tears."

"I love you, Deb. I do."

"Let's save that I do for the ceremony, okay? But the feeling is oh so mutual." Deb pecked a kiss on Sam's cheek. "Let's get 'er done, babe."

During the ceremony, Liz chose a simple story of love and shared some observations regarding the couple, the temporal journeys through injury in reference to sickness and walks on the beach in health. The traditional vows had been modified somewhat. Sam and Deb recited how they would support the other, their relationship, and their own individual needs and growth, with communication being a necessary guide to that path. Sam choked through her recitation. Deb's gentle squeeze of her hands helped her through.

By some sort of magic, Monty had found two beautifully hammered, matching bands for their rings. She instructed Sasha how and when to hand the ring to Sam, and Peg held Deb's ring for Sam's finger.

At the end of the service, Sam and Jeff were almost sobbing, and Sasha was pointing at them and giggling. There was a definite "whoop" from the group when Deb and Sam kissed, and neighbors on their porches clapped.

There were hugs before everyone began walking or driving the few blocks to the reception at Bull's. Bottles of champagne and hors d'oeuvres dotted tables. Shiny mylar balloons floated around the room. One of Deb's favorites there was playing DJ, and dancing ensued. Deb's softball crew was there, and Jeff had invited some of his and Sam's buddies from back in the day.

Friends greeted the couple as they entered. Deb signaled the DJ to play their dance song, "Inside These Arms," from a Marti Jones CD, *Match Game*. After giving the couple time for their private dance, everyone joined them. Even Deb's boss, Jim, cut a rug. Most of the songs were from their era—disco, Captain and Tennille, Doobie Brothers, Beatles, and a string of eighties tunes. Peg's gruff, smoker's squeal sounded more like a howl when she heard Gerry Polci's voice leading the Four Seasons in, "Oh What a Night." Peg grabbed Deb's arm and they stole the floor.

The staff began preparing for their normal crowd at seven, moving tables back out onto what had been the dance floor, and the DJ left. Lots of folks stayed, but Tom, Sagal, Sasha, and some of the cousins left. There was more time to visit as the crowd thinned.

"It's so weird not having my own place here anymore. I mean, with Mom gone, there's not the same anchor." Sam's eyes welled with tears yet again, and she began crying. Jeff joined her in a hug.

"Hey, now." Deb pointed to herself.

"Uh, if you don't remember why we're all here...you're now married to a wonderful woman who lives right down the street." Monty's face displayed disbelief as her thumb pointed over her shoulder in the direction of Deb's house. "I don't know of a stronger anchor for you than that, Sam. And Jeff, pretty sure you already love Deb as much as we do." They all laughed, and Sam laughed the hardest. Deb hugged her, laughing and shaking her back and forth.

"We'll load up the gifts and drop them at Deb's," Liz advised.

"Thanks, y'all." Sam hugged them all as they left.

Sam and Deb walked out to the ocean before heading back. As they stood on the sand, Sam leaned back into Deb's arms. She felt so loved, so content, so complete. Deb pulled her hand.

"We should walk back."

"I know, but I'm enjoying your arms around me."

"Plenty of that for later."

"Deb. We're married," Sam whispered as they strolled back to Deb's place.

"It's almost too good to believe. I didn't realize I could feel so strongly."

"I didn't either. A whirlwind...I mean, this is a lot for a year."

Deb squeezed Sam's hand. As they walked into the house, they saw the table covered with unopened gifts.

"Oh crap."

"What?"

"I just noticed the guest books." Sam heaved a sigh. "Between the funeral and our wedding, we're going to be writing enough thank-yous to cramp our hands for a month." Deb chuckled and pulled Sam to the bedroom. Sam was too overwhelmed to think of anything but decompression.

"You need a shower." Deb adjusted the knobs and slowly undressed Sam. Her body reacted to Deb's soft, slow touch. She shivered as Deb reached around her to work her panties down, and she relaxed into Deb's arms. They kissed, and Deb walked Sam backward into the shower stall. Sam began sobbing as the water flowed through her hair. Deb had removed her clothes, and she bathed Sam. She rinsed her off, turned off the water, and put a towel around her. She dried her and led her to the bed. Sam slipped under the covers and onto her pillow. "Look. It's my pillow, Deb. Mine. At your house."

"Yes, it is. And it's our house now." She smiled as Sam pulled her hand to join her.

"Be there in a minute," Deb whispered. After her shower, she settled into the bed beside Sam, and almost before Deb's head hit the pillow, Sam heard her slow breathing.

I love this woman. She put her arm around Deb's shoulder, and exhaustion pulled her into sleep as easily as it had Deb.

Chapter Thirty

"IT'S FUNNY"—DEB SLOWED their walk to the ocean to watch the sun rise—"I still feel as if we're dating. But we are really married."

"I can't believe how comfortable I am in thinking of it as our house. Hope you feel the same."

"I do feel the same. Look, we'd better get back to meet Liz and Monty."

"Yeah. Monty will be starving. She's as bad as Tom and Sasha."

Liz and Monty were waiting for them at the restaurant, Monty sporting a huge grin. "Y'all have a big night when you made it home?"

Deb laughed. "I'll say. I fell asleep the minute my head hit the pillow."

"Before!" Sam laughed too. "But we did get up and sit on the beach this morning to watch the sun come up. Such a beautiful day."

"Don't worry, Sam. Monty and I will take care of everything back home. You just stay here and focus on Deb's surgery and recovery."

"But the hemlock treatment. I was supposed to help."

"Aw shoot, Sam. Nancy, Monty, and I will take care of that."

"And our group's birthday get-together. We're going to miss that too." Sam frowned. "I've been looking forward to that."

"All you need to do is tell us where that ice cream churn and the recipe are. We're 100 percent capable of doing that," Monty chimed. Liz pushed her shoulder.

"Monty." Liz chided. "Sam, we will certainly miss you and Deb, but Thanksgiving's not too far away. The rest of the group will get to meet Deb then, if not before."

Sam's lassitude returned, knowing Liz and Monty wouldn't be there with her. She was so grateful that Jeff was going to be around. As she considered that, her phone buzzed with a text.

Awake. Ate here. Tom n Sasha stayed. We ate together. They gonna dip in pool b4 checkout. I'm ready tho.

K. Give us a few. (smiley face emoji)

* * * *

"What would we do without your helping us?" Sam asked as Jeff wrote gifts and givers on yet another list.

"So many lists, so little time, right?" Jeff chuckled. "It's better to get it over with, so to speak...this one?" He held up a beautifully handwoven basket. "I'd say mountain house rather than beach house."

"Agree." Deb said.

"I know exactly where we can put it. Hey, milestone here. We only have five more thank-yous from the mom list."

"I should have helped you with that one, Sam, but thank you for letting me help with this list instead." Jeff feigned wiping his forehead. "Whew." They all chuckled but continued working. "Guess what, ladies? It's five o'clock somewhere. I'll make us some yummy frozen beverages, okay?"

"Oh yeah. I vote for that." Deb raised her hand.

"Will you make some of your special spring rolls—you know the ones. With the uncooked wraps."

"Summer rolls. That's a great plan. I'll run out and pick up the ingredients before we start on beverages."

"Likely a safer plan," Deb added.

Shrimp summer rolls, a cabbage and carrot salad, island beverages, and my two favorite people. What better life could there be? Sam enjoyed sitting on the porch, noshing and talking. She was content, peaceful, loved. It was as if all three of them had known one another for years.

* * * *

It was Tuesday. Deb's cyst removal was scheduled for ten. Jeff and Sam accompanied Deb to the surgery center.

"Ms. Martin," called the young woman in scrubs. Deb and Sam stood. "Come with me."

"You sure you don't mind waiting here? I'll be back in just a few minutes," Sam asked Jeff.

"Sure. That's why I brought this magazine." Jeff smiled at them. "Good luck, Deb." Deb just nodded, and they disappeared behind the double doors.

Deb changed into the requisite gown, her clothes were bagged and given to Sam. All the typical preop preparations were done: an IV, verbal and written consents, including consent to share information with Sam. Sam waited to meet this Cammy Gates and hoped she was as skilled as Deb and Dr. Moore had indicated.

When Gates walked in, Sam knew immediately this was the surgeon. The air of confidence was unmistakable, but she was not exactly how Sam had pictured her. She was taller than Deb, and beautiful, even with her hair thoroughly tucked under her surgical cap. Her eyes were as green and bright as Monty's, and her smile captivating. No wonder everyone thought Gates was all that and a side of fries. Sam was totally mesmerized.

Gates smiled and rested her hand on Deb's shoulder. "Deb, I'm sorry to see you again under these circumstances." She turned to Sam, "You must be Samantha. I'm Cammy Gates. It's nice to meet you." Sam nodded. Gates sat down on the visitor's chair and looked at them both. "The surgery is routine. You both know that. What we find may not be. You both know that, also. After surgery, I'll come talk with you, Samantha. Then Deb, I'll come back and talk with you as soon as I think you can process what I have to say. By then, you will have probably heard the information from Samantha. There's no need to worry until we get the molecular report back, but I don't think it's going to be much different from what the biopsy showed. Deb or Samantha, do you have any questions for me? If not, Deb, I'll need to move your gown to the side so I can mark the surgical site, okay?"

"We're good," Deb said, looking at Sam. "Right?"

Sam nodded. "Yes. This is what we were expecting."

"Okay then." Dr. Gates marked the site after verifying the cyst by feeling.

"I think I can go right through the same scar tissue, Deb. I want to keep your scarring to a minimum." She stood and shook both of their hands. Sam was impressed by the handshake, although she considered that she was only mesmerized by the surgeon's beauty.

"Thanks, Doc." Deb left the room and the nurse smiled and followed, saying she'd be back with the sleepy-time drugs.

Sam found Jeff in the waiting room where she had left him. She blew out a breath as she sat. She wasn't the praying type, but she silently said a few words. Jeff reached and patted her hand, as if he knew what she was thinking. She leaned her head on his shoulder.

"I'm glad you're here. So glad." Jeff nodded and squeezed her hand.

"It's going to be okay. Routine...okay?" Sam nodded the response to his question.

At eleven, Dr. Gates strolled through the waiting room. She walked to Sam and squatted in front of her.

"Is it okay if we share information within earshot of this gentleman?"

"Oh yes. This is my brother, Jeff. Deb wouldn't mind at all."

"Hi Jeff. It's nice to meet you. I'm Cammy Gates, Deb's surgeon. Deb and I go back a ways."

"So I hear," Jeff responded. "Deb has done nothing but sing your praises."

"That's nice to hear." She turned toward Sam. "Just as we expected, Sam. Routine procedure. The cyst seemed all-contained in a capsule. I think that's a good sign. We took some samples of the surrounding tissue and nodes. Patho's already checked, and they didn't find anything weird in the margins, so that's encouraging. Sam, they'll probably call you back in thirty minutes to sit with Deb. Recovery should be minimal, but the nurse will explain the discharge restrictions."

"Results, Doc?" Sam asked.

"My guess is a couple of weeks before the detailed genetic testing results are in, but the initial pathology should be back in a few days. I'll talk with Tina, and your appointment to discuss both results will be with her. Recovery will give you follow-up info and the appointment dates before she's discharged."

"Of course. Thanks so much, Dr. Gates."

"Dang," Sam whispered as Gates exited through the double doors.

"Just like you, you letch. Looking at her ass in those scrubs. Shame on you." Jeff laughed and pushed on Sam's shoulder. Sam shrugged.

A nurse followed quickly behind the doctor, and she led Sam back to Deb's recovery station. "She's been awake for a few minutes, taken some ice chips. She's dozing again. You can expect that for the rest of the day. I'll be back in a few." The nurse disappeared behind the curtain, and Sam sat in a chair next to the stretcher. She reached and took Deb's hand.

"Hiya," Deb said softly, eyes opening and closing. Sam stood and kissed her forehead.

"You feel okay?" Sam asked as she held her hand. "The doctor came out and spoke to us."

"Yeah? I think she may have come by here, but I'm not sure. I thought I heard her voice, but she might have been walking by." Deb smacked her mouth. "It's so dry. Can you hand me a few ice chips? It's okay."

"She said you'd just taken some. You sure it's okay?"

"I think so. I just want to wet my mouth. I don't want to try to drink." Sam handed her a spoon with three chips. Deb took them in and teased, "Don't try to choke me now."

Sam popped her arm lightly. "Quit it." She leaned across the stretcher rails and kissed Deb. The nurse walked in and caught them. She smiled. "Deb told me y'all were just married. That's sweet."

Sam considered the nurse must have thought it was unusual for older couples to marry, but she wasn't sure that's how she meant it.

"Thanks," Sam said, deciding to take it at face value. "It's one of the good things that comes with the experience of age." The nurse smiled again, nodded, and made a couple of notes on the computer.

"I'll be back within ten minutes." With that, she disappeared behind the curtains again. Sam peeked at Deb's dressing. It was a flat, white, non-stick pad covered by a clear adhesive strip. Very tidy looking, with only a small spot of blood barely soaked through. "Looks good, babe. They probably gave you a local that won't wear off for six hours or so. Just a guess, though."

"Okay. I think I'll sleep until she comes back. You'll stay, though, right?" Deb squeezed Sam's hand. "Oh, but Jeff. Is he waiting?"

"I'm not going anywhere. Count on that. And Jeff is fine. He's reading." She leaned and kissed Deb's head again.

Within the hour, Deb had already walked to the bathroom, changed into her clothes, and they had removed the IV access. She was waiting for the discharge instructions. The nurse popped back in, explained her instructions, and handed Sam a prescription for five pain pills in case Deb needed them. The appointments for test results and follow-up had been scheduled, and she called for Deb's wheelchair. Sam headed out to retrieve Jeff and the car.

Deb was subdued for the remainder of the day, napping a good bit, some of it on the porch. Sam and Jeff worked on thank-you notes for a few recently received gifts and memorials and enjoyed cocktails. At five, Deb asked for something real to eat. Jeff made grilled cheese sandwiches and tomato soup.

"Can we keep him, Sam?"

Jeff laughed. "Oh, I think you'd tire of me."

"Not if you rebuilt my dock and pier the way you suggested when we were enjoying those island beverages." Deb chuckled and closed her eyes again.

"And you must be in some sort of drug-induced state." He chuckled. Deb just smiled, eyes closed.

"I think you're finally waking up a little." Sam assisted Deb into the upright position in the lounge chair.

"It doesn't hurt...more like a pressure." Deb lightly touched the surgical dressing. "Is this thing bulky?"

"Nah. Typical postop dressing. You're still numb, so it probably feels weird. Here, take these."

Deb took the two over-the-counter pain relievers, and Sam made a cold pack for the incision area. Only twenty minutes had passed.

"Is it bedtime yet, Sam?"

"It's six-thirty, but you're going to be sleepy. If you wake up in the night, we'll try that cold pack again."

Later, when she turned in, Sam slept alongside Deb. She knew it was for her own comfort more than for Deb's. If she could feel Deb, then she considered Deb was safe.

Sam woke the next morning to the smell of coffee. It was eight-thirty. She had no idea how she could have slept that late, nor how she could have slept through Deb's rising. Deb was sitting on the porch with Jeff, both drinking coffee. They seemed to be having a heavy conversation. Jeff's hands were moving, indicating some sort of spatial feature. Sam poured herself some coffee and opened the porch door to join them. "Hiya," Deb said.

"That's a lot perkier than the last time you said it to me," Sam teased. "I can't believe I slept this hard. Did you get up during the night?"

"Once. I used the cold pack and slept on the couch until this morning—"

"Oh, Deb. No."

"I didn't want to bother you. And I slept fine. I feel only a little sore, but really, I feel fine."

"Okay, okay," Sam said.

"Yeah, she had the coffee brewing when I woke up," Jeff added. "We've just been chatting away out here. And the heron was here when we came out."

"I'm so glad you were able to see it too." Sam's eyes welled with tears, and Deb took her hand and kissed it.

"Jeff has been suggesting some ways to rebuild the pier. From what he's described, I think we'd absolutely love it." Sam smiled at her brother. "He's promised to send us some plans. I'm going to do it, Samantha. It would be so nice to have easy access to the water here again.

"We've also been talking trips. I told him we're going to Maine. Then how we're taking a big road trip after Maine. It dawned on me that we could get one of those truck camper inserts. Then we can stay in the truck if we want to or need to. It's easier to park. And we can stay in our friends' driveways easily."

"Why not? There are a couple of places here that sell them. We can start there," Sam recommended.

"Can we go today? I don't have to do anything but walk around and look. And Jeff said he wouldn't mind looking at them, so he'll go with us. Okay?" Deb sounded so excited, Sam couldn't have turned her down.

Sam stood up, put her coffee on the porch rail, and kissed Deb. "PDA be damned." She kissed Deb again.

Chapter Thirty-One

"HARD TO BELIEVE IT'S been an entire week since Jeff left." Sam stood looking out toward the water.

"I can't believe how much I miss him too. I told him I'd try to talk you into visiting him."

"Huh. You did, did you? Even if we could go, it would be another year or so."

"You know, at the airport, all of us, including Tom, Sagal, and Sasha….so many tears. How can someone who brings such laughter into our lives bring so many tears?"

"It is ironic, isn't it?"

"And now, we have that slide-in camper with the nice touches he added."

"That was just crazy…crazy in a good way."

"He's so creative, Sam, and generous. It was such a treat to meet him, and to be able to just hang out for a good visit."

"It was." A few minutes passed in silence. "But we'll soon be traveling. I know we've had to change our plans a bit because of the postop visits and results, but I can hardly wait."

They would go to Sam's home in Suches first, then Maine, then a road trip heading west and down the coast. They'd hit Route 66, here and there, and come back across the country in a zig-zag pattern.

"Me too." Deb said. "I can't wait to bike along the Eastern and Katy Trails."

"That'll be so cool. And I look forward to seeing old friends and seeing new things," Sam said. "It's the best sort of trip I can imagine."

"Just that pesky final appointment. The one I dread the most."

"I know." Sam dared not harp on the appointment where they would learn the results of the molecular testing and the recommendations for treatment. She suspected she knew what the recommendations were going to be. And Deb was likely not going to take those recommendations. *For better or for worse. Don't forget that.*

* * * *

Sandy waved at Deb when she was bringing another patient back. Her gaze was warm, and Sam thought maybe bad news wasn't coming, but she had to admit that she would have smiled at Deb if she had seen her sitting in a waiting room. She couldn't rest Deb's results on a chance smile.

"Geez." Deb sat straight up with her hands on her knees.

"Try to relax, babe." Sam whispered, resting her hand atop Deb's.

Deb picked up a magazine, thumbed through a few pages, put it down, and resumed the position.

"Babe," Sam whispered again. "You realize that is the fifth time you've done that?" She rested her hand on Deb's arm. "I know you're anxious." Sam herself tried not to think, period. Finally, Sandy called Deb back, and Sam followed.

"Everything is pretty much what I expected." Dr. Moore looked at Deb while she rolled her chair around the desk to face them and sat. "I suspect other cysts may form, or cancer may be present elsewhere at some point. You know I recommend one of the oral agents, at minimum."

"I know, Doc, but you know how I feel, however ill-advised. I'll agree to surgeries for cyst removals, but hell, I've felt good...for the past two years...good."

"But Deb—" Dr. Moore started.

Deb held her hand up to interrupt. "I'll continue once, or twice, yearly films, but I want nothing to interfere with my pretty normal life."

Sam shrugged and Dr. Moore stood.

"Okay, Deb. I respect your decision. Sandy will set up your usual follow-ups. I guess that's that."

"Tina, you know I appreciate everything you and Cammy have done and do for me. Please don't take this as disrespect. It's nothing of the sort."

"I know that Deb. You know I know that." She gently pulled Deb into a hug. "See you in six months. By the way, congratulations." She pulled out of the hug and extended a hand to each of them. "Y'all go have some fun for me, okay?"

Later, as they sat out on the porch, Sam ran her hand down Deb's arm. "What are you thinking?" she asked.

Deb let out a sigh. "That I hope you don't regret being with me if one of these cysts comes back."

"You realize that I married you, right? I married you when we knew that might happen. I'm not going to sit here and tell you it'll be all smiles if it happens, but I'm *with* you. I can't imagine *not* being with you. And I'm not going to dwell on your not being here with me. I'm just not. So please stop worrying."

"Do you remember that first night you came up here?" Deb asked.

"You mean that night you kissed me and I went home? And thinking of you made me come? Yeah. I remember. How could I ever forget that? Jesus."

"I wanted you crazy bad. Can't believe I let you leave." Deb sighed.

Sam stood and stepped to Deb's lounge chair. She tilted the head back and rested her knee between Deb's legs, holding herself just above Deb. "So, let's go inside." She leaned and kissed her. Deb moaned softly and pulled Sam's weight onto her. "This is not inside," Sam whispered. "PDA. Remember?"

They retreated inside. Deb pushed Sam backward until she was at the bed. Deb leaned to pick Sam up.

"Stop!" Sam said firmly. Deb pulled back, startled.

"Your incision, remember? You can't pick up or bear too much weight yet. I'll pull myself up."

"Then, get on with it. What are you waiting for? It's been two weeks since we've fooled around, you know." Deb teased.

* * * *

The morning light streamed through the window, a beam zeroing in on Sam's eye. Her head was resting on Deb's unaffected shoulder, just as it was when she'd drifted off to sleep. Deb was stroking her shoulder, lightly. Sam slid her hand from Deb's waist down to her hip. "Mm. This is nice," Sam said softly. "Hey, guess what?" She seemed to have suddenly remembered something good.

"Hm?" Deb responded quietly.

"We get to do this every single day." Her kiss was soft on Deb's shoulder. "By the way," Sam whispered, "was it one of your bucket list items to render me useless last night?" She kissed Deb's shoulder again.

"Oh, no. Not at all. That's on the top of my *Daily To Do List*," Deb responded. Sam lightly slapped her arm. Deb chuckled and pulled Sam into a tight hug. Sam rolled on top of her and they kissed.

"Hey, you may want to save this for later. We have a lot to do today, you know. And if you don't get up, we're going to be here quite a while."

"Ugh. Spoilsport...all right," Sam conceded. She rolled off and headed for the shower.

"Hey," Deb called. "How can someone have captured me this way, and at this age? I feel instantly turned on and yet so calmed by you. That first time you smarted off at me. It caused me to look at you, and when I did, that was it." Deb touched her scars and drew her finger along the new incision. "I was dead inside before."

"I'm glad you don't feel that way now. I love you, you know. Just the way you are. Want you. Just the way you are."

"I just can't believe it sometimes. It's almost too much." Deb wiped tears from her eyes.

"I'm going to jump in the shower. Okay?" Sam drew the back of her hand softly across Deb's cheek.

"Yeah. I just want to rest a little longer. I'll shower when you're done."

* * * *

Sam had left her robe open as she walked into the bedroom, towel drying her hair. "Not up yet?" she teased. She climbed onto the bed and settled on top of the sheet covering Deb. She cupped Deb's face in her hands and lowered her lips onto Deb's for an intense kiss. As they kissed, Sam ground her body against the sheet. She grunted softly into Deb's mouth. Then she pulled back to speak.

"I think I would be perfectly happy to kiss you all day long. Your mouth is beyond description...*hors catégorie*, as they say in the Tour de France."

Deb pulled Sam's head back toward her for another kiss, their tongues caressing as their bodies thrust against the other. Sam lightly took Deb's bottom lip with her teeth before she kissed her again.

"Yeah. All day long. See. We're not too old for this are we?" Deb whispered before a guttural sigh.

"Not too old, indeed." Sam whispered.

Deb knew they would be postponing any plans for the day. No one was expecting them. They were officially on their honeymoon. What difference did it make when they started their road trip? They didn't need to find a reason for their delay. The goal was to live life to its fullest during whatever time they had left. No matter how long that was. And they were doing just that.

The End

About Ann Tonnell

Ann Tonnell is a retired RN, having worked in management most of her nursing career. However, her first career was typesetting and composition. It was not until retirement that she found inspiration to capture stories in writing. She lives with her wife in a small community in the North Georgia mountains just yards from the Appalachian Trail. She is a DIY dabbler and avid cloud admirer.

Email keepintouch@anntonnell.com

Website https://anntonnell.com/

Facebook https://www.facebook.com/ann.tonnell/

Instagram https://www.instagram.com/anntonnell/

Twitter https://twitter.com/anntonnell

TikTok @anntonnellauthor

Note to Readers:

Thank you for reading a book from Desert Palm Press. We appreciate you as a reader and want to ensure you enjoy the reading process. We would like you to consider posting a review on your preferred media sites and/or your blog or website.

For more information on upcoming releases, author interviews, contests, giveaways and more, please sign up for our newsletter and visit us at Desert Palm Press: www.desertpalmpress.com and "Like" us on Facebook: Desert Palm Press.

Bright Blessings

www.ingramcontent.com/pod-product-compliance
Lightning Source LLC
Chambersburg PA
CBHW051136020726
47501CB00005B/1540